TALES OF THE WHITE SPIRE

Book One: Daemon

Jason J Lynch

Copyright © 2024 Jason J Lynch

All Rights Reserved

No part of this publication may be reproduced, distributed, or transmitted in any form or by any means, including photocopying, recording, or other electronic or mechanical methods, without the prior written permission of the publisher, except as permitted by U.K. copyright law. For permission requests, contact the author Via Amazon's Author page.
The story, all names, characters, and incidents portrayed in this production are fictitious. No identification with actual persons (living or deceased), places, buildings, and products is intended or should be inferred.

There are a few thank you's I really should mention.
Firstly, a huge thank you to Steve Leigh, my first proof-reader and motivator, fuelled, most likely, by simply wanting to know how the story ended. Also, my Niece Jennifer Lynch, for her help, encouragement, tea, advice and understanding. Check out her children's and young adult fiction.
To the army of online webpage writers and advisors whose help in self-publishing a book is invaluable, thank you all.
To my wife and daughter, for simply putting up with me constantly moaning about this silly book I wanted to write.
And you. For reading it.

Jenny

Love
Jason J Lynch

CONTENTS

Title Page
Copyright
Dedication
One   3
Two   7
Three   14
Four   15
Five   25
Six   31
Seven   41
Eight   47
Nine   55
Ten   63
Eleven   68
Twelve   75
Thirteen   79
Fourteen   84
Fifteen   90
Sixteen   97
Seventeen   102
Eighteen   108

Nineteen	114
Twenty	119
Twenty one	128
Twenty Two	135
Twenty Three	143
Twenty Four	152
Twenty Five	159
Twenty Six	170
Twenty Seven	179
Twenty Eight	188
Twenty Nine	195
Thirty	203
Thirty One	214
Thirty Two	225
Thirty Three	234
Thirty Four	243
Thirty Five	250
Thirty Six	260
Thirty Seven	267
Thirty Eight.	277
End	279

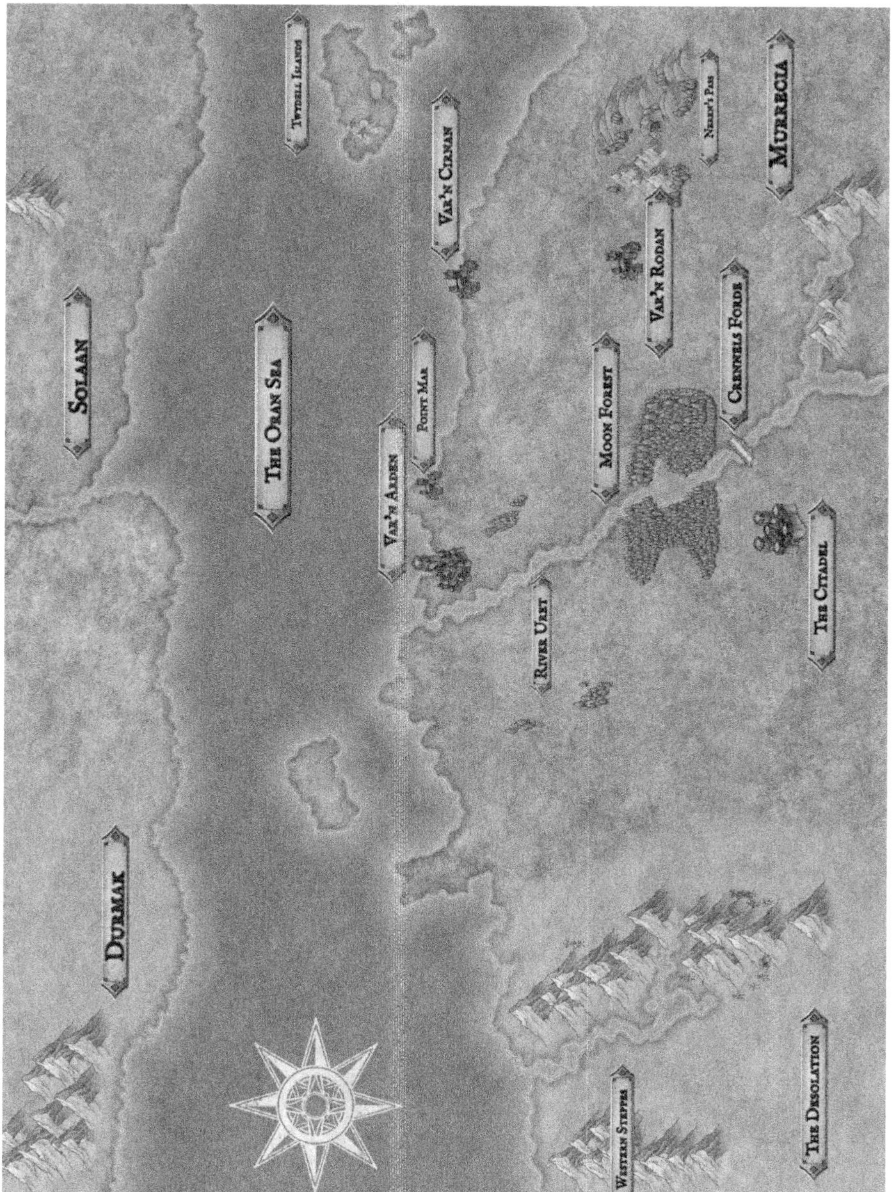

Durmak
Solaan
The Oran Sea
Twydell Islands
Var'n Arden
Point Mar
Var'n Cirnan
River Uret
Moon Forest
Var'n Rodan
Neren's Pass
Crennels Fords
Murrecia
Western Steppes
The Desolation
The Citadel

"......Papa...?"
"Yes, my son?" he answered.
"What am I?"
"You are... my son." He said quietly.
The boy thought for a moment.
"Papa...?"
"Hmm?"
"Where did I come from?"

ONE

Twelve Summers Ago.

The flames in the wall sconces danced and flickered as the last of the magic crackled across the dim basement chamber. The air was thick with the tang, cloying in the back of the guards throats as they watched, fascinated. Eyes wide and fearful.

Fian stood, straight as a spear, his face thin and lined with exhaustion, a wan smile on his lips. It was a long, demanding spell, calling on the magic from the depths of the otherworld itself. Not an everyday spell.

But then, this was not an everyday occurrence.

When The Queen had presented her plans two moons ago, he'd thought her touched by madness, at first. After all, such practices had been outlawed by The Great Seat for some time. Although, he was never one for adhering to the laws of the Mages! And he knew better to voice such thoughts out loud. So he began to think on it. Plan on it. And now, that plan had finally come to fruition. He allowed himself a small degree of smug satisfaction. And the timing was excellent, allowing for accelerated growth, everything should be ready in time.

Now for the test.

He turned to the overstuffed shelves on the back wall, jars and wooden boxes jostling for space, and retrieved a small, dark brown box. He placed it on the bench next to his creation and took out the small, glowing orb with a pair of wooden tongs in his gloved hands.

This would be the ultimate test.

Loshin was watching intently from the side, silent. His face unreadable.

Fian placed the orb in the hands of his creation. The reaction was immediate.

And shocking.

"Shit…" he heard Loshin mutter.

***

Queen Isiarus paced back and forth along the back wall of The Great Hall. The sun had melted into the Oran Sea some time ago, casting longer and longer shadows across Var'n Arden until night claimed the skies, the White Spire jutting upwards in the darkening gloom like a great, crooked tooth. Isiarus's patience had worn away to almost nothing as she waited for news from Fian. His assurances had given her little comfort, it had to be said. Results were all that mattered now.

The huge, dark-wooden doors at the far end creaked open, and Loshin swept in, the doors closing behind him, pulled by unseen guards. The Great Hall held a mixture of servants and guardsmen, mostly chattering aimlessly. Loshin's entrance had set them into hushed gossip. He strode across the polished floor, his long black robe sweeping the wood behind him.

"It is done, Highness." He announced with a bow of the head, dappled light from the wall sconces bouncing off his bald dome.

"…and?"

Loshin swallowed.

"It…does not work, your Highness"

The whispering stopped. The pacing stopped.

"Explain." She said through gritted teeth.

Loshin swallowed again, and she waited whilst he wiped the sweat from his over-large forehead with a cloth.

"The Orb causes…" he searched for the word. "…damage"

"What sort of damage?" Queen Isiarus turned and headed for her ornate throne on the dais at the far end of the great hall. Settling her lithe form into it, she pushed a lock of jet-black hair from her face and poured herself a much-needed goblet of Solaanian red with her right hand. She would not suffer the shame of using her left, withered as it was. She drank deeply, as Loshin mumbled and muttered about the scaring to the hands, the scales that formed, how exposure could kill it. She couldn't help but wonder how it had *failed?*

Everything had been conducted according to the scriptured texts of the great books. Everything! How could it not have worked? The scriptures were clear enough, translated from the ancient Dermal Texts by her best scholars. Her father had been laid to rest in the basement vault now for scarcely three months. If he were here, he'd say...

Actually, he probably wouldn't have said anything. Just look at her with those sad, disappointed eyes. Like the ones he used when she caught him glancing sideways at her withered left arm, thinking she hadn't seen. And she never let on. She just stored the memory away for a later date.

Like now. When everything was in place to rectify things. To make herself whole again. This plan had been a long time in the making.

And now she had nothing to show for it?

Damn that stupid mage. She would decorate the gates to the White Spire with his head!

She became aware that Loshin had stopped explaining and was awaiting her instructions. She met his gaze.

"Destroy it. It is useless to me now." she said dismissively.

Loshin bowed his domed plate once more. "Yes, Highness." Isiarus watched as he backed away a few paces before turning and heading for the door. She fought the urge to scream in frustration.

***

He descended the great staircase, thanking all the gods that things hadn't gone the way he feared they would. The last person to upset Queen Isiarus had his head decorating the outer wall for a month! He'd been watching the whole experiment with a mixture of fascination and disgust. It was an arduous spell, that much could not be denied. The kind of dark magic this had called for was not something every mage in the great seat could master.

Not that they were permitted to anyway!

Now, he mused as he entered the basement chamber, he was tasked with what to do with this...thing! He searched the dark, dimly lit chamber in the deepest bowels of the White Spire and found the *face he was looking for.*

"Aleas?" He called to a tall, bearded cavalry soldier who stood, deep in conversation with two of his unit. The man turned and stiffened abruptly.

"Sir?"

"I have a job for you…"

A short while later, Aleas cantered through the gates as they creaked closed behind him, reins in his right hand, a large brown sack held across his lap with his left. As the tall, twisted White Spire fell away behind him, he turned south and headed for the Moon Forest.

TWO

Present day.

It sat silently, high in a tall, thick tree.
Watching.
Waiting.

"Fuck me, it's dark in these woods…" Jared mumbled. He glanced over his shoulder at the undergrowth for the umpteenth time, seeing new threats in the shadows.

"Settle down, you fucking girl!" Mikael shot back without turning round.

Mikael was in the lead. Mikael was always in the lead. They'd crested the rise of gentle hills to the north some hours ago, the horses jittering as they entered Moon Forest on Mikael's insistence. Bored probably. Now, deep withing its embrace, light barely penetrated the thick, dense, canopy above, dropping the occasional leaf or twig on their brown, mottled leather tunics and breeches.

This stupid forest was getting the better of all of them, although Mik wouldn't admit it. Jared wiped a bead of sweat from his nose and looked up warily to the forest canopy. He'd mentioned the "Daemon of the Forest" on more than one occasion. Usually sitting around the fire they'd made. Usually well into their cups too, to be fair. But still, he'd argued. Surely a fire was a risk with such monsters abound? That had gone down as well as Spatz's cooking!

He looked to the left as a twig snapped somewhere in the distance. Jared spotted a crow take to the wing and let out a sigh

of relief. Bloody Moon Forest was spooking them all. Jared wasn't entirely sure what they were looking for if he was honest with himself. Lord Pehl had sent them out some days ago from camp. Instructions from The Witch Queen
herself, no doubt. Jared chuckled to himself as he followed Mik and Spatz through a knot of large oaks.

Suddenly a crash above startled the horses. Jared managed to calm his chestnut gelding as a white shape, tangled amongst the twigs and leaves it had collected in the fall, plummeted to the forest floor.

Still, it sat silently.
Watching.
Waiting.

They circled her, whooping and calling and taunting.
And threatening.

She'd tried on more than one occasion to spread her wings, their white feathers dappled with mud and leaves she'd collected as she crashed through the forest above. Wincing, she let out a curse from the forest floor.

"Come on sweet cheeks. We won't 'urt ya much!" grinned Mikael, the short, stocky of the three. His two, taller and thinner companions jeered back. Jared couldn't believe their good fortune at coming upon a real live one! Up close and personal! Her blonde hair, pulled up in a loose bun, was billowing in the morning breeze. It took his breath away. Her ivory tunic dress, mud splattered though it was, was still cleaner and better than anything he had ever seen in his twenty-one name days.

It had been a long, hard ride through the Moon Forest, Mikael's constant complaining only equalled by Spatz's stomach! A simple scouting mission it may have been, but Jared had had enough. They would definitely have a bit of fun with this stuck up bitch. Nothing less than they deserved, after all they'd done, he reasoned.

The Avian spun as best she could from the ground, trying to face them all at once.

"Leave me be, vermin!" she spat.

"Come on, darlin'." Spatz laughed, grabbing his crotch. "I got a nice present here for you."

***

The Beast sat high on a thick, knotted branch, hoping against the nature of fighting men that things would not go the way he knew they would. He could feel it in the pit of his stomach. It did not sit easily with him to watch idly as things got nasty, but it would do him little good to be spotted now, after so long hidden. His Father would not be pleased at that. Not that much pleased him at the best of times.

But he had vowed to stay away from people in general. People were complicated. Difficult.

Dangerous.

Plus, if recent events were anything to go by, he seemed cursed by nothing but bad luck.

"Bring that thing near me, and I'll bite it off!" she snarled from the ground. Loran grinned. This was a feisty one. Not like some he had watched.

"Come on girly. No need for that! We're only gonna have some fun. One way…"

There was a hiss of metal as daggers were drawn.

"…or another…!"

It landed amongst them. Before they could recover their surprise and weapons were used, all was chaos. It lashed out at the nearest, gangliest soldier, long cruel talons ripping Jared's throat out in a spray of red. Gurgling, Jared crumpled to the forest floor as it turned to Spatz who charged in, dagger raised. The beast batted his hand aside, and ripped out spatz's stomach. Blood and entrails tumbled to the dirt, and spatz followed.

It turned to Mikael and folded its black leatherette wings in across it's grey, muscular back. Long black talons jutting out from its large grey hands, it stepped menacingly forward as the colour drained from Mikael's face.

"Fuck me." Mikael mumbled, dropping the dagger and raising his trembling hands.

"Enough, enough!" he spluttered. "You have her. We were only gonna have some fun. No harm done, eh girl?" He backed away a step.

The beast reached out and took Mikael by the throat, lifting him into the air. He stopped struggling as the blood and breath was cut off from his head. The beast closed his hand and crushed the soldier's neck like he was crushing an egg.

As he let Mikael's lifeless body drop, the thing turned to the girl cowering on the floor, who let out a scream and covered her head as the thing strode toward her. She waited for the blow, but nothing happened.

She uncovered her eyes to find the beast looking at her with his head to one side.

"What are you doing?" it asked in a voice deep and liquid, like molten rock.

"I... erm..." she stammered. "I thought you were..."

The Daemon lowered his hands to help her up. The Avian took them warily, noting that the claws were now safely tucked away in the tips of his large fingers. It pulled her easily to her feet. She winced as a jolt shot up her wing.

"I mean you no harm. My name is Loran." It grumbled, dipping its head.

"I am Daynar. Princess of the Citadel, and Daughter to King Pyrus." She announced, raising her chin slightly.

"I don't know where that is..." Loran lied as he turned and unfolded his wings.

"You cannot leave me here!" she spluttered, eyes wide. "I cannot fly. I am injured" she gestured to her left wing. Two primary feathers were missing, and the joint was at a curious angle.

"So? Take a horse. They won't be needing them." He said, nodding to the bodies on the loam covered ground.

"I cannot. We don't use animals."

"Not even for Farming?"

"No. I can't ride that…thing." She said, wrinkling her nose at the very idea of clambering onto a sweaty animals' back.

"Well," said Loran, "I suggest you walk quickly. This is not a safe place to be, as you can clearly tell." He turned and headed for a clearing to depart.

"Please…" she whimpered.
He turned.

"Can't you carry me…?"

***

The scouting party of four crested the hill north of the Moon Forest and passed the outer sentry position, nodding a greeting as they rode on. They entered camp, passing rows of tents, campfires and cooking pots dotted at uneven intervals.

They reigned in at the large central tent.

"Yeah, fuck that. I'm not tellin' 'im. You tell 'im!" the eldest of the group gave the item they were carrying to the youngest. Wide eyed, he gulped and entered the tent.

Two men were bent over a large table, a map spread across it. Both dressed in a cuirass of boiled leather, the elder of the two, long dark hair and beard streaked with grey, pointed at the map and mumbled a command to Caris, his younger and shorter shield man. Conversation around the table stopped abruptly.

"Report?" The elder man snapped.

"Um. Dead, my Lord."
Pehl raised his eyebrows and waited.

"We found them in the forest. Terrible mess it was." The young soldier rambled on. "Blood and guts everywhere. Torn all to pieces they were, and…"

"By?" interrupted Caris.

"No idea, Sir. No tracks, no trace, no nuthin'." He shrugged. "We did find this though.…"
He threw the long, white primary feather on the table in front of them. It was dappled in mud and leaves.

And blood.

***

The young scout closed the tent flap behind him and headed for the nearest cooking pot and a flagon of ale, his companions full of questions. Inside the tent, Lord Pehl examined the long, white feather on his table.

Were they getting braver? Those bird-brained Avian bastards were never afraid of getting their hands dirty, that was for sure.

But this? This was something else entirely.

Maybe Pyrus was finally growing a pair! He'd seen the Avian King only briefly, and then from a distance.

But Pehl had little doubt that he'd changed since they were small. His memory of that time was scarce.

But not *that* scarce!

"What does it mean, my Lord?" asked Caris. He picked up the white primary feather, turning it in his fingers and wiping the blood off on his cuirass.

"Who knows." Mumbled Pehl. "But I do know I'm hungry. Have some food sent in."

"Yes, My Lord." Caris dropped the feather back down, then turned and headed for the tent flap.

"And send my son in." Bellowed Pehl after him.

***

Caylen trudged through camp toward his Fathers tent. More summons. More mundane nonsense no doubt. Perish the thought of something he could really get his teeth into!

By the gods, he was fucking bored! He could do nothing right for his father of late, temperamental old shit that he was becoming. This Path they had been on for what seemed an eternity was becoming an obsession.

As he trudged past a campfire, he overheard tales from the young scout who had returned. He'd heard the same story earlier, only this time there were more embellishments of his meeting with Father. More shouting, angrier words. The usual stuff that accompanied soldiers and ale. He was sure some of it were true, nonetheless. He'd had enough shouting matches with his father to know that the old man's temper could turn like the tide. Mostly in his direction.

Caylen entered the tent as his father was ripping the leg off of...actually he wasn't quite sure what it was.

"You sent for me?" he yawned

"I did. Time to get your hands dirty, boy."

Caylen raised his eyebrows.

"Time to attack out feathered friends..."

Caylen grinned and grabbed a leg of whatever it was they were eating.

THREE

Deep in the moon forest, a dappled grey mare was tethered to a tree, happily munching on the grass growing around its roots. A campfire burned merrily away, a pot of rabbit stew bubbling on the spit above it as the fire pushed away the twilight.

Aleas knelt on the ground and opened the brown sack. With a slight hiss of steel, he unsheathed his dagger. A crow cawed in the distance, and the trees above rustled with the gentle northern breeze that had followed him all afternoon.

He stared down at it. The wind and his breathing the only sound.
Until it let out a soft cry. Until it looked up at him.

Aleas lowered the dagger to the ground. Thoughts of his past, present and future flooded his mind. His time as a soldier. His family that should have been.
Elise.

What would she say, if she were here now, watching him? Would her large, green eyes stare at him accusingly? Would she tut in that disapproving click she always did, like when he forgot to thank a street vendor, or belched in public without thinking?
What would she think of him?

Damn it all, he was a soldier now. That life was over. He'd made the choice, after what happened. He alone. And he was a fucking good soldier.
So why couldn't he get her face out of his mind...?
Aleas stared at it for what seemed an age.

"...Bollocks..." he finally mumbled, and wrapped the package back up, leaving its head clear.

FOUR

They were high. Higher than she'd flown before. A chill of gooseflesh raised on her skin, a slight shiver running down her spine. She tried to ignore the pain screaming from her wing joint. Daynar looked up at the Daemon and took in the sight before her.

It was tall. Very tall. A good couple of heads taller than her father, King Pyrus, easily. Its skin grey and scaled across its huge back and shoulders, down the arms and legs, muscles large and taut. Hairless, it had pointed ears, a ridged forehead and two small black horns atop its head. Large black claws jutted out from the ends of his hands and feet. She took in the muscular thighs, and the single loincloth covering his 'area' as mother would have said, a bone handled dagger at his belt. Loran had lifted her easily, the muscles in his arms and back barely tensing as he cradled her to his grey scaled body like a child holds a pup. She looked over his shoulder at his large, midnight-black wings, stretched out behind him like a corsair's sails.

Daynar turned her attention forward again. The flat, crescent-shaped tree line of the moon forest that its name came from was far below them now. To the south, the white, cannulated walls of the Citadel stretched out. The Market square was in the process of closing up, and she could just make out people heading to Old Gillen's Tavern. The round, ruddy faced taverner would be quipping jokes and listening to the day's tall tales, no doubt. Daynar closed her eyes and tried not to think about the reception they would receive.

It was not her fault. That's what she'd say.
It was not her fault that her mind was so full of thoughts and

images of…
No.
She couldn't say that. Definitely not. She'd have to make something up, that was all. She certainly couldn't admit what she was really doing out above the forest. Alone.

Spying.
She cursed the forest, the outcasts and her stupidity.
Mostly her stupidity.

Yet another occasion when she had disobeyed her father and regretted it. But she felt more and more trapped of late. Her brother Isaac had no such problems. His attentions were on his studies and the temple elders.
How could she have spent so much time, peering through the trees, her heart quickening, breath catching in her throat at the sight?
How could she not? She'd known it was wrong for a while, to feel the way she did, but something about it felt so… right.

***

Loran looked far below him at the Citadel as they passed high over its pale outer wall, guarded by archers along its length. Each wore a highly polished breastplate that wrapped around their wing roots at the back, and greaves of steel. Plumed helms covered their long blond hair. At the corners the wall was broken by tall towers, each topped with a huge crossbow that shot an arrow longer than a man. Loran glanced down at the wall guards, some shielding their eyes against the evening sky to see who or what was flying in overhead, far from arrow range.

He'd watched these people before, fascinated. Even heard tell of this place once or twice from Father. Tales and myth mostly. Fables and yarns, doubtless to keep him away. As he was kept away from most things.

But the Moon Forest was empty and quiet. So very quiet. Despite all these beings' faults, he'd envied them as he watched from the forest, his keen eyes seeing smiles and camaraderie. His sharp ears picking out talk, and laughter.

He wasn't used to laughter.

And now, for his conscience, here he was about to let people see the "Forest Daemon," or whatever such hokum they were calling him lately.

He would often sit high in the tallest, thickest trees, listening to merchants, thieves, vagabonds, and soldiers cantering through. Children who ventured to the moon pool to bathe. How scary he was. What they thought he looked like, which seemed to change on a daily basis.

I should have let them have her, he thought ruefully. Knowing full well that he never would have.

***

"We can't find her anywhere, Sire!" Remus removed his plumed helm and ran a hand through his long blond locks.

"Well, she must be exactly somewhere, doing exactly something!" Blustered King Pyrus. He looked skyward as flocks of soldiers flitted about the sky in various directions searching parts of the Citadel that had been searched already. King Pyrus smoothed his own hair, his own blond hair streaked with grey and tied at the neck with a white band.

"I'll try the Great Temple again." Remus started off toward the domed structure at the heart of the Citadel.

"The Acolytes are searching it still. Try the Medical rooms again." Commanded the king.

"Aye, Sire"

Damn that girl and her fool adventures. Too much of her mother in her, no doubt. Too proud and haughty to be told how she should behave. As a princess of the Citadel was expected to present herself. And now, only the gods knew where she could be. If those outcast thieves had hurt her…

Somewhere in the distance a child screamed. Sky soldiers shouted and gestured to the king. He turned toward where they were pointing.

Loran landed amongst them.

More children screamed and ran, soldiers landing, some running. All bearing arms. A hundred bows were turned on him from the battlements of the wall, lances bearing down on him from the ground.

"HOLD!" King Pyrus yelled.
All was still for a heartbeat.

"This young lady is injured." The Daemon rumbled. "She will need assistance?"
King Pyrus pointed to the Medical building without taking his eyes off the thing in front of him.

Loran strode to the long, single storey building with a red cross on its roof. He took the three stairs in a single stride and kicked open both double doors.

Malaner the healer turned to the doors, the child seated in front of him staring wide eyed, his scraped knee all but forgotten.

"She is hurt." Loran nodded to her left wing. "The wing is broken, and some feathers are missing." Malaner nodded his thinning blond head and gestured to a bed along the back wall, his eyes never leaving the beast towering over him. Loran lowered her gently and she winced as her wing joint sent fresh jolts of pain down her back.

"Can you help her?" He asked, backing away, careful not to knock the myriad of bottles and jars off the shelves on the wall with his wings.

"Should be able to. The primary feathers will grow back in time. Wing will need setting though." The healer mumbled, looking closely.

"How did this happen? What have you done to my child, you monstrous animal…?" Thundered King Pyrus from the doorway, wingtips twitching in rage.

"Father, no!" Daynar said. "He helped me. If not for Loran I would have…" she left the sentence unspoken. King Pyrus cleared his throat. Loran looked beyond the old king at the two winged warriors in the doorway bearing lances. They were facing in, watching him intently.

"Yes, well…" said King Pyrus. "I'm sure you're a very busy…" he cleared his throat again. Whatever this thing was, it clearly did not belong in his Citadel, with his people. Outsiders were not welcomed at the best of times, and then usually only traders.

"You cannot let him leave now, Father! It is nearly nightfall." Daynar protested from the cot bed, wincing again as Malaner tried to reset the wing joint.

"It is not a worry, Princess. I can see perfectly well in the dark." Loran took one last look around, nodded, and walked to the door, the guards parting quickly to let the towering Daemon through.

***

"She will be ok?" Loran asked once outside. his voice low and rumbling.

"Yes." Said the old King. "And now you must leave. You cannot stay here."
Loran turned and headed to the market square, taking in his surroundings.

Low, single storey dwellings shot off in various directions from the central square, torches flickering on the walls every twenty or so paces, casting their pale orange glow across the stonework. Directly in front of the market was a large high towered palace, guards in plumed helms bearing lances outside the large main gates. Opposite this, across the square was a large, white building with a high, domed roof of opaque glass and a pillared entrance. Loran could almost sense a low, deep power from within. Outside this there were more guards, only these ones were different. They wore no armour that Loran could see, only long ivory cloaks over their tunics, gold thread woven in detail at the hems and fastened with a golden clasp. They were completely bald, no trace of blond hair at all.

And they were wingless.
He'd watched this place many times from the treetops. It seemed

to be all the things that the Moon Forest was not.
He didn't belong here.

Loran turned to find King Pyrus looking at him, eyebrows raised. Without a word, he took to the air, great black wings stretching wide, the Citadel falling fast below him. He took in a great gulp of air as if breathing for the first time. Ah, but it felt good to be up here. Away from people, winged or otherwise.
He wasn't really an admirer of people.

He took one last look at the Citadel, tiny now. Fledgling children and adults alike were watching from the ground, guards following him from the battlement wall. Loran turned north, back towards the Moon Forest, hungry for its seclusion.

He skirted the western edge of the great treeline, the vast painted scrublands of The Desolation coming into view off to the west. Well, his view anyway. Far superior to anything or anyone else. He shivered slightly at the memory of his time there in hiding. From those that would harm him, and his father. He turned back toward the trees when something caught his eye.

Horses. Three riders coming through the forest, and not slowly, carefully, as he might have expected at this twilight hour. But quickly.
Very quickly.

Loran stopped flapping his great black wings and stretched them wide, gliding soundlessly over the treetops. To his right, far on the other side of the forest, his sharp eyes picked out three more riders.
Galloping.

He swooped slowly to the west, The Desolation all but vanished in the darkening light. As he swept toward a great, wide tree trunk, Loran stuck out his hands and feet to absorb the impact. The claws on his huge fingers and wide, splayed feet extended to grip the gnarled trunk as his wings folded in.

In the distance, on the edge of the forest was a small camp of soldiers. Three tents, a couple of wains pulled by great bull aurochs. Campfires, horses. And men. With sharp ears, he picked up laughing, jeering, the usual camp noises he had heard as he'd watched, ever hidden, from his treetop in the past.

But why, or more importantly, where? Where were those riders heading at such speed in the dark? They must be scouts surely, but at sundown? It made little sense. The camp, at least, showed no sign of moving off just yet. Loran looked over his shoulder, tracing the path both sets of horses seemed to be taking.

With wide eyes, it dawned on him that both paths came out of the woods either side of the same place.

The Citadel.

***

"You foolish, spoilt girl!" King Pyrus raged from the foot of her cot bed. "What in the name of L'shaan were you thinking, bringing that…thing here?"

"I had little choice father. "Mumbled Daynar, her head lowered. "I was injured. Loran…"

"…Should never have seen you, or any of us. How are we expected to protect the purity of our people when you put yourself at risk by…"? He trailed off, furrowing his eyebrows.

"What exactly *were* you doing?"

She mumbled, and stuttered about exploring the forest, her father running a hand through his greying blond locks as she apologised for clipping a tall tree. The soldiers. Loran.
King Pyrus shook his head slowly.

"If your mother were here…"
Well, she's not, thought Daynar.
Thanks to you.

"She needs to rest, Sire." Malaner said from the corner of the room. Pyrus harumphed, but conceded, nonetheless. He bent forward and kissed his daughter on the top of her sweat stained blond hair. As he left the low building, he posted two guards on the door.

Isaac was waiting for him a few spans from the steps. The king caught his sons eyes and nodded with a wan smile.

Isaac smiled back enthusiastically, his mop of curly blond hair billowing gently.

"Thank all the Gods I won't have such problems with you flying off and getting into trouble, my boy." He said quietly.

"I'd have trouble flying anywhere, father." chuckled Isaac, motioning to his wingless back.

"You're nearly ready for your vows?" they fell into step together, heading across the square for evening prayers at the temple.

"I am." He said, with as much conviction as he could muster. He tucked his hands into his ivory cloak, trimmed with black, as were all novice acolytes. Soon, as he took his vows to guard the Seraph, they would shave his head, and he would receive his cloak of ivory and gold. The King looked to his right and spotted Remus heading toward them.

"Excuse me, my son. I will join you presently." He said with a smile.

A smile that disappeared as Isaac headed toward The Temple.

"Sire....?" Remus began.

"If that thing, whatever it was, ever sets foot in our Citadel again, Lord Commander...." He hissed.

"Yes Sire?"

"Kill it!"

Remus Held his Kings gaze a heartbeat.

"But Sire...?"

"Kill It! How can we be expected to protect the purity of The Devine Gift with such monsters invading our walls? Your orders are clear, Lord Commander. If it returns, I want it dead."

Remus gave a curt nod and headed toward the crenulated outer wall to make his rounds, as he did every evening before prayers.

Pyrus watched him leave, then turned and followed his son to The Temple. He would do whatever it took to protect the divine gift, whatever the cost. His path was clear, as was his fathers before him. He had travelled too far down it to be interrupted now.

Purity was everything. Everything they had strived to protect and promote was at stake, and he would not see it threatened.

***

The over-large dark wooden doors swung inward on invisible hands, and the tall, painfully thin form of Loshin appeared in the arched doorframe.

"Her highness will see you now." He announced, turning on his heels and clipping back into the throne room.

About bloody time, thought Pehl. Although he had long since learnt to keep such slips of the tongue to himself. He still shuddered at having witnessed some of her Highnesses more colourful ways of disposing of those who had annoyed her. Or had simply outlived their usefulness.

She wasn't known as The Witch Queen for nothing, although it seemed to him that her mage did more of the magicking than she ever did.

He rose from his hard, wooden seat out in the corridor. I feel more like a youngster every time I see this cursed woman.

"Ah, my Lord Pehl. How are things progressing?" she was sitting in a high, ornate chair, on a raised dais at the end of the room. Her midnight black hair pulled back into a high ponytail; her sharp nose raised slightly as if the air had an unpleasant smell. Pehl came to a stop in front of the throne, and gave a polite nod, Sande and Rhyl either side of him following suit, Sande's long brown plait spilling over her shoulder.

"As well as can be expected, your highness. These things take time, obviously."

"Time is a luxury I am fast running out of if I am to perform the ritual according to the ancient texts. I have waited long enough as it is. Timing is everything, you understand. Everything!" she snapped.

"Yes indeed, your Highness. Alas, it has taken longer than I anticipated to train my warriors and get them ready for an all-out assault on The Citadel. To rush it would mean almost certain slaughter. I have not spent these last twenty years in hiding to watch everyone I care for cut down like crops." Sande reached out and touched his hand with her own in warning.

"Watch your tone, outcast. I am not a patient woman. And I've been more than patient wating to convert this useless appendage into something worthwhile." She said, nodding to her withered arm. "And I will get what I want, sooner rather than later."

"Indeed, Highness. I meant no disrespect." He nodded again. Tiptoeing around this woman's ego and temper was something he had grown accustomed to. She took a long sip of dark red wine, replacing the chalice on a small table to her right.

"Besides, I wouldn't have thought those winged idiots would give you too much trouble?"

"Don't underestimate them, your Highness. It seems they're getting braver in recent times." He told her about the blood-spattered feather his men had bought from the forest, having found the three blood-soaked bodies of their colleagues. She listened with a disinterested air.

"Yes, yes. I'm sure you can handle them. Just get me what I want."

"And I have your word? My men and I will be looked after? Taken care of properly?"

"Yes, my Lord, as agreed." She picked up the goblet again, smiling.

"Trust me."

FIVE

Evening prayers had finished, and King Pyrus was making gentle chit chat with several ladies from the Citadel. Isaac was looking more like an acolyte each day. He must be very proud. And what of Daynar? No suitors yet?

No, no suitor brave enough to put up with her. He smiled and gave the same pleasant answers he always gave. Plenty of time for that. The usual nonsense. His daughter's apparent disinterest for suitors to be bound to was something of a sore point between them. It seemed she had little interest at all in being bound to another. Making his excuses he left quickly, heading toward the forum building that adjoined the medical one. He would meet with his generals before stopping in on Daynar.

Isaac trotted down the stairs and joined his father.

"Off to see Daynar, Father?" he fell into step alongside.

"No, not yet my son. Business to attend to as usual. We must strive to fortify our defences in case those rebels get any more ideas. Daynar's attack was just the start, I fear."

"And what of the Daemon? He was certainly something." Pyrus stopped and rounded on his son.

"Yes, but I'm not sure what, exactly. Nor do I wish to find out. That thing must never be allowed back here again."

He started off again toward the forum.

"But Father?" Isaac protested, hurrying to catch up. "I don't think he means us any harm."

"Really? Expert on such monsters, are we? Required learning in the Temple teaching halls, is it?" he snapped.

"Well, no but…"

"You of all people, as a Novice, should appreciate the need to protect all we are, and all we stand for here, Isaac."

"Yes father." He conceded, dropping his eyes. Pyrus shook his head imperceptibly. Isaac was still so impetuous, and at times even naive.

So unlike Meryl.

There was a rush of wind from above, and Loran landed in front of them both. Armed guards came rushing forward, and archers from the walls turned and trained their bows on the Daemon for the second time that day.

Up on the battlement wall, Remus stared down at the towering grey form in front of the King, and the only remaining Prince. To his left, an archer looked across at him.

"Do we loose sir?" he asked, arrow notched, and bowstring taught. Remus didn't answer at first.

"Sir?"

"Hmm?" He turned to the archer. "No. Hold position. It's too close to the King." Word was passed along the walls, and arms quivered slightly as bowstrings remained taught.

The hairs on the back of Remus's neck stood on end.

On the ground, guards with Lances were standing in a circle, weapons trained at the Daemon like a dozen porcupine quills, ready to advance. As king Pyrus began to bluster, Loran pointed to the Moon Forest to the north.

"Soldiers." He rumbled

"What? Where?"

"Two scouting parties outside the wall and a dozen or so camped in the woods."

Remus rushed over, panting from the hasty decent of the west tower stairs.

"Sire. Stand back." He slid his sword from the scabbard on his weapons belt.

"It seems we have a raiding party on our doorstep, Lord Commander. Take a dozen men and dispatch with the scouts outside."

"That won't be necessary…" Loran said quietly.
Isaac noticed blood drip from Loran's claws and splatter on the stone floor of the square. Loran met his gaze, almost apologetically.

"I see. Well." Began Pyrus.

"You should go." Urged Remus. Loran looked from Isaac to the plumed helmet of the Lord Commander of King Pyrus's Army. They held each other's gaze uneasily.

Finally, Loran nodded.

"No."
All turned to look at King Pyrus.

"You've seen fit to give us this warning, the least we can do is offer you some food and drink, and rest for the night?"

"But Sire?" began Remus. "What of the raiding party?"

"They are well bedded down for the night. They show no signs of moving out just yet." Said Loran, turning to the King. "My guess is they'll attack at first light."

The king nodded his agreement and turned to his son.

"Isaac, why don't you take our friend here to the feast hall and find him some food and drink, hmm?"

"Er, yes Father…" the young novice said, a blank look on his face. As he wandered off toward the entrance to the Palace of Sh'Bal, Remus sheathed his sword and leant in close to the king.

"But Sire, you orders…"

"Yes, I know, Lord Commander. But it seems his acute night vision may come in handy tonight. And with any luck, if he sticks around tomorrow, Pehl's brigands will kill him for us!"

***

As they walked off together toward the palace's feast hall, Loran towering over the young novice at his side, an uneasy tension built between them.

What do I say to him? How do you start a conversation with…well, that? It's not like anyone listens to me anyway, not much. Not since Meryl perished.

"Erm. Father seems to have had a change of heart?" he stammered, not daring to lift his eyes to the Daemon at his side. Faces in windows gawped open mouthed at the strange sight heading toward the palace, children pointing and staring.
Loran turned his face away from the youngsters quickly.

"Not really." He said, his voice low and liquid. "Your Father is hoping I am killed on the morrow."

"What makes you say that?" Isaac now raised his eyes and looked at Loran, who tapped his pointed ear with a large, squat finger.

"You can hear them? From here? Really?" Loran nodded in reply, smiling for the first time in a long while at the youngsters awestruck look of wonder.

"My hearing and eyesight are much stronger than yours. Smell too. Fresh bread, if I'm not mistaken?" he said, nodding to the feast halls doors.

"Yes, more likely. And a trencher of fine stew to go with it. Do you eat stew, erm, what do I call you?"

"My name is Loran, and yes. I eat most things. Except people, contrary to what most believe."

Isaac laughed, and Loran joined him, a low rumbling chuckle, relaxing a little despite the glares aimed in his direction.

"If you don't mind me asking, why are you without wings, my young friend?" Loran asked, nodding to his back.
Friend, Isaac thought. No one calls me that.

"I am a novice acolyte of the temple. We surrender our wings in order to guard the Seraph."

"Seraph?"

"Yes, the Seraph is a dark-magic orb of power that gives us our gift of flight." He nodded a greeting to two passing ladies in white, blonde hair pulled back into ponytails. They simply stared up at Loran.

"So, you have given up this gift?"
Isaac nodded as they walked.

"Does it not hurt?"

"Oh, I was but a bairn. I expect so, for a while." He answered with a sudden faraway look in his eyes.

"You did not make this choice freely...?" Loran stopped suddenly.

"Well. no, but..." Isaac was unsure how much he should tell this stranger, especially as he had asked himself these questions many times before, in quiet moments of contemplation in the temple. Times when he should have been praying or meditating. Or studying. And questions he had long since stopped asking the King. His father had made his choice long ago, little knowing that Meryl would cross the bridge as he did. And now, the prospect of Daynar the spoilt daydreamer becoming the queen was almost laughable. But what choice did they have if things were to continue as they did?
Father certainly wouldn't have wanted me to be king.

"...it is an honour." He said as proudly as he could. Many times, he'd wondered what he might have become had this honour not been bestowed upon him at birth. It would have been nice to be given the choice, but it was an honour. Yes. Definitely an honour.

"I do not understand how this "Gift" is given by this... Seraph?" They continued walking toward the Feast Hall.

"The divine Goddess L'Shaan bestowed our gift upon us using The Seraph when we were created for her purpose." He said, almost reciting the scriptures word for word.

"Purpose?" Loran pressed him.

"Aye. We were her army during the century wars. The wars of Gods and men and beasts. We were set free by her when the Supreme God Vororr was victorious. The scriptures hang in the Temple." Perhaps they could have a quick look before the king got wind of it. He still wasn't too sure just how at home he should make their new visitor. But then, father did say to make him welcome! That's all he was doing, surely?

They entered the two great, dark doors of the palace, the

guards on the doors watching them uneasily. As they entered the feast hall all conversation stopped.

Loran sat alone at a long, empty bench, his wings draped over the back, as Isaac went to fetch a bowl of fresh bread, and two dark trenchers of stew. He sat opposite his new companion, totally ignorant of the sideways glances they were getting. Isaac stared at the Daemon sat across from him in wonder.

"Where are you from?" he asked at last between mouthfuls of stew. Had he been in the temple he would have earned himself a cuff on the ear from one of the elders for talking at mealtimes. Suddenly that seemed less important somehow.

Loran laughed gently and broke off a piece of bread.

"I'm not really sure, I'm afraid. I have asked the question many times of my Father, but his answer is a little sketchy at best."

"Father? You mean there are others like you?"

"No, my friend. I call him my father, as he raised me and cared for me. Taught me to survive. As a father teaches and cares for a son. But I am not of his birth, or anyone's that I know of."

They ate in companionable silence, Loran finishing sooner than the novice. He placed his huge hand over his mouth, as if to belch, then seemed to think the better of it.

As they left, Isaac nodded to the guards on the door. They returned it, watching them leave.

"Let's find you a bed for the night, shall we?" Isaac headed off to the side street on his left.
Loran did not follow.

"Something wrong?" he asked, returning to the Daemon's side. Loran was looking at the temple, its domed roof lit from inside, two temple acolytes guarding the door.

"It's in there." He said quietly. It wasn't a question.

"Yes…"

"I can feel it. Power. Energy." He looked down at the young Novice.

"I must see it.

SIX

The two acolytes on the doors were unsure at first what action to take. The novice alone was strange enough at this late hour. But being accompanied by a huge grey Daemon seemed to leave them stumped. They protested and blustered to Isaac as they entered. Loran ignored all three of them and walked, unchallenged, into the temple.

There were rows of wooden benches arranged either side of the central aisle, with a white, raised dais at the head. On it was a column of bronze about waist height, to a normal person at least. Floating above this was the Seraph.

Suspended in mid-air, the Orb was larger than he expected. About the width of a horse. It's white-blue light flickered and pulsed with a web of dark magic energy, like a million ants crawling across its surface.

Loran stared at it blankly. All thought of Isaac, the acolytes, the king, were gone. Any thought seemed gone.
There was just the Seraph.

He could feel its energy pulsing deep within the base of his skull, pushing against his chest like an ocean wave. Could hear the gentle but incessant hum coming from it, like a thousand angry voices buzzing inside his head. And something else. Something he couldn't quite put his finger on.

Darkness. That was the only word he could find. A darkness that seemed to pull at him, deep within. He was aware of voices, raised and urgent, but far away. Of people. Of Isaac. But at the same time, of nothing.
Nothing but the Seraph.

***

Brianne walked into the temple, as she did most evenings. Mainly to avoid people and small talk. Only this time something was wrong. Very wrong.

She stared at the back of the Daemon, great, black wings folded in across his wide, muscular back. She'd heard people gossiping in the square about this strange intruder, but dismissed it as fantasy. She tightened the white scarf around her bobbed, blonde hair and strode forward to where Isaac was frantically trying to shake Loran from his reverie.

"What's he doing?" She asked the young acolyte. The Daemon was only a span from the Seraph now.

"I'm not sure. He insisted on seeing it but..."
Loran stretched his hand out.

"NO!" they shouted in unison.

Loran looked down at this new intruder for the first time, and Brianne caught her breath at his bright blue eyes. She'd expected them to be black, somehow.

"You must not touch it. It will kill you." She took his arm, Isaac the other, and they steered him outside, the acolytes still fussing and flustering.

Once outside the temple doors, Loran seemed to waken from his trance. He smiled slowly at her. Her hair was bobbed and covered with a scarf, ivory tunic dress edged in dark red.

"The Gods only know what you're grinning at, you idiot!" she raged. "You could have been killed. No man may touch the Seraph and live."

"I am not a man" he said quietly, his voice deep and thick.

"No. That I can plainly see. Nevertheless…"

"We should get you to a bed for the night." Isaac insisted. Loran looked down at his new friend and nodded.

"Where are you putting him?" Brianne asked as they strode off together.

"Twenty-three. Its unoccupied at present."

"Very well. I'll see to it. You should get back to your

studies." Isaac conceded unhappily and stuck out his hand. Loran looked down at it and frowned.

"You shake it!" Isaac laughed.

"Why?"

"I don't know. Just good manners, I think. Here. Like this." He shook hands with the Daemon. "I'll no doubt see you on the morrow."

Loran watched the young novice acolyte walk away toward the temple and turned to his new companion.

"Brianne." She said simply and started walking off toward the side street Isaac had headed toward earlier. Loran followed, catching up within a few strides of his much-longer legs.

"So, are you a warrior too?" he asked, somewhat awkwardly.

"Hah!" she scoffed. "Women are not warriors around here, more's the pity. No. I am a tutor. I tell the Fledglings about our history, and traditions. Numbers, letters. The usual stuff I suppose."

"That's good. Isn't it?" they headed down the side street, dark now but for the wall sconces every twenty paces or so. A few quizzical looks from windows, but Loran appeared not to notice. Brianne paused a beat.

"I suppose so, yes."

"But you'd rather be something else?"

"Sometimes. But we all must perform our given roles to the best of our ability."

He was quiet a moment.

"I see…"

They stopped outside a squat, brown, single storey dwelling with a white door. Unlike it's neighbour's, there were no flowers. No drapes at the window. Inside was a table and chairs, and a bed.

"It's not much, I'm afraid. But it will give you somewhere to rest until the morrow."

"It's perfectly adequate, thank you." He said with a small

nod of the head. Brianne turned to leave, then stopped at the door.

"Why are you helping us?" she asked without turning around. "Not that we aren't grateful, but I'm curious. Why? Why now, when we've been at war with Pehl for so many years?"

"Because you need it." He said simply. There was silence for a beat.

Brianne turned to look at him.

"You're not at all what I expected. For a Daemon." She smiled.

"Nor you I. In truth, despite what I told your princess earlier, I have watched your people from afar for some time. Your customs and ways seem strange to me, as I must to you."

"You're not as scary as I thought you'd be. You know, listening to the stories and tall tales."

"I'm not naturally violent, despite appearances. Unless I'm forced to be." His said, his smile fading somewhat.

"Well," she said turning to leave. "I must let you rest. Until the morrow, Loran."

"Until then, Brianne." He smiled again as he said her name.

She held his gaze a beat, then closed the door behind her. Loran rushed to the window to watch her walk back up the darkened alley. He smiled again, in spite of himself.

***

Josten stamped his feet and gave his wings a quick flutter against the cold night air. He stood alone on the south wall, the nearest guard to him at the southwest tower. Remus and his bright ideas! But then, he supposed, it made sense to send most of the guards to the north wall where the raid would most likely come. His breath steamed in front of him, and he warmed his hands on it. K'Lahl was fast approaching, the rains threatening daily and preparations for The Festival of L'Shaan had not really begun in earnest. Still so much to do. They could ill afford to get bogged down with recent events.

And, by all the Gods, had recent events been busy? Certainly, he'd seen nothing like it in his thirty-four summers. He stretched his wings and gave their white tips another flutter against the chill night air, checking his sword and looking over his bow for the twelfth or thirteenth time. This cold could easily freeze a sword in its scabbard.

The Daemon! Actually here? He shook his head at the thought of it. After the speculation and argument as to whether the thing existed at all, or was but a myth, the great grey monster was actually in The Citadel. And he'd actually seen it! Striding into the feast hall with that short streak of a novice prince for company, of all people. Sitting, bold as you like, stuffing his face.

He should have gone over, said hello. He'd wanted to, all the lads on his watch jeering him on but his nerves had got the better of him. Pop always said he should speak up more. Be more forward, lad, he'd say. You can't afford to let others…

A noise behind him made Josten swing around, reaching for his sword.

"Gods, Kall. You nearly got your stupid throat cut!"

Kall stepped out of the dark corner into the light from a wall sconce and snorted a laugh.

"From you? That'll be the day, Jost!" chuckled the youngster.

In truth Kall was a much quicker swordsman than Josten, having proved his mettle on the training corner many a time. Josten had always preferred the bow himself. If nothing else, it gave him an excuse to fly and fight, which he always thought was a natural advantage to a winged warrior, after all. Sadly, not everybody shared his ideas.

"So? What brings you to the wall?" he asked.
Kall was quiet a beat.

"You must be kidding? Now? With so much going on, you want me to turn a blind eye? Tonight, of all nights?"

"I just need half an hour, friend, that's all!" He pleaded to the older warrior, tugging his dark cloak around his tunic, wings sticking out the slotted back, almost luminescent in the dark night.

"No"

"But Jost...?"

"No. Remus will have my hide if you're caught. And yours too, you half-wit. Where do you keep going at such a late hour that's so damn important anyway?"

"Just half an hour, I promise. Give me that at least, eh?"

"I must want my head looked at." He shook it and sighed. He did, in all honesty, quite like the young pup. Impetuous, and sometimes foolhardy. But seven hells of a swordsman. And one he'd like at his back in a battle.

"Half an hour, then I sound the alarm." He turned away as Kall stepped up onto the wall, stretched his wings out, and fluttered down the wall to the ground.

I'll have an ale or two at Gillen's out of him for this, thought Josten.

***

Kall landed softly on the damp grass, and scurried away to the south. He headed to a clump of large bushes, The Citadel large and dark behind him.

"You're late!" she hissed.

"I know. I can't just slip out the main gate, you know! Have patience."

Sande strode toward the winged warrior, his hood up, shrouding his blonde locks and sharp features in shadow. She jabbed her spear in the ground, threw her own hood back from her long, dark ponytail and melted into his arms, their lips meeting in a long, breathless kiss.

"By all the Gods, I've missed you, my love" she sighed.

"It's only been a couple of days, my sweet." He smiled a large, boyish grin at her.

"A couple of hours is too much, Kall. Can't we get away from all this?"

"If only, my darling. If only."

They'd talked about it many a time. In truth they both knew if would scarce ever happen. Pehl, for all his faults, probably would let her leave and find her way in life alone. After much arguing, cajoling, bribery, threats and pleading!

Pyrus, on the other hand…

"I don't have long." She whispered. "Caylen is preparing for the morrow. You will stay safe, won't you Kall? I couldn't bear it if anything happened to you because of me, or…" Her eyes moistened.

"Now, now. None of that." He wiped a tear away and kissed her again. "We both know the risks. We've spoke of this often enough. You do what you must. And so will I."

"I love you so much…" she breathed as she melted into his arms again.

***

Isaac nodded his greeting to the acolytes on the temple doors and slipped inside. The temple was dark and deserted. He crossed the floor as quietly as he could, staring all the while at the seraph.

Trying to see just what had mesmerised the Daemon so.

It seemed to take over his very being. Isaac had not seen that reaction before from an Avian.

But then, Loran was anything but an Avian!

"Isaac?" Eral the temple elder called from across the aisle. Isaac cursed under his breath.

"What brings a novice here at such a late hour?"

"I wanted to check a couple of texts in the temple vaults, if I may?" he swallowed hard.

"And it could not wait until the morrow?" Eral crossed the aisle and stood in front of him, his thin yellow hair matching his thin expression. He raised his eyebrows and waited.

"I have many lessons tomorrow and I fear the moment may be lost to me. I will be but a short while." He pressed, hoping that the elder would not refuse the King's son, novice or not.

Finally, Eral relented, standing to one side.

"Very well," he said, "But only a short while. I have preparations to make before morning prayers."

"Thank you, Eral." Isaac yelled over his shoulder as he darted into a door in the corner of the temple.

Inside was a stone spiral staircase leading down. Isaac descended slowly. He'd only been down here in the vaults a couple of times and much preferred the main library in the forum. The room was dark and dank, and smelled of old water. Thick books lined every wall, a caged off section separating the rear.

He spent more time than he meant to searching various tomes and textbooks.
Surely, there must be something on beings of Loran's kind somewhere. There had to be.
He couldn't be the only one ever!

Finally, after an age, he closed the last book and rubbed the bridge of his nose. It was a wonder old Eral hadn't come down to chase him out before now. Hopefully, he'd forgotten Isaac was even there!
There had to be something from the ancient texts that mentioned…

Isaac looked up at the end of the dimly lit chamber. The closed off section was forbidden to all but the temple elders. It was never locked, the threat of expulsion deemed enough to discourage the nosey.

Isaac crossed the floor, his heart thumping, and opened the cage door as quietly as he could, listening for footsteps on the stairwell.

He chose a thick, ancient Dermal text. Translating dermal to his native tongue wasn't easy, the curly, cursive script melding and blurring as the hour got ever later.
Isaac stared at the page he was on for a long, long time.

***

Kall fluttered down the inside of the wall to a dark alleyway and took off his cloak. Folding it, he hid it behind the barrels at the rear of Gillen's tavern and walked out, turning left into another alley.

Brianne was standing in front of him.

"My lady? What a pleasant..."

"Spare me, halfwit! Are you mad? You know full well what goes on here this night and yet you risk all by meeting up with your mercenary little lover? You could have been taken as hostage. Anything could have happened that would risk the Citadel"

"Keep your voice down." He hissed. "I've been but half an hour, no more. Nobody knew I was even there. "

"I did."

"There are no spies in Caylen's camp that she knows of."

"That she knows of! The whole point of spies is that you don't know, fool!" She stuck her hands on her hips.

"Enough! I am not a fledgling child to be lectured by you, my lady. Turn me in if you must, but there are more important secrets to be kept than mine, I think. No?"

She held his gaze a beat, then stepped aside. Kall strode past her down the dark alleyway to his dwelling. She watched him go, cursing quietly.

Loran stepped back into the shadows of his dim, sparse room as the winged warrior swept past his window. This Citadel was becoming more interesting by the day!

He'd been awake since she left, and to hear her voice again was almost making him giddy, angry though she clearly was with this warrior. He'd sat in a hard wooden chair, it's back low to allow his wings to fold over the top of it, thinking on what he should do. Whether to leave or stay. His very existence seemed cursed to the point of ridicule. Maybe the Gods were having a joke at his expense. Thoughts tumbled in his head, Faces, he'd known, now gone.
Because of him.

In truth, he'd thought long and hard on whether or not to

simply take off and leave these people to their war. It was not, after all, his battle to fight. But the loneliness and quiet of the forest had left him needing company more than he'd realised.

He knew he wouldn't sleep this night. Not here, at least. Soft beds were for soft, normal people. He'd taken to the floor in the end, staring at the roof and listening to the conversations he could pick up from inside the room. He almost wished he could light the fire, although he didn't really need the heat. But the sound and flame would be something familiar to him.

Something else father had taught him.

"Rub them together quicker, my boy." He'd say. Watching, ever watching. Never an angry word or a scold as he's heard other men scold their children on trips through the forest. He wished the old man were here now to ask advice from. But Loran had made his choice a while back now, to keep the old man safe. Even if that meant staying away from him. Scared riders with flame and spear from Var'n Rodan would find only a tired old man, and no silly Daemons. Old wives tales, myth and nonsense. That's all. Nothing to be scared of here. Be about your business now.

He would not allow his father to perish because of him as others had.

Loran stared at the empty fireplace, waiting for sunrise.

***

"You sit quiet, now." Murmured Aleas, taking the reins of his horse. "I'll be back soon."

He'd left it as safe as he could, here in this secluded corner of the forest. This was a risk he had to take.

And he had no choice but to take the risk. He needed provisions, come what may.

He only hoped he could get in and out unseen.

He mounted his horse and headed toward Var'n Arden.

Back to The White Spire.

SEVEN

The wan morning light was spreading fast across the open grasslands between the Citadel, nestled on the backs of the river Uret, and the edge of the Moon Forest. Archers lined the northern wall, standing shoulder to shoulder, wings pulled back to allow room. Breastplates and greaves chinked as bowstrings were checked and rechecked.

All except the centre tower. That was deserted, but for one.
Loran.

He had risen well before the sun, broken his fast on some fresh bread and cold meats from the feast hall and taken up position. The space around him had quickly cleared as men found somewhere else to stand, fearful of the giant grey Daemon whose presence many still did not understand.
He wasn't sure he understood it himself yet.

Loran watched the forest intently. He could make out the men within its treeline. Just. Plus the wain he'd seen yesterday, and horses. He could just about hear those whinnying and snorting from here.

What were they waiting for? Loran turned and took in the winged lancers waiting in the square. Did this warband know they were expected?

***

"What d'you mean, they aren't there?" yelled Caylen. Rhyl took the eyeglass down, blessing the day he'd won it in a game of bones from two Solaanian sailors at Point Mar.

"I can see horses milling about. But no men. They just aren't there!" Ryhl checked through the eyeglass again just in case his vision was playing tricks on him.

Caylen swore under his breath. He would have them bloody flogged when he found them. Idiots! Where had they disappeared to?

"Ok, well, we can't wait for them. We'll attack as planned." A murmur of disapproval swept through the camp as people began shifting around uncomfortably.

"What?" He glanced around as some avoided his gaze.

"Well…" began Sande, "We planned to have our flanks protected. This changes…"

"It changes nothing."

There was uneasy silence for a few beats.

"As you wish." She conceded with a sigh. Caylen trusted Sande's opinion more than most, it was true. But damn it all, he was Pehl's first born and only son, and he would lead this attack as he damn well wished. And he wouldn't have anyone say that Caylen had not the leadership skills of a horse fly! He knew only too well what some thought of him, not least of all his own father.

"Mount up!" he yelled. They broke off and headed for their horses, adjusting boiled leather armour and swords at hips. Sande looked at the white towers of the citadel.

"Stay safe, my love." She whispered.

***

Loran watched the treeline intently. Here was a soft clatter of armour as Remus joined him.

"Anything?"

Loran met his gaze briefly and shook his head. Remus swore under his breath and turned to leave, his wingtips fluttering in frustration.

"You should go. We can manage. Us Avians have dealt with these scum a time or two." He said without turning round. Loran looked at his back, his own reflection twisted and contorted in the gleaming plate.

"That would not please your king, as we both know…" he

said quietly.

Remus turned and stared.

"It takes more than swords and arrows to kill me. Fortunately." Loran said with a thin smile. He turned back to the treeline as Remus trod down the first step.

"But I am grateful for the warning, nonetheless." The Daemon rumbled. Remus turned, nodded, and continued down to the wall.

He got four steps.

"Ready your men." Loran growled.

Remus swore and rushed down to the wall and shouted "NOCK!" at the top of his lungs. Along the line, men reached for arrows from slung quivers, nocking them on bowstrings as the word was passed along the wall.

From the treeline, horses sprung free, galloping in an arrowhead towards the wall. A wain followed them, pulled by two Bull Aurochs. On the back was a giant catapult.

"Wait…" warned Remus. Just let them get closer. Arrows loosed now would be a waste. Let them get close enough to feel it. He turned and held a hand up for the Lance men in the square below. They spread their wings and waited. lances held high. Remus turned back to the treeline, then bought it down. Hundreds of arrows loosed in an arc toward the riders. Horses fell, snorting and screaming, riders tumbling to the ground. Some rode on, their riders fallen, eyes wide in panic. Caylen's horse crumpled, its front legs giving way and Caylen tumbled over its neck to the ground. He stood quickly, taking in the scene around him, searching for his round shield, his eyebrows furrowed in puzzlement.

He held his own hand aloft and bought it down. The wain stopped a hundred or so spans from the wall and the catapult was winched down and loaded. Caylen waited.

He did not have to wait long. Lance men appeared, from over the wall as expected, but from the sides. On foot.

Lances bared down on Caylen's warband, pointed death

advancing toward him.

Caylen swore under his breath.

"NOW!" he screamed.

The wain driver, now manning the catapult, reached for the release handle.
With an ear-splitting crash, the catapult collapsed in the centre, an explosion of wood and rope, shards and splinters littering the ground. At the centre of the chaos stood a towering grey Daemon.

"Fuck me…" muttered Caylen, his eyes wide. He reached for his sword as the lance men began skewering his fallen riders. On the right flank, Rhyl batted aside a lance bound for his midriff, ramming his round shield boss into the Avians face, feeling a nose crunch beneath it. He sliced his sword across the Lance man's neck, a river of red flowing as he crumpled to one side. Rhyl ran on a few steps, then stumbled to one side as another two lance men headed in his direction.

This was crazy. There were hopelessly outnumbered.
On the left flank, Sande had taken a lance to the shoulder, thankfully grazing off boiled leather plate, but by all the Gods did it hurt! She cursed and swung at the lance man, who had stepped away, her sword slicing empty air.
Caylen rushed towards the Daemon, sword ready. Six fallen riders joined him, raining blows down upon the monster at their midst.

Inside the northwest tower, Brianne watched in horror as Loran disappeared in a sea of bodies and sword blows. She held her breath, still unsure what prompted her to ignore the warnings of the Lord Commander to stay clear.
She shouldn't be hear.
She couldn't not.

On the ground, the sea of men burst outward, bodies falling around as Loran exploded clear, great grey muscles flinging men away like rags. He spread his wings wide and took to the air briefly, dropping two to their deaths from a height.

Wings folded in, he dropped on a horse and rider, crushing both, then rolled away and stood in time to bat aside a sword from a foot soldier and rip out his throat. Snarling like a trapped animal, Loran hurtled at a group of ten or so soldiers who were trading blows with Avian lance men and sent them scattering like rats.

Brianne let out the breath she'd been holding.

Caylen recovered his senses, standing to look at what was left of his father's only catapult. Rhyl had warned him against using it, but it seemed like the perfect plan. Only now...

"Fall back." He screamed.

They scattered for the treeline, some mounting loose horses and pulling comrades into the saddle behind them. A great cheer went up from the wall as Caylen's raiders retreated into the relative safety of The Moon Forest.

"Should we give chase, sir?" asked the Josten, standing at the side of Lord Commander Remus.

"No, we've made our point for today." Remus watched as Lance men fluttered back over the wall to land in the square below.

Inside the northeast tower, Isaac had also been watching this strange Daemon who called him friend. He'd had to turn away from the window as shards and splinters of wood clattered against the tower wall, then let out a similar breath as Loran had burst free from a sea of swordsmen.

Isaac felt strangely hot and cold all at once. He looked down at the spreading curtain of red on his tunic, a shard of glass longer than his arm embedded in his chest.

Sounds seemed distant, like when he'd bathed in the moon pool and dunked his head underwater. Like his brother used to. He missed his brother.

Isaac sunk to the floor.

***

Up on the wall, Kall let out a silent prayer of thanks to any God who'd listen as he watched Sande gallop back to the safety of the forest, her high, brown ponytail swaying from side to side.

"Should have given chase. Could have cut the bastards down." Muttered Josten, walking up beside him.

"We fought them off, didn't we? Isn't that enough?" snapped Kall, instantly regretting his mouth.

"Bit touchy, aren't we?" Josten raised his eyebrows.

"Aye. Long day."

"Go and take a breather, Kall." He didn't wait for Kall to agree, turning to walk to the centre tower, where Remus stood talking to the Daemon. He was determined to talk to this great beast before the King sent him off again.

Josten walked up the east steps as Brianne walked up the west.

"Oh, fuck it…" he muttered.

EIGHT

"My thanks, Daemon." Remus said with a curt nod. Loran nodded in return, and the Lord Commander turned to leave, pausing at the stairs.

"I'm still not sure why." He said quietly.

Loran said nothing for a few beats.

"Why not just watch us struggle, knowing that the King wants you dead?" he turned and faced the Daemon.

It's what he would have done. What Remus had expected, to be sure. For the Daemon simply to fly off and watch the carnage from a distance.

"As I said. It takes more than swords and arrows to kill me. Besides, you seemed to need it." Loran smiled.

Seemingly satisfied, Remus removed his plumed helm and tucked it under his arm, then plodded down the stairs to the wall.

Loran turned and beamed at Brianne's arrival. She in turn smiled back, stopping somewhat awkwardly in front of him, her wings fluttering slightly.

"I feared for you, for a moment." She said, suddenly aware of the heat radiating from her cheeks, flooding her neck.

"No need, my lady. I'm perfectly well."

"I am glad. Perhaps we can get to know each other properly, if that meets with your approval?"

"You should not get too close to me, My lady." He said, thin lipped. Brianne furrowed her brow.

Steps from the wall drew their attention as Remus returned to the centre tower.

"My lady." He nodded. "I've just received word from Malaner. Prince Isaac is injured. It doesn't sound encouraging."

***

They both landed in front of the squat medical building, pushing aside the door guards to enter.

Malaner looked up at them gravely and shook his head.

"I can do nothing for him. He's lost too much blood." Malaner said, wiping his hands on a cloth. He walked away to check on a lance man who was bleeding from a leg wound.

Brianne looked down on the small, pale figure of the novice acolyte. His tunic was virtually red from the wound, the stench of blood acrid and tangy.

"…I think I can." The Daemon mumbled.

She looked up at Loran.

"Can what?"

"Help him." He looked from Isaac to Brianne. "At least, I know someone that can."

It would mean returning to a place he'd not seen in nearly two summers, but in the short time Loran had spent in his company, he'd grown quite fond of the young novice. Besides which, this needed to be done.

Come what may.

"I don't understand, Loran. Who?"

"We need to take him from here. And quickly." He turned to the healer, who shook his head again.

"He'll never survive being moved." Malaner stressed.

"He might if you pack the wound as best you can, and I carry him. I'm faster than any of you."

"You'll do no such thing!" thundered King Pyrus from the doorway.

Brianne curtsied hastily as the king strode into the medical room.

"What nonsense is this? Lady Brianne?" he bristled. Brianne looked from her king to Loran and back.

"Loran can help him, Sire."

"Can he, indeed?"

"I can," Loran insisted, "But I need to go now. Before it's too late."

The king stared at him blankly.

"Let me help him. Please!"

"If you think for one second, I'll let you take him anywhere… He's my only remaining son!"

"Then trust me." Loran said through gritted teeth, holding the King's gaze.

"Sire. We're wasting time." Malaner said from the side of the cot bed as he packed the wound.

All was still for a beat.

Finally, Pyrus stood to one side.

Loran swept the young novice up and strode from the room without another word.

"I'm coming with you." Insisted Brianne as she rushed out after him.

"If you can keep up." With that Loran sprang into the air and headed north.

Brianne took off after him.

***

"You fucking idiot!"

Caylen stared at the carpet covering the tent floor whilst his father ranted, rage and spittle flying.

"How could you have been so fucking stupid? And who, for the love of the Gods, thought it was a good idea to take my only functioning catapult for a simple raid? All you had to do was teach them a lesson, not try to take the Citadel single handed. Moron!"

Pehl backhanded a goblet, sending it and its contents clattering across the carpet. Caylen fought back the urge to counter, choosing instead to continue studying the floor some more.

He could never please his father, no matter how hard he tried. And all he did was try.

All he seemed to do was get in the way.

An uneasy silence settled over the room.

"What happened to the scouts you sent to guard your flanks?" Pehl turned and picked up another goblet, filling it with Solaanian red.

"Slaughtered…" Caylen mumbled. Rhyl had told him as they returned how he'd seen the bodies as he led the attack against the lance men. He still couldn't work out how they had readied so many archers in such a short time?

"Really? They are getting brave! And how exactly did they destroy my catapult?"

He'll never believe me.

I'm not sure I believe it, and I bloody well saw it! Bold as you like.

"Well?"

"They have… help." Caylen raised his eyes at last and met his father's disapproval.

"Help? What help?" Pehl took a deep gulp of wine.

"The Forest Daemon." He held his father's gaze. Let him call me a liar. I know what I saw.

"Get out, you arse."

"I'm not jesting, Father. Ask any of us that returned. It's bloody monstrous. And they have it working for them." Caylen said, pointing toward the south.

A polite cough came from the tent flap as Caris entered.

"Forgive me, My Lord, but Tialla is here."

Brilliant.

That's all I need…

"Finally. Some common fucking sense. Go and get some food before I part your empty head from your shoulders."

Caylen turned to leave, barging Caris out of the way.

"And send in your sister, now she's here." Pehl yelled after him

***

Loran landed heavily in the large clearing between the small, squat wooden shack and the river Uret, bubbling toward the Moon Pool in the distance. Brianne landed a full minute later, breathless from her flight where Loran had barely broke sweat.

What in the underworld are we doing here, on a farm? she took in her surroundings. There was a large paddock with three horses happily munching at the grass, a dark wooden fence keeping them in. A few large, flat boulders sitting on the riverbank.

And nothing else.

She couldn't, for one second, imagine anyone here being of help to a dying acolyte.

Loran was at the door already. He folded in his wings and kicked it twice.

It was opened slowly by an old man in a black shirt and trews, his long hair going grey and a small greying beard. He had his sword up, ready to repel any raiders. He lowered it when he saw who was knocking, the Avian mounting the three steps behind him.

"Loran!" he beamed.

"Hello, Father."

***

"Put him on the bed. Gently now!" said the old man, rifling through the cupboards to fetch cloths.

"What happened?" He asked over his shoulder.

"Raid." Loran said simply. "He was in the wrong place at the wrong time."

"Loran tells me you can help him?" Brianne said from behind him.

The old man looked up at her for the first time and smiled thinly.

"Oh, hello, my lady." He said. Then his face took on a grave look.

"I can, yes. But there will be consequences. These things are never easy. It involves a dark magic, and he may not be exactly the same after."

In fact, I can almost guarantee it.

"Do what you must. He is the king's son. Please!"

"A Prince, eh? Well, I'll do what I can, but neither of you can remain in here. You must wait outside."

Brianne looked for a moment as if she would stand her ground, then seemed to think better of it. Slowly, she nodded, then turned and headed outside.

"Horses need hay…" he called as he closed the door on them both.

***

He couldn't help but smile. By all the Gods, it was good to see him again. And with such beautiful company, too. He needed to ask him how he'd been?
Where he'd been?
First, to the task at hand.

He examined the wound, cutting away the red stained tunic with a short knife. The figure on the bed moaned as he looked, probing and prodding, eliciting a fresh wave of scarlet.

"I know, my friend. I know…"

Could he take the risk? It would certainly cure the young man's wound, If his knowledge of the dark magic was correct. And he would most surely die otherwise, his blood loss being what it was. He noted the young man's pale, almost ashen face.

And he was a Prince, after all.

Nothing else for it.
Questions.
There would most definitely be questions. He would have to deal with those later. The consequences of this would be impossible to hide.

He crossed to a tall wooden cupboard in the corner and lifted a key on a gold chain from around his neck. Stooping low, he unlocked the left-hand door and took out a huge, black bound book, with a cursive symbol of gold on its cover. He placed that on a table, then stooped again to retrieve a small vial, and a small dark-brown box about the size of his hand.

He opened the book and found the page he needed.

"Now then, my young friend. This will most surely sting like a thousand angry hornets, but I'm afraid it must be done."

Isaac didn't respond.

"You understand?" He bent low to the acolyte's ear. Isaac mumbled something and the old man nodded.
I'll take it you do, he thought.

He took a deep breath, then opened the vial and poured a black viscous liquid over the wound, lazy wisps of smoke threading up.
Isaac moaned louder.

Next, he opened the box and used a pair of wooden tongs to take out the small, white-blue ball inside and held it over the novice's chest.
Tiny tendrils of dark-magic energy buzzed across its surface.

He began reading from the tome, chanting from the ancient text. Long incantations from a dead language tumbled from his mouth as the ball fizzed and crackled. The old man squeezed the Tongs as hard as he could.

With a loud crack, the tiny ball splintered, and a small blue glow erupted across Isaacs skin. The old man stepped back as far as the room would allow.
Isaac screamed.

***

She watched, fascinated, as Loran grabbed a huge box-like pile of dry, golden grass and carried it into the paddock as if it were a bag of secondary feathers. He dropped it into the centre and all three horses stuck their faces into it.

She'd often watched the trader's horses from Var'n Rodan or Point Mar that her father dealt with, snorting and whinnying as their wains were unloaded. Always the same ones. Very few traders would deal with the Avians.
She was never entirely sure why.

She silently cursed herself for the umpteenth time for not standing her ground in there. She should have stood up for herself, as she had almost all her life.
Almost.

Moreover, she should have stayed, to keep an eye on

things. But dark magic, or whatever it was? That was something she knew little of. So, If Loran trusted this man enough to call him father, well. That was good enough for her, too.

Loran stood watching the horses eat for a few moments, then headed out across the damp grass toward the babbling Uret. Brianne watched him all the while.

He headed into the river and bathed his feet, wriggling his wide, splayed toes, his claws extending and scratching at the riverbed for purchase. He smiled and opened his huge black wings, the leatherette membranes casting long shadows across the water in the late morning sun. He threw his head back and closed his eyes against the sunlight.

Brianne watched him all the while.

Until Isaac screamed.

NINE

"……Papa…?"
"Yes, my son?" he answered.
"What am I?"
"You are… my son." He said quietly.
The boy thought for a moment.
"Papa…?"
"Hmm?"
"Where did I come from?"
This again. He couldn't keep putting the boy off. Inquisitive minds will keep asking until they're satisfied. And this was a most inquisitive mind.

Aleas was mending a fence post. He'd cut away the old, dry hemp rope and tossed it on the grass. With a new piece tied in place and looking sturdy enough for now, Aleas nodded, satisfied, and beckoned him over.

The boy splashed happily out of the water and joined him to sit on a large flat rock at the water's edge. Aleas took out his pipe, tapping the contents out on the rocks edge.
The boy watched, ever fascinated.

"You, my son, were born to an evil Queen. A vain and power hungry woman who wanted you, not for a son, but to get something she really needed."

"So, this Queen is my mother?"

"Of sorts…" this is going to get complicated. Should have just made something up.

"She had you created, if you like, from a dark magic energy from deep within the underworld. To steal something for her. Only that's not going to happen now. So, I've got you instead." He nodded, happy enough with his answer.

"So...you're not my father?" the boy looked up, crestfallen, at the only family he'd ever known.

"I raised you. Protected you. Taught you, fed you, clothed you. Sort of." He shrugged. "I think that makes me your father, yes. Maybe not of blood, but in all other things, it does." He said, filling the pipe from a small bag.

The boy thought on this for a long while, his brow furrowing, eyes lost as his mind wandered. Finally, he decided this answer met with his approval and smiled a wide grin at his father.

"Talking of clothes, I think we need to get you some new trews made, my boy." He looked down at the tattered ones he had on.
The boy was growing so damn fast.

"Papa?"
Aleas met his gaze and raised his eyebrows in question.

"When am I going to get to use these?" The boy asked, stretching his black wings out as far as he could, almost straining to make them larger. Not that they weren't large enough to support his weight already.

"Soon, Loran," Aleas said, standing and stretching. "Soon."

***

Aleas opened his eyes and watched his son, now fully grown, standing in the river as he had done as a youngster. He shook his head. He'd finally gave up on the trews after about ten pairs, such was Loran's growth rate.

The loincloth had been a last-minute idea. Still, it worked, he thought with a smile.
I haven't seen that dagger before, though...

"Is she still in there?" Loran splashed up the riverbank and sat beside the old warrior. Aleas took a long drag on his pipe and nodded, blowing smoke out over his shoulder.

They sat quietly for a beat or two, the river, the trees and the horses the only sounds. A far away splash as a wayward fish came up for air, no doubt. The grey mare in the paddock whickered.

"Where did you go…?" Aleas asked at last, looking into the distance.

"The Desolation." He said quietly.

Aleas rounded on him, aghast.

"What the fuck were you doing in *that* barren scrubland? Nothing there but prairie wolves and old bones."

"Exactly. No prying eyes. No nosey villagers with swords and fearful wives to contend with." Loran looked out over the river again.

"We could have dealt with them easily enough." He took another long drag on his pipe.

"No. They would have killed you to get to me."

They were quiet another beat.

"I missed your company, my son." He said, looking up at the horizon.

"And I yours, father."

Aleas chuckled quietly.

"You used to call me something else." Aleas said.

"Papa seemed a little…" he searched for a word. "Childish?"

"Not to me, my son."

Loran nodded, standing and looking back at the small shack. Aleas followed his gaze.

She had been an awfully long while.

***

Tialla and Pchl ate and drank together, swapping stories and tales. She, of her time in Solaan, across the Oran Sea. Fighting. Learning.

He, of his deal with Isiarus.

"So, you trust this witch?" she asked between mouthfuls.

He shook his head sadly.

"No, not really. In truth I am waiting for her to double cross us, but we're left with little choice. If her Mage is to be believed, we do not have the spells or knowledge to unlock the secrets of the Seraph." He refilled both cups.

"And what of Caylen?" that spoilt brat of a brother would never amount to much, of that she was certain. He'd skulked off after the failure of his raid on the Citadel without saying much to her at all. They were never close as children, especially after losing Mother.

"He'll be back, I'm sure."

"So, what are your plans now?" she peeled a piece of fruit while he thought for a second.

"Regroup, keep training. Build another catapult I suppose, now that one's truly buggered."

"I have a better plan." She swept a lock of red hair back from her face and smiled as Pehl eyed her carefully.

"What plan?"

"Suppose I were to show you a way to build much better, more efficient siege engines with less wood and much less time? You could take the walls in a few weeks, when the rains come, and they can't fly. They will be forced to face you on the ground. Even the odds a little." She sat back, trying not to look smug.

Caylen faced them on the ground, remember? It did him little good."

"You are not Caylen..." she said, sipping her wine.

"I'm intrigued, my girl. Where did my daughter learn of such things?"

"Well, I didn't spend all my time in Solaan fighting and fucking. I did learn something along the way."

Pehl laughed.

Perhaps her return was timed just about right. Maybe now, he'd realise that the best man for the job was his daughter.

***

Brianne closed the door behind her quietly. Her face

blank, her eyes distant.

Loran watched her intently. Aleas was scratching a grey horse's nose over the fence, his eyes on her.

"What do I tell the king?" She said at last.

"Tell him the truth. That this saved his life. Was the only way, really." Said Aleas, abandoning the horse and walking over to join Loran.

"Aye," Loran said. "What choice was there?"

"He will not see it that way. Of that, I'm sure." She walked down the steps to the grass, almost in a dream.

"He'll be furious with me."

"Why? T'was not your doing, but ours. I'll return with you both. To explain." Loran said.

"What if he wants things put back the way they were?"

"Is that even a possibility?" Aleas couldn't believe for a second that a king could do that. To his son? Surely not.

"No!"

They turned and looked at the open door, Isaac standing in its frame. He stepped onto the porch on unsteady legs.

"You should be resting, young man." Said Aleas. "How are you feeling?"

"Like I've been stabbed." Said the novice. "He can't take them away from me. You won't let him, will you Loran?" he begged the Daemon.

"No, I surely wont, my friend. Want to give them a try?"

"Are you kidding?" he beamed, stretching his new white wings out as far as he could, billowing in the breeze like bedsheets.

"I can't wait!"

***

Aleas sat on a bench on his porch, Brianne beside him watching the afternoon sky. The clouds had grown dark of late as the torrential rains of K'lahl grew ever threatening. They'd disappeared quickly from sight, Isaac slowly getting used to supporting himself on his new wings.

They had grown quickly, that was for sure. Hours, where normal Avians took months for the downy new fluff to give way to more mature feathers. Yet another "Side effect" Aleas mused. Besides the obvious wound healing. The questions had been surprisingly few yet, such was their shock.
He had a feeling that was about to change.

"You haven't yet explained how you did this. I know little of Magic, dark or otherwise. We don't even have a Mage." She said, as if reading his thoughts. Her eyes were never off the sky.

"The orb I used is like a smaller version of the Seraph you guard. It can heal wounds, and restore that which has been taken, according to the books. It seems to have given back more than I thought it would, although I suspected this might occur. Dark magic is not an exact art, my lady."

"Brianne, please." She smiled at him, his kind old eyes lost in thought.

"How do you know of the Seraph? Or Dark Magic at all, for that matter? I thought only the Mages were privy to such things?"

He met her gaze, his face unreadable.

"I was a Mage. In another lifetime."

Brianne was silent, waiting patiently.

"When I was but seventeen summers old, my pa took me in the wain to the Mages Seat in Var'n Cirnan. There I spent eight long years with the Elders learning nothing spells and magic and darkness. I thought nothing good could come of my time there. Until I met Elise."

"Elise?"

He smiled at the very thought of her, the very name on his lips. He'd had women since, various brothel whores and harlets in taverns across the land. Hers were the only lips he had ever kissed.

"Elise and I met at Point Mar. I was to meet a galley coming in from Solaan with a shipment of lettun gran for the Master mage. She was waiting for her uncle."

He looked at a point on the horizon.

"Her hair was the colour of the sunset, her eyes green as the grass in summer."

Aleas looked at her.

"I'd never seen green eyes before. Or since. She was breathtaking."

He was quiet a long moment. Her face filled his mind.

"She was trampled by a horse. A thief, I think, making off with some merchant's money, no doubt. Stole his livelihood and my love." His eyes were wet with the memory.

"All those spells and I could do nothing to help her. That day I left The Mages Seat and joined the nearest cavalry unit I could find. Fighting for Queen Isiarus."

"The Witch Queen?"

"Aye…" he said solemnly. "The Witch Queen. Buried myself in a soldier's life. I was good at it, too, after near on twenty-three years a soldier. Till he came along." He nodded to the sky, where two pinpricks of dark were barely visible against the clouds, getting larger as they approached.

"How did you come to look after Loran?" she asked, looking back at the sky.

"I wasn't supposed to look after him, I was supposed to kill him. I expect that's a job you give to a twenty-odd year veteran." Brianne looked at him sideways. "Didn't have the heart. In truth, when I saw those big blue eyes, it reminded me of her. Loran was the name we would have given our son, had we been blessed."

They'd talked of it often, in quiet moments. He could almost hear her soft lilted accent talking of the plans she had. A quiet cabin like this one. Horses like those in the paddock. Children.

He turned at looked at her puzzled expression as she no doubt tried to do the sums in her head.

"How long were you in the cavalry for?" she asked.

"I know, it doesn't quite add up, does it? Thing is…" he said as they landed some distance away, "…Loran is only twelve summers old."

TEN

The Century Wars
Year five.
The Holy City of Lianna
Durmak.

High in the holy tower of Lianna palace, Vororr, God of Honour stood with his back to L'Shaan. She'd been pleading with him for what seemed a ten night. He flexed his muscles, the thin, evening light catching his rippled and knotted torso, and ran a hand over his bald, dark skinned head.

As Supreme, his was never going to be an easy lot. They ruled over these people, yes, but they did not control them.
And they did not control each other, more was the pity.

"I must remain impartial, L'Shaan. You know this." He turned and met her gaze, suddenly needing a drink.

She tossed her impossibly dark mane of hair and stuck her nose in the air slightly.

"This cannot continue, Vororr. Myla and Betris have been fighting off these Wraiths for five long years, and still Blaise continues to create more." She held out her hands, pleading. "Something must be done, I beg of you."

Vororr sighed. Myla, Goddess of hunting and fighting had an army to rival any in the lands at her beck and call. They had been trading blows with these creatures endlessly, much to no avail. And Betris, God of strength could crush almost anything with those muscles.

"What do Blaise and Rotaldir hope to gain from this

conflict?" he strode over to the ornate throne and settled into it, finally pouring himself that drink. She sidled across the smooth wooden floor to stand before him.

"Blaise has her reasons firmly within envy, my Lord. She and I have never been close. As Goddess of the Mages, she seeks to overthrow me. This she does by getting her mages to create these… monsters." A shiver ran down her back, the thought of those half wolf, half bat creatures snapping at her neck. Had her Avian army not plucked her to safety? Well…

"As for Rotaldir? His reasoning is quite clear."

"It is?" Vororr sat forward in his thrown. It certainly wasn't to him.

"He means to overthrow you, my Lord." She gave a self-satisfied smirk as Vororr sat back.

Does he now? Rotaldir was cruel and ambitious, but never reckless. He was the God of the Otherworld, keeper of the bridge, and was meant to be welcoming those who crossed it.
Not trying to get his Supreme to do so!

"I must give this some thought, L'Shaan. I'm sorry, but for now you must hope to defeat them without my assistance."

"As you wish, my Lord." She sighed.

***

Goral bought his sword firmly through the neck of a wraith as the giant creature's dripping teeth snapped towards his neck. The head rolled away and the torso collapsed, blood pouring from it. He turned and ran a hand through his long, blonde locks, surveying the battle.

Avians were engaged everywhere, some on the ground, some rolling around the sky, trying to get some purchase on their quarry. The wraiths were not an easy foe, that was for
sure. Most wounds seemed to just annoy them. Removing the head was effective, but little else.

He hawked and spat. The ground here was arid and dusty, the heat cloying. He had little clue why the Gods had chosen this desert shithole as their battlefield, but his was not to reason why. He hoped against hope that they were making good ground against these things. These Wraiths.

Still, it was fortunate that the Mages could not use their magic against the Gods directly. And so far, Goddess Blaise had them far too busy creating Wraiths to even make a dent in the armies of L'Shaan and Myla.

The God Betris needed no army. His strength was equal to a century of men all on its own. Even the beasts seemed to place him in awe. Goral looked across at the mighty form of Betris, muscles as thick as tree trunks, a long spiralling tattoo down one leg, as he commanded a pride of lions to attack. The lions ran off toward the enemy wraiths, most falling foul of the giant beasts' huge teeth. Three lions had gathered around a single wraith, a coordinated attack at its neck and legs. The beast fell amid a flurry of roars and fur and blood.

On the crest of a hill some distance away, the Goddess Myla gave orders to her army. The men, all dressed in scarlet and white, looked up at her, red hair fluttering in the breeze, as she gave commands.

Goral shook his head and flapped the sand from his wings. They clearly loved her and would fall on their swords for her in a trice. All he had was dissent and arguments from his Avians.

And they felt like his Avians. L'Shaan's army they may have been, but he alone was responsible for their wellbeing, their morale.

Their very lives.

He was not the oldest among them, that was certain. But as others had looked to him in the past, he had become an unofficial leader of the Avian army. Something he and Nadya had argued over relentlessly, it seemed.

He watched as another wraith fell from the sky.
Half bat, half wolf.
Wretched creatures.

***

Rotaldir watched alongside Blaise with a mixture of fascination and disgust. These creatures her mages were creating were indeed a strange thing. And they were turning them out at an ever-alarming rate.

They were deep in the darkest part of Blaise's Castle. The candlelight danced off her blonde hair as she watched her mages work, incantations tumbling from their mouths as their hands weaved and twisted into sacred formations. The animals they were melding with humans shrieked and howled and thrashed against it, all in vain. The humans seemed numb to it all, meekly accepting their fate.

One after another, a fresh Wraith plodded from the room.

"It is marvellous, is it not?" she turned to Rotaldir as he wrinkled his nose, watching with wide eyes.

"That is not, alas, the word I would use." He hissed. He ran a hand over his grey, leathery skin, large talons of yellow skimming his head and turned to her, taking in her lithe form. Imagining, not for the first time, how she might look unclothed.

They were taking a risk, he and she. This plan to take Vororr's place had seemed foolhardy at first. But the more she purred and cooed about it, the more real these plans seemed to be. It appeared possible that they could, indeed, overthrow Vororr.

He could actually become Supreme.

They needed Torna. His sly, devious plans and mischievous ways would be the final straw to break Vororr's hold over this realm. He was, after all, God of cunning. Not a title one gets without reason.

He had argued much with Blaise about the need to include Torna in all things. She wasn't as sure as he, that much was certain.

They never did get on that well, it had to be said. She seemed not care for his short stature, or his sharp, pinched features and long, dank hair. And it was clear she didn't trust him one tiny bit. She'd said so, many times. But such misgivings must be set aside if they were to be victorious. The pious ways of old should be a thing of the past now, surely? The time was right for a new beginning. A different set of rules.

The time was right for Rotaldir to show his true worth.

Another fresh Wraith plodded from the room, and another peasant was plucked from the many cowering in the corner, awaiting their destiny. A young girl this time, no more than twenty summers *old. She cried and begged as they dragged her across the floor, her struggling finally subsiding as she accepted her doom.*

The young girl said a silent prayer to Vororr as a short, stocky mage came forward and sliced a dagger cleanly through her neck. She collapsed in a stream of blood.

Blaise smiled. Rotaldir did not.

ELEVEN

On the northeast outskirts of the Moon Forest, tree cutting had begun in earnest. Caylen watched, ever more sullen as Tialla spent several hours, with parchment and ink, explaining her designs to the best of her father's builders. At first they laughed. As he knew they would.
As did he.

After she'd backhanded the first man brave enough to give her a smart-arsed comment, the laughter stopped.
Perhaps these ideas weren't so stupid after all. Perhaps they deserved a second look.

So, many grumbling men stripped off their leather and sword belts and got to work. Cutting, sawing, chopping.
Building.

Watching it all was Pehl, a proud beam on his face as his daughter gave orders and instructions to various people.

It was bloody typical. Typical of that bitch to come strutting in here with her big ideas and her stupid fucking plans from some foreign shithole. Ideas she no doubt stole from someone smarter than herself. What did she know of war, of battle, and leading men? What did she know of the training and planning they'd done?
What did she bloody know of anything?
And now, here she was fluttering her eyelashes and earning fathers ear all over again. While he'd done his level best in a difficult battle and made to feel like a bloody child. Through no fault of his own.
All over again.

***

Isaac stood in the centre of the Forum, its oval table of dark wood surrounded by the city elders. At its head was Pyrus. Pyrus stared at his son in disbelief for some time as their story was relayed. Still, he said nothing. Silence hung in the air, the room thick with tension as Isaac studied the ground before him.

Behind Isaac, Brianne and Loran stood at his shoulders. They'd said nothing since they returned, except to explain the details of this apparent miracle. Without really explaining much at all, at Aleas' request.

"No." said the King finally. "This cannot be allowed. Only the Goddess L'shaan herself may bestow the divine gift. No Mage or suchlike can give back that which has been sacrificed."

"What stands before you would suggest otherwise." Rumbled Loran at Isaac's shoulder.

"This is all your doing. Had you not arrived here…" thundered the King.

"Your son and daughter would both be dead…" Loran growled.

Uneasy silence settled upon the room once more.

"And what now, hmm? What role is my son to play, seeing as he cannot fulfil his duties as an acolyte without the sacrifice of flight?"

"And whose sacrifice was it?" Loran yelled back. "It was not a choice he made. Let him now choose his path for himself."

"What path is there? What is he to become?"

"What about a prince, and the next King?" said Isaac calmly.

All eyes turned to Isaac, virtually silent up to now. He'd stood, head hung as the expected joy of this cure turned to rage and anger at the return of his wings. He silently chided himself for expecting anything else from the King.

His wings still caught him unawares sometimes. Twice he'd spun round, thinking somebody was standing at his shoulder as he walked, yet it was merely his wings he could see from the corner of his eyes.

More than twice, he'd knocked over something in Aleas's shack.

Now the idea of him being king was a very real one. And from his father's face, not one Pyrus relished.

"…Or is that what bothers you?" He spat, raising his head. "That your only remaining son, whom you thought safe and off your hands in the path of the acolytes, might actually succeed you?"

"Give him a chance to show his worth, sire." Said Brianne. "He may surprise you yet."

The king stood abruptly, his ornate chair toppling backwards to the forum floor with a loud clatter. He rounded the table in a few quick steps to stand in front of them.

"You, my lady… I haven't even started with you." The king thundered, pointing an accusing finger at the tutor.

"Touch her and I'll kill you where you stand." Growled the Daemon.

Pyrus met his gaze and bit back his words. A murmur went round the table, and one city elder stood. His thin blond hair almost white with age, he fluttered his wings and addressed the King.

"Sire. It would seem that what is done is done. There is no precedent for sacrificing the divine gift twice," said the elder, chuckling at his own joke.

I'd love to see you try, thought Isaac, staring up at Loran.

"Perhaps we should give the young prince some time to adjust? To find his feet, and his wings, hmm? And in time, to find his true calling." Again, murmurs of approval went round the table as the man sat.

Pyrus sighed, turned and walked back round to the head of the table. He stooped to retrieve his chair.

"Very well. You may find a room at the palace. You," he jabbed a finger at Loran. "I want you gone. Now."

"I will help the boy settle in and adjust, then I will leave."

"Good enough." Said the elder before the King could

bluster any further.

***

"I cannot thank you enough. Or your father. You will tell him for me, won't you?"
They stood outside the forum building. People were looking, pointing and whispering. But not at Loran this time.
At Isaac.

"I'll tell him. Although I think your smile was thanks enough, my friend." Loran clapped him on the shoulder.

"So, what *will* you do now?" Brianne asked, tightening her ever-present headscarf.
Isaac looked around at the people watching.

"I don't know, to be honest. Answer questions for hours, most likely. I'll see if I can help with the preparations for K'lahl. There's still much to do if we are to be ready for the feast.

"K'Lahl?" Loran furrowed his eyebrows.

"The downpour. It lasts for weeks. We must prepare, gather what food we can and batten down for the storm." Brianne looked skywards at the darkening gloom.

"Why?" he asked, genuinely puzzled.

"They cannot fly in the rain." Said Isaac.

"We." She corrected.

"Oh yes. I'd almost forgotten. Seems I've only just got them and now I must get used to not using them."

K'lahl was something Isaac had simply known about, up to now at least. He'd never really had much to do with preparations, as an acolyte. And there was the feast of L'Shaan to prepare for at K'lahl's end. Now, with no real role as such, he was determined to get stuck in with helping. A prince should be willing to roll up his sleeves and help out.
Meryl had always said that.

***

Daynar embraced her brother, tears welling in her eyes. She'd sought him out in various places before finally catching up with him, helping to carry sacks of grain into the store behind the palace. Preparations for K'lahl were well under way now, with wains of grain and barrels of honey wine and ale being unloaded, and Isaac seemed to enjoy being useful.

"I thought you were dead. They all said you couldn't be saved. But here you are. And look at your lovely wings. How…?" She stumbled over questions as he stumbled over answers.

"So, you've become pretty friendly, you and this Daemon?" she linked arms with him as they walked back toward the Palace.

"I have. He's…remarkable." Isaac shook his head in awe of a creature feared by all, yet who had shown him more kindness than his own kin.

"Well. You're not the only one. I gather Brianne is quite taken with him too." She looked around her, almost to see if anyone were listening. Gossip had been rife in the ladies meeting hall, the feast hall. Just about everywhere.

"Oh, I don't know…" Isaac said, his cheeks reddening visibly.

She was quiet as they walked, arm in arm, wings touching. In truth she had worried endlessly about seeing him with his wings intact. When they'd bought her the news she was, at first, elated.

Then came the inevitable question.

She swallowed.

"So… I expect you'll be King now, when father crosses the bridge."

He stopped and faced her.

"That's a long way away. Besides, I'm not sure father would want that. We both know he thinks me a fool."

"I'm sure he doesn't, Isaac."

They started walking again, the palace of Sha'bal looming large in front of them.

"And I'm not sure I would want it."

They stopped again.

"Oh, tell me you'll think it over, please. I've been dreading the thought of ever becoming queen since Meryl crossed the bridge. Please say you will."

"Well, I didn't expect this. I was expecting more of a fight, to be honest."

"No. Queen is not a title I relish in the slightest, actually. Far too much responsibility." She stuck her nose in the air again. She felt the need to help people more and more of late, that much was true. But not to make decisions that would govern the Citadel as a whole, or the Avians in it.

That was a role she could suddenly envisage her brother taking up.

***

Brianne finished washing herself down, her hair wet and slick. The last couple of days had left her drained, and a nice hot wash followed by a hot tisane would do wonders to restore her to normal.

Almost.

She wasn't even sure what normal was now. So much seemed to have changed. She pondered over the last day or so as she shook the water from her wings.

All she could seem to think of was him.

He dominated her every thought since returning. The way he'd helped young Prince Isaac. A Prince now, an acolyte no longer. Flown with him. Stood up to the king for him.

And for her. She surely wouldn't forget that anytime soon. She had little doubt he would have carried out his threat there and then had it been needed.

It wasn't.

But she couldn't allow herself to get too lost in this... whatever it was. She could never allow others to get close to her. That was more complicated than ever, since...

A loud rap on her door startled her from her reverie. Who could be calling at this late hour?

"Yes?" she stood on the other side, a towel hastily wrapped around her.

"It's Loran." His low, liquid voice rumbled through the door.

Brianne cursed. She couldn't let him see her now, not like this.

"Erm, just a minute…" she looked around the room in panic. Her eyes fell upon her gown, its back cut low to allow her wings to protrude. She put in on and quickly wrapped a towel around her wet head, covering it completely.

Brianne opened the door a couple of handspans. Loran had his back to her, his enormous frame and black wings filling the gap entirely, blocking any light from the wall sconces outside.

He turned and smiled at her.

"Forgive the intrusion, my lady. I came to take my leave of you before I depart."

"You need not apologise." She smiled back. "Besides, I thought we were past formal terms now, surely?"

"Brianne." He nodded once.

"Depart?" Her smile dropped.

"I fear I have outstayed my welcome, yet again. The young prince is getting stronger and more confident by the hour, preparations for your feast at the rains end are well underway and your King has made it very clear that I am as welcome as a bad smell."

She chuckled, holding his gaze.

"Will I see you again?"

"I'm sure of it." He said. Loran held her gaze as he stepped backwards from her door down onto the stone walkway. With a nod, he spread his huge, black, gossamer wings wide and leapt into the air, disappearing from view almost immediately.

She held the door open a while, nodding to a passing lady without noticing who it was.

Quietly, she closed the door.

TWELVE

During the night, the ever-threatening sky finally burst, a torrent of rain coming down in great sheets and bouncing off the stones that lined the market square of the Citadel. Archers and Lance men pulled their cloaks tight around them, buttoned up at the front, a flap in the back between their wings. Guards in doorways cursed and shuffled back, trying to gain some respite from the deluge. Time and again they'd pleaded with the Lord Commander to arrange some kind of shelter from K'lahl at sentry points.

Always it was ignored.

Far to the northwest of the Moon Forest, Pehl looked up from his cot as the rain made a sound unique to rain on a tent roof.

He closed his eyes and smiled.

***

"Enough, woman!" Rhyl screamed against the howling wind, horizontal rain lashing one side of his face. "This is fucking madness…"

Tialla had been training the warriors hard for a week now. The siege ladders she'd created were met with a mixture of mirth and disgust in equal amounts and had been ready just as the downpour began.

Now was the time to learn how best to use them.

"No." she rounded on him, her red hair sopping and stuck to her face. "Again."

The ground was a quagmire as wheel ruts and footprints made more mud. The going was hard. Rhyl had little doubt that these ridiculous ladders would be hard enough to get used to in the height of summer, let alone during the downpour. He watched as two more teams of men pushed the wain uphill toward the makeshift wall Tialla had insisted they create. As they neared it, the ladders were raised, and in one swift movement, long lengths of timber slotted into place to keep the ladders at an angle.

The wains hit the wall, and wedges of wood were placed behind the wheels. Two men scuttled up the ladders swiftly, followed by two more.

"Better." She grinned, clapping Rhyl on the shoulder. "We're nearly ready. What say you, father?"

Pehl looked on from behind her, pleased at her progress and determination. He'd been as sceptical as the men, it was true, at some of her ideas. Caylen's pouting and protesting helped little as usual. Pehl had finally lost his patience and tasked his son with making another catapult. That should keep him busy for a while.

"Good." He said, meeting Rhyl hopeful gaze. "Again."
Rhyl's shoulders dropped.

***

"You've done well, Tialla. I'm proud of you, and the progress you've made."
They were seated in his tent, food spread before them. Caylen hadn't joined them.

"If your mother were here, she'd be gloating now of how women should be in charge!" they both laughed at the memory. Ellen had been gone six years now, illness wasting her away from the inside. The sack of skin and bones they buried was not how Tialla wanted to remember her mother.

"Thank you, father." She said, picking up a husk of unleavened bread.

"For what?"

"For believing in me. Trusting in me." She took a bite.

"I'm not sure I did, at first. But your ideas deserved merit. Your trip across the Oran Sea was a trip worth taking. You've learned much. And I've seen you training with the others. Your skills with a sword have improved vastly."

She'd bested some of their best swordsman on many occasions, her fighting style fluid and twisting where theirs was solid and staid, just as she outclassed about everyone with a bow. Caylen had tried twice to best her with a sword.
Twice she'd put him on his arse.

"I think we're ready." Pehl said, taking a gulp of ale from a wooden flagon. Tialla nodded. They were as good as they would get, that was certain. Whether it was enough, only time would tell.

"We'll gather in two days. We'll be ready. Then we can crush the winged scum and finally end this."

"What about the other problem? How do we move that?" she asked, sipping her own ale.

They had both given that much thought. In truth, it seemed neither of them were entirely sure it *could* be moved. However, once they took the citadel, its location could be secured and then its removal would be Queen Isiarus's problem and welcome to it. As long as her father and his men were taken care of.
Pehl assured her that the queen had given her word, after all.

***

Line upon line of horsemen sat in the saddle, cloaks pulled tight over their boiled leather against the rain. Horses snorted and whickered in frustration. To the flanks, four siege ladders sat ready, tethered to teams of Bull Aurochs.

Pehl sat in the centre, straining his eyes against the darkness of early morning. The rain was incessant, as was Caylen's pouting. He sat four rows back with the newly built catapult. The basic design had been updated to Tialla's specifications. Caylen had resisted to urge to find fault and just got on with building it for once.

Tialla sat next to her father, her dark blue sable cloak edged with fur, pulled tight over her sword. Her father had attempted to get her to wear some kind of protection, but in vain. She could move far better without it, apparently. Something else she'd learnt from her time in Solaan.

"Move out." Pehl shouted, kicking in his heels. The line moved with him, and slowly the warband gathered pace, siege ladders rattling in protest as they trundled across the forest floor. The path through Moon Forest was wide enough for them. Just.

Pehl kicked his heels in again, and his horse fell into a trot, the rest of the warband doing the same. A chill ran up Pehl's neck like a feeling of being watched. He looked over his shoulder briefly, seeing nothing but trees and the blasted rain. This damn forest was spooky enough in the daylight, but in this thin light everything looked menacing.

High in a tall, thick tree, Loran looked on closely.

THIRTEEN

King Pyrus rose early, as was usual. He broke his fast alone, Isaac having taken to avoiding his father's uncompromising glare and Daynar not yet awoken. Today was not one he looked forward to. The forum session that loomed promised to be a difficult one. Rumours were abound that more and more, Avians were questioning the very beliefs that this life of theirs was built upon.

He would steel himself to protect all they had fought for. Whatever the cost. His father had drummed that into him as a youngster. Years of long, drawn-out speeches, he'd heard a thousand times. How L'Shaan had bestowed the gift upon them, and them alone.

How Pehl and his like had nearly caused its ruin.

Damn that foolish woman and her Daemon friend. This uneasiness would not exist had he not appeared.

Damn them.

Pyrus left the Palace of Sh'Bal and headed for morning prayers.

***

They exited the shelter of the Moon Forest, its darkness foreboding, into the relative light of the greying morning. The rain was continual once out of the protection of the forest canopy, the thin dawn light barely enough to see. The flanks spread out wide, the line forming a wide arrowhead. Horses foamed and snorted, bathed in sweat.

At the head of the line, Pehl's heart was pounding, the blood in his ears as loud as the horses' hooves around him. He drew his sword as the imposing walls of the Citadel grew in front of him, slabs of dark against the dawn sky.

Pehl raised his sword, and the line halted. The siege ladders moved forward until close enough to be untethered and moved by hand.

Rhyl stood one side of the leftmost ladder, Dellin's large hulking form stood the other. Behind them, two more warriors stood at the rear. Pehl cursed as the horses whinnied, quietly begging them to keep silent.

Dellin nodded to Rhyl, and they pushed the ladder to the wall, feet slipping in the wet grass, mud covering the soles of their boots. Like a well-rehearsed dance, the chocks were in place, the ladder raised, and the supports locked into place. Two warriors climbed the ladder as quietly as they could, while Rhyl drew his sword.

Josten stood on the crenulated wall, his cloak tight around him against the rain. He shook the water from his wings and walked slowly along the wall. He'd spent the last three night-watches constantly wondering where Kall kept disappearing off to. He'd given up asking, and Kall had stopped his nightly trips over the wall.

A thump stopped him in his tracks. He peered over the wall, to see a ladder against it, a warrior near the top. Jost drew his sword, leaned over and stabbed down into the man's neck, blood flowing down his boiled leather. He watched the warrior topple sideways, another below him taking his place.

Josten stood, put his horn to his lips and blew hard.

***

Sat in the centre of the line, Pehl muttered a curse under his breath as a horn blew out across the morning. He'd hoped they would get more of a jump on these idiots than this.

He was forced to watch, helpless as a new-born, until his warriors took enough ground inside the Citadel to get the gates open.

Or they came out and faced him on the field.

He hoped it was the latter. Surely, he would lose less men that way?

On the left-hand ladder, Dellin's hulking form hopped over the battlements, and raised his sword as two winged warriors ran at him. He blocked as the first Avian chopped down at his head, stepped back and parried as the Avian thrust towards his chest. Dellin stepped inside the Avian's guard and headbutted him on the nose, feeling bone crunch beneath skin. As the Avian stepped back, his vision momentarily clouded, Dellin sliced his throat open. He crumpled to the floor as the second ran in behind him. Dellin batted his sword aside and thrust his own into the Avian's groin. Blood flowed down the Avian's legs, and he staggered back, toppling sideways like a felled tree. Dellin ran towards the central tower, desperate to get to the stairs. Getting the gate open was paramount.

Behind him, Rhyl was busy trading blows with a tall, thick set Avian with flowing blonde locks jutting out from his helm. Behind him, another warrior was stepping over the battlements, barely getting his feet on stone before an Avian stabbed him in the chest, ripping his sword free, a torrent of crimson flowing down his boiled leather. The Avian turned his attention to Rhyl, running up behind him just as the warrior was slicing open an Avian throat.

On the ground, Caylen had assembled the catapult, now a much quicker process after Tialla's changes. It was loaded with stone and rocks, and Caylen nodded to the man standing at the lever. He watched in horror as a giant arrow, as long as the man himself, buried itself into the man's chest, exploding out the back and pinning him to the ground. Caylen swore, looking up at the corner towers as the giant crossbows were reloaded.

On the far-left flank, a horse screamed and collapsed as a giant arrow buried itself in its side, toppling its rider in the process.

Caylen ran across and pulled the lever.

The catapult erupted, coiled power releasing and hurling rocks and stones over the wall, knocking archers to the floor.

"Yes" Pehl fist pumped the air,. "Now, get the fucking gate open!"

"Patience, Father. Patience…" Tialla said, smiling proudly alongside him, nonetheless.

The catapult launched a second time, aimed at the far-left corner's giant crossbow. Avians on the wall swore and ducked for cover as a rainstorm of rocks and rubble clattered over them, one falling to the floor with a large cut across his temple, his helm dented like an old pail.

The far-right corner crossbow launched its giant arrow, burying itself through a rider's chest and out the other side. He slid to the floor silently, his horse bucking and trotting away.

"Come on, come on." Pehl mumbled, desperate for the squeal of the portcullis rising. Archers on the wall knocked and loosed.

"Shields!" he screamed, pulling his own round, black shield from his saddle behind him and raising it. Arrows thudded into the wood, one clattering off the boss. Three riders fell, one with a leg wound, two dead.

Inside the central tower, Dellin descended the staircase, disembowelling the guard running up toward him, yet to get his breastplate on. Rhyl followed behind, the stench of blood and entrails assaulting his nostrils.

***

Loran watched intently from high in the treetops. His wings were twitching in frustration as he fought the urge to assist yet again. After all, he kept telling himself, this was not his fight. The king had made it plainly obvious that he was unwelcome. Who was he to interfere in matters that did not concern him?

It was not his fight.

And yet something niggled at him. Something he hadn't felt before.

Guilt.

Isaac was in there. He had grown fonder of his young friend than he'd realised, and after seeing his life saved, would not see it wasted again.

Brianne was in there too.

***

King Pyrus came rushing out the temple doors, the sounds of battle coming from the wall. He looked to his right to see Lord Commander Remus running at the wall, hastily fastening his breastplate.

"Lances!" Remus bellowed as he fastened his helm under the chin. Men were running from the barracks at either side of the wide central square, lances drawn hastily from a rack on the wall. The rain was falling in sheets, great squalls pummelling the square. Pyrus ran toward the Lord Commander, who was shouting orders.

"Remus!"

"Sire!" he gave a curt nod, turning and shouting more orders. "They knew just when to strike us! This rain is going to get us all slaughtered."

"Indeed." The king said.

There was a harsh, high-pitched squeal from the central tower. They turned and looked as, almost in slow motion, the portcullis gate began to rise.

"Shit" they mumbled in unison.

FOURTEEN

They poured through the gate, horses snorting, and swords raised.

"Lances!" yelled Remus again as Avians hastily formed two lines with lances aimed at the enemy. Rows of pointed death. Horses screamed as they poured into the line, some dismounting their riders, some being ridden to their end. Dismounted riders engaged Avians as swords met swords, and lances were thrust into black clad warriors.

On the wall, Josten nocked and loosed at warriors streaming over the wall, one toppling face first on the stone as another took his place. He nocked again, releasing the bowstring as the warrior ran towards him. The warrior raised his small, round shield, the arrow thudding into the wood. Josten cursed and stepped back a few paces, making a desperate grab for his sword.

A sword appeared next to him, piercing the man in the throat. He fell forward, gurgling and coughing as blood flooded his neck. Josten looked up at Kall's face, nodding his thanks. The young avian grinned, shaking the water from his wings, and ran towards the next unfortunate victim. Along the wall, more archers were forming up, shooting down to the riders still waiting to get through the open gate.

Yet more lance men formed two wide flanks, closing in as more riders streamed through the open gate, most falling on the rows of dark metal-tipped lances. The stones on the market square were slick with blood, the endless rain diluting it as it continued to fall in heavier and heavier squalls, bouncing off the stones.

Outside, his horse whinnying in frustration, Pehl

watched helplessly as his men fought to get through the gate on horseback. Barely room for three abreast, it was an irritating process.

"This is taking too bloody long." He yelled through the rain at Tialla. She turned and nodded, feeling their element of surprise slipping ever further from their grasp. She turned her horse and yelled at Caylen to raise the catapults aim. Caylen shot her a dark look, but cranked the handle, nonetheless. The catapult groaned in protest as it was raised at the front. Caylen pulled the handle.

In the market square, a storm of rocks fell as the lines of lance men managed to hold their own against a sea of horse-mounted warriors. Most of Pehl's warband soon found themselves unseated or skewered like tunnel rats. Those that made it to their feet were on equal terms with Avian swordsmen, as the clash of steel mixed with the screams of the dying.

Rhyl ran across the square from the exit to the gatehouse, which sat at the foot of the central tower. A tall avian turned to meet him with an almost manic smile. Rhyl raised his sword as the Avian chopped sideways at his head, the blow jarring his arm. He thrust his own sword out, only to glance off the Avian's steel breastplate with a loud clang. Rhyl stepped back a pace, and parried a thrust towards his abdomen, turning his sword and slicing up through the Avian's upper arm. He smiled as a thin line of red appeared.

They circled each other slowly, looking for an opening. Rhyl lunged at the Avian's groin, but his sword was turned away as the winged swordsman blocked. Rhyl stepped to the side to avoid a thrust to his chest, raising his own sword to block. The Avian bought the pommel of his sword up and smashed it into Rhyl's mouth. He stumbled back, tasting blood, white light clouding his sight. Rhyl hawked and spat onto the ground, looking back up just as a sword pierced his stomach, white-hot pain flooding his gut. He felt hot and cold all at once. The Avian ripped his sword free, and Rhyl crumpled to the ground.

Outside in the downpour, Pehl's horse jittered about impatiently as the sounds of war and dying drifted over the wall in equal measure.

"It's time." He said to Tialla, her own white mare equally unsteady. She nodded, and they kicked their heels in to spurt their mounts through the gate.

A great crash behind them startled both horses, Tialla's mare bucking and unseating her. She fell backwards into the mud with a loud splat, cursing. Pehl turned his horse around.

Loran stood up from the centre of what used to be a catapult, shards and remnants falling from his wet, grey skin.

Pehl stared, words failing him. His horse whinnied and jittered, and he fought to calm it as best he could.

Loran stared at the old, black clad warrior as Pehl ran a hand through his greying black locks.

"So, my son wasn't lying. You actually do exist!" he said, turning to see Tialla sitting up in the wet grassland, cursing again.

"I do." He said simply, his voice dark and grating.

"You know nothing of the fight you are involving yourself in, Daemon. Nothing!" Pehl bellowed. Tialla stood and grabbed the reins to her own horse, stepping back up into the saddle.

"Perhaps not, but I would see this violence end. It solves nothing." Loran stepped out of the crumpled catapult and stretched his wings out.

"Fine words from a creature that destroys my catapult at every chance." Pehl laughed. "You want to know of violence? Of hatred and of evil? Then look to the King in his castle. Ask Pyrus of his betrayal."

A squeal from the portcullis drew their attention, and Pehl watched in misery as the gate slid back down into place with a loud, metallic clang. Pehl cursed.

"Father…"

Pehl looked at Tialla. It didn't need saying out loud.

The morning was lost.

"Retreat." He bellowed across the grassland, the call being

passed along the line. As horses turned and galloped for the forest, Pehl turned to Loran and stared at the Daemon for what seemed an eternity.

"Seek me out, when you know of what you speak, Daemon."

He turned and kicked in his heels.

Loran looked to the Citadel as the last remaining sounds of steel on steel faded.

***

He landed in the square, with the central tower behind him. The downpour was coming ever harder now, falling diagonally. Guards were helping their wounded comrades to Malaner's medical building for attention. In the corner, a suffering horse was put out of its misery with the slice of a dagger, fresh blood mixing with the old on the flagstones, quickly diluted by the constant rain.

"Loran?"

He turned to see Daynar walking up to him, her dress sopping and stained with blood.

"Oh, it isn't mine, thankfully." She said, following his gaze. "I've been helping out in the medical building."

"I see. That's good to hear." He said, somewhat bemused. Obviously, her brother Isaac's insistence on helping out was having some effect on them all. "It's good to see you on the mend, Princess."

"I can't believe you came back." She said quietly.

"I can." said a voice behind him. He turned to watch Brianne walking toward him. Loran beamed at her, his eyes cobalt blue in the late morning light. All thoughts of Daynar were lost as he watched her.

"I knew you'd return." She said, nodding a greeting to Daynar, who turned and walked back toward the squat building with a thin smile on her face.

"You knew more than I, then." He chuckled, despite the death surrounding him. They held each other's gaze for a while. The smell of blood and bowels assaulted his senses as they stood for the longest time.

There was a sound from the distance. Loran looked over her shoulder, past her rain-drenched wings to the square in front of him.

An Avian was crouched on the ground, stooped over the body of a dead, black-clad warrior, his hands on the man's chest, his head low. Loran thought, at first, that he was stripping the man of his armour, or weapons. Father had told him, on more than one occasion, that was commonplace in war. Then the sound came again.

Crying.

The Avian was sobbing. Loud, gut-wrenching sobs of grief wracked his body as he crouched over the enemy.

Loran waked past Brianne to stand at the man's side.

"You weep for your enemy?" he asked at last, unsure if he should interrupt him or not.

"...not my enemy..." the man managed between gulps of air, fresh tears streaming down his face.

"I don't understand..." began Loran. He trailed off as the man looked up. Loran looked from the tear-streaked face staring up at him, to the lifeless one on the ground.

They were the same face.

He stared in disbelief for an age. They were identical in every respect, save hair colour. The dead warrior's lank brown mane where the Avians golden blond locks were.

"Kall?" Brianne walked up behind them, the sight robbing her of further questions.

"What is this?" mumbled Loran. "What goes on here? Witchcraft? What dark arts are to blame for this? Are you a Mage?" He thundered.

The Avian stood and chuckled through his tears.

"Oh, you poor, innocent fool." He said, wiping his face on the back of his hand. "Look around you. Look for the first time and see with better eyes."

Loran raised his head and looked around the rainy market square, head and shoulders above everyone else.

Bodies were strewn across the square, the drenched flagstones running red with blood, a murder of carrion crows feasting on the fallen.

Loran's eyes widened.

Every one of Pehl's warriors had long, lank, brown hair. Every Avian was Blonde.

Every one of them.

He looked back to the man on the floor staring up at the dark grey sky, then to the Avian beside him, his eyes wide and questioning. Kall smiled bitterly.

"Have you never heard of identical twins before?"

FIFTEEN

"We found each other about five years ago, Rhyl and I. Pure accident, really. I was flying over the woods as he was riding through it. When I landed, it took my breath away. My own face. My own twin brother. That's how I met Sande."

"Sande?" Loran raised a ridged eyebrow.

"His lover." Brianne said with a hint of scorn.

"Yes." Kall rounded on her as they walked across the battle-torn square. "Yes, I love her. And I don't give a shit who knows it."

"One of them?" Loran asked. Kall simply met his gaze. Loran looked around at the bodies again.

"And everyone else? All brothers?"

"Brothers, sisters, nephews." He shook his head. "Sons and daughters…"

"But all Avians?" Loran asked.
Kall nodded sadly.

"But why? Because their hair colour is different?" Loran could feel the rage boiling within as they started walking again. Damn this stupid feud. And for what?
So much death.

"It is written in the scriptures. There was a large tapestry on the back wall of the temple. I doubt you noticed it, distracted as you were…" Brianne half smiled with a hint of sarcasm.

"Scriptures be damned." Spat Kall. "Bollocks to all of it."

"So, what? These people were cast out? When?"

"At birth, mostly." Said Brianne, almost matter of fact. "Their wings are clipped, and they are left in the forest. It was assumed for a long time that they were simply taken by Sayer-bears, or Prairie Wolves. It would seem that Pehl has been rounding them up for years. We all thought him long dead."

They reached the palace doors, the guards standing firm this time.

"And what of Pehl? Where did he come from?" Loran met the guards steely gaze before glancing down at Brianne, her headscarf sopping with rain.

"From here." She said. "He's the Kings brother…"

***

Pehl stomped into the tent and kicked a stool across the floor with a loud curse. Tialla followed, stripping off her wet, mud-covered cloak and dropping it onto a chair. She filled two flagons with ale and handed one to her father cautiously.

"Damn that stupid, interfering monster. Where in the Gods did he come from anyway? Why is he helping them?" he thundered between sips. Tialla said nothing, choosing instead to sit silently, sipping her ale.

"Where did that fool brother of yours go?" he wondered aloud, his rage subsiding eventually.

"I sent him into the Moon Forest to see if he could round up any stray horses. We need all we can get." She said, her head low.

Pehl mumbled an acknowledgment and sat heavily in his seat, kicking off his riding boots.

"You shouldn't be quite so hard with him, Father." She said. "He only tries to please you."

Pehl raised an eyebrow, and slipped off his leather overshirt, scratching idle at his shoulder blade.

"He can help me best by doing as I ask." He grumbled. "My Brother must be paying him." He slammed down his empty flagon. "That's the only reason I can think of for that…creature to be sticking his grey, scaly nose in."

"Perhaps." She nodded slowly. "Either way, we must decide what comes next."

"We're not giving up just yet." He said, refilling both flagons. "Next time, we won't fail. Next time, it's all-out war."

***

Pyrus had settled back into his ornate chair in the palace's main hall, having listened patiently to Remus' report. Numbers dead, numbers wounded, numbers of enemy slain.
So many numbers.

He sipped on a goblet of Solaanian red as he listened, imagining the discussions that would take place within the forum later.
More damn discussions.

Remus had some good ideas, though. Ideas that merited thought. Things they could do for next time. And there would almost certainly be a next time. Pehl wouldn't give up now. His father's weakness for his youngest son had almost been their undoing on more than one occasion. They were getting better. Stronger.
Should have killed him as a baby, thought Pyrus. Better for everyone, really.

Remus droned on as the king's thoughts wandered.

A crash outside the door interrupted Remus momentarily, the Lord Commander picking up where he left off. Another crash. Shouting.
Remus stopped and looked over his shoulder at the doors.
Yelling.

The doors were kicked open, and Loran picked up a guard by the throat and flung him through the doors and up the central aisle like a sack. He skidded to a stop in front of the King. Loran shrugged the other three guards of as though they were an ill-fitting cloak and strode into the hall.
Claws bared. Teeth bared.

"You!" he stabbed an accusing talon at Pyrus. "This is your doing. All of this." Loran snarled, marching forward. Remus drew his sword and stood in front of the king.

"You know nothing of…" began the King.

"I know enough to know a pointless massacre when I see it. They are your own kin! Your own flesh and blood. And you cast them out of your precious Citadel like scraps from your feast table? And you call me a monster?" Loran bellowed, echoes reverberating from the walls.

"They are not worthy!" yelled Pyrus, standing. "It is written in scripture. None of dark hair shall inherit the divine gift of L'shaan. You expect me to defy the Goddess herself?" Pyrus threw up his hands in despair and sat again.

"Damn your goddess and your scripture. It means little to a child scarred for life at birth and cast into the woods to be dinner for the wolves." Loran roared, wings fluttering in anger.

"It is not your business." Said Remus, sword raised.

"It is wrong…" said Loran quietly. ".. and you know it!" He stared at Remus, then King Pyrus.

Loran turned and strode from the room, the guards parting hastily to let him through.

***

Well, that went well…" said Brianne, falling into step as Loran strode across the square in the rain. Loran simply humphed.

"What exactly did you expect? For the King to simply agree and say 'Yes, oh wise Daemon, I'll abandon the doctrine I've been taught since birth and accept the outcasts with open arms?' Highly likely…"

"Will there ever come a day you do not scold me with sarcasm, woman?" he turned to face her.

"…doubtful…" she smiled thinly. Brianne clicked her fingers. "That reminds me, I have something for you."

"Really?" they fell into step again.

"Yes. Follow me." Brianne led him across the square to a large, wide alleyway. At a small white door, she took out a key from her ivory tunic dress and went in. Loran thought it good manners to wait outside until asked in. Father always tried to teach him good manners. Manners cost little and matter much, he would say.

She emerged a few seconds later with a black package, tied with white ribbon. Loran knotted his ridged eyebrows, puzzled.

"Short Trews. I had the seamstresses make them from the

stretchy material we use for the fledglings. That will prevent your scales from ripping them, and they should move with you as you grow. Assuming you do grow anymore."

"Thank you." He said quietly, taking the package from her. He untied it and held them up, nodding his approval. He moved a hand to undo his loincloth.

"Erm. Perhaps you should change in private?" she laughed.

"Oh. Yes. Of course…" he smiled. "Thank you again."

She stood to one side, and motioned him in. He stepped into her rooms, almost a mirror of the one he last slept in. Except the furniture was cleaner, neater. White, where the other was bare wood. Immaculate, yellow drapes hung across the windows, and the room smelt of roses. He stepped further in, and the door closed behind him.

Loran undid the belt around his waist, and the loincloth slipped to the floor. He felt strange, being naked in her room. Untying the white ribbon, he slipped the black trews on.

They felt odd at first. Clingy. Almost suffocating. They stretched over his scales and over-large thighs, reaching down to his knees. He bent his legs up one at a time, awaiting the familiar tearing of fabric that would send his father into another mood. Nothing.

Loran couldn't help but be impressed. He picked up the belt, and slipped it through the loops around the waistband, then attached the dagger to the belt.

His dagger, now.

Loran fingered the blade, then sheathed it into the scabbard. Taking a last look around, he opened the door and stepped out, holding the loincloth.

"Perfect." She said with a grin. The rain had abated somewhat. Less angry, like the energy had gone out of it. "Perhaps you should show them to Isaac. He'll be glad to see you again, I'm sure."

"I will." He said. "And you?"

"I'll see if I can help with the clean-up. I'll find you later."

Loran nodded. Watching her turn and walk up the alleyway, he spread his wings, shook the water from them and took off, heading for the medical rooms.

He found Isaac, knee deep in bandages and blood and wounded Avians. Looking less like a prince of the Citadel than it was possible to look.
Looking every inch a man.

***

Brianne spent the next half an hour in the grassland outside the wall, helping a team clear away the wooden debris and general mess that had been left. The dead horses were dragged by auroch to be burnt, the smell of charred flesh and hair making her eyes water.
She checked them all for their colouring as discretely as she could. None were suitable.

She walked toward the woods, picking up a long length of timber. More kindling for someone, she thought.

A noise caught her off guard. Like a scream, only not Avian. Nor human. She squinted, shielding her eyes against the damn rain, and peered into the forest.

A handful of paces into the woods was a grey coloured horse, speckled with black spots. It lay on its side, head lolling, tongue drooling. A long spear from the crossbows had pinned it to the ground, its legs sopping with rain and blood.

Brianne crept up to it. She couldn't just leave it to its fate. One of the horse traders her father regularly dealt with had told her that.

"Always put them out of their misery, my girl." He'd said once when she was but a fledgling.
She knelt by its head.

"Shhh. Easy now. Easy." She stroked its nose. "Time to cross the bridge, my friend." She picked up a rock, the horses eyes widening in panic, its legs kicking.

"Easy now." She whispered.
The sound of wood snapping behind her startled them both. She turned to find a tall, skinny outcast with unkempt curly hair and

a vicious grin standing over her.

Caylen cracked her across the temple with the pommel of his sword, and she crumpled across the panic-stricken horse.

"Stupid fucking bitch." He mumbled as he sheathed his sword and dragged her over to a copse of dense trees where he had four horses tethered together. Heaving her up, he slung her over the back of a large chestnut gelding, her wings drooping across her face like wet bedsheets. The horse on the floor snorted, and Caylen walked over to it, unsheathed a dagger and cut its throat without a word. He mounted the lead horse and headed back to camp.

SIXTEEN

The Century Wars.
Year fifty seven.
The Holy City of Lianna.
Durmak.

"Come on," yelled Goral, "Keep pushing them back." The wind whipped his words away, sand blasting their faces. They were high on the hills overlooking the Holy city, the spires of Lianna Palace twisting into the air to his left. On his right, the River of Light cut the land in two, running down to the Oran Sea in the distance. Beyond the river sat Solaania, ancient and passive.
Above him, the skies were full.

He and his shield man, Easton, stood watching, shouting commands and still unsure that they could be heard above the gusts coming from the wilderness.
How he hated this barren sand heap.

Easton took off his helm and brushed a hand through his mop of dark, unruly hair. The summers had merged into years, the years into decades. And still, there seemed no end to these Wraiths.

"You'd think they'd run out of victims…" he mumbled, not for the first time.
Goral nodded.

Yet seemingly, they did not. He shielded his eyes with his hand and peered into the distant sky. Great swarms of wraiths were headed this way.

"Second century!" yelled Easton, spotting the threat. Below his position a hundred Avians launched themselves into the air. They joined the first hundred, already twisting and turning about the sky, wrestling with the huge hunks of muscle, teeth and wings, intent on *tearing every Avian they saw into pieces.*

The first century had split into two flights. At Easton's suggestion, the first flight of fifty would take the Wraiths head-on, stabbing at the giant creatures as a distraction for the second flight, that would dive at the wraiths from high, slicing their swords at the necks of the creatures. It had worked well enough.
At first.

Now, though, the creatures were getting wise. They too had split, most heading toward the Avians, some staying back to catch the second flight on their descent. He cursed under his breath as a dozen or so Avians were torn to pieces on their way down, giant teeth tearing them into piecemeal. Of the first flight, twenty had fallen, the remaining thirty stabbing Wraiths through the mouth, then taking the beasts' heads.

He watched as a wraith fell, his head landing some feet from him.
Goral and Easton stepped back as a Wraith landed at their feet, roaring and rushing at them, maw snapping for Goral's head. Easton drew his sword and stabbed at the beasts flank. It turned and snapped at his arm, missing by a hairs breath.
Goral brought his sword cleanly through the Wraiths neck. The head tumbled away, the body crumpling.

***

Easton handed Goral a trencher of cold meat and vegetables. He nodded his thanks, then simply sat, staring at it.

He didn't feel sure how much more of this they could take. Goddess Myla's army sat way to the east of them, beyond Lianna Palace. L'Shaan had kept them back to guard their precious palace. These wars were relentless, and he felt weary.
Bone weary.

"Why not get some sleep, if you're not hungry?" Easton asked as he sat beside him. The tent flapped angrily in the desert wind, the hill they were camped beside giving them little shelter.
Something else there seemed no end to.

He picked up a piece of meat and stuffed it in without truly

tasting it. He should sleep, really. But his nights were fitful and restless of late. Outside the tent, he could hear the distant roars of the wraiths. They didn't attack in such great numbers during the darkness, thankfully. He chewed on an orange vegetable of some kind, it's taste tangy and salted, his mind wandering to the battles to come in the morning.
If only he could keep the damn things asleep.

***

Torna stood at the head of the large, glass topped table. A map of the realm spread before him, marked in various points with ink to denote their position and the enemy's.
Enemy.

It still felt strange to think of his fellow Gods as enemies. They had, after all, ruled and lived among these mortals for centuries together. Blaise had always been cunning, some might say untrustworthy. She, like himself, would not hesitate to use any situation to her advantage. They had never been close, but they had worked together well enough.

Rotaldir, on the other hand, was not so subtle. God of the Otherworld he may be, but he was blatantly ambitious and jealous in equal measure. Torna found him nothing short of

unpleasant, both to look at and to talk to. That voice. Slithery and insipid, like his grey skin. But Blaise was determined to see him take Vororr's position as Supreme.
So be it.

He would throw in his lot with them, supplying them with suggestion and strategy. He would prove invaluable to them, that he may benefit from the outcome of this war, would it end in their favour.
And if it did not?

Then he would use that to his advantage also, demonstrating to Vororr his loyalty and worthiness by being instrumental in their downfall. His cunning and deviousness would be put to the ultimate test.
His very existence depended on it.

***

Goral awoke suddenly to find Easton standing over him, his hand shaking his Commander by the shoulder.
His face grave.
"Goral? There's someone here to see you." *He whispered, standing.*
Goral shook himself awake.
Who could be visiting at this late hour? It seemed only minutes since he fell asleep, although he suspected it was much longer.
"A visitor? Who?"
"L'Shaan."
It took a moment for the words to sink in.
The Goddess?
Here?

This didn't feel good. No wonder Easton had woken him. He would not have done so lightly, knowing how sleep had evaded him of late.
"Show her in," *he hastily stumbled to his feet, shuddering his wings.* "at once."
The tent flap was pulled aside, and the Goddess herself glided in, nose in the air slightly, candlelight shining of her dark mane.
"My Lady." *He dipped his head in reverence.*
"I hope I'm not intruding too much, Goral?" *she said, taking a seat in the only wooden chair available.*
"Indeed not, My Lady." *He cooed.*
Not that it would have mattered much if she were.
"How can I be of assistance?"
"I have been thinking on how we may best turn the tide of these battles if we are to be victorious."
"I see." *He said slowly.*
"And I can see a time where the beasts may be vulnerable."
Goral swallowed. He had a nasty feeling he knew what was coming. An idea he and Easton had talked over and dismissed several times before.
"They sleep during the night, only attacking in very small

numbers. We should locate their resting place and destroy them while they slumber." She said, smirking as if it were so obvious they should have thought of it already.

They had.

Easton had suggested it almost every time he and his century commanders sat around this very tent.

And every time, Goral dismissed it.

"We have discussed this plan already, My Lady. It is far too dangerous for us to undertake. We would be spotted from afar and would never make it to Blaise's castle."

"Goddess Blaise." She corrected. Goral harumphed.

I'll be damned if I'm calling her that ever again, he thought.

"Well, now, it seems a pity that you feel unable to undertake such an obvious opportunity for fear of dying for your Goddess's cause." She let the words hang between them.

He would not stand for his men to be branded cowards. Not after all they had given.

"Might Goddess Myla's armed men not be better placed to undertake such a task?" He ventured. It made sense to him for Myla's army to sneak around Blaise's castle during the night-time hours, slaughtering every Wraith they could find, than for him to risk his precious Avians in such a venture.

"No."

No explanation. No justification or reason.

"I see."

He saw only too well.

He and his Avians were deemed expendable.

SEVENTEEN

Queen Isiarus screamed in rage. The messenger that Pehl had sent in his stead shuffled nervously about as she ranted, hoping against hope that he was too insignificant to simply murder out of pure spite.

Fortunately for him he was correct. He scuttled out at Loshin's nod like a scurrying rat.

"They will do better next time, Highness, I'm sure." Loshin said at last. She glared at him a beat, then sat with a sigh.

"Time is fast running out, Loshin. You know that."

"I'm aware, Highness." He said with a nod. "Fian assures me all is prepared. All he needs now is the Seraph."

She poured a glass of wine and sipped it silently, her withered left arm cradled in her lap.

She simply couldn't afford to fail. The last failure had been embarrassing enough, after all the trouble and time spent creating that "Thing" that Fian assured her would be able to take the Seraph from the Avians.

Fian was lucky his head was not adorning a spike before now.

Had he not been instrumental in locating the Seraph, after the years they had spent searching Durmak for its apparent resting place, she might have felt differently.

She could not fail again. Everything depended on that damn Seraph. She would be whole again. Complete. And more besides, if Fian had read the scriptures correctly.

She would be a Goddess.

***

"What do you hope to gain by keeping me prisoner?" Brianne ranted, tightening her headscarf.

She stood in Pehl's tent, rain pooling about her feet. Her

wingtips were tied to prevent escape. Tialla eyed her uneasily.

"I'm not sure yet, my lady." Pehl said wearily. In truth, he had little clue what use she would be, or what Caylen was even thinking, bringing her back here. A point he would be making with his son soon!

"You will be fed, and looked after while you're here, have little fear. You may be of use as a bargaining tool of some kind."

"A bargaining tool for what?"

"All in good time, dear lady," he said. "All in good time." Pehl nodded to the guards, who led her away.
Damn!

"She's a feisty one." Said Tialla. "I like her."

"Splendid!" Pehl shot back, standing. "Perhaps you can plait each other's hair." He paced about, muttering to himself.

"Relax, father. She may be of use yet, as you said. It will do no harm to keep her a while." Pehl raised an eyebrow. It was unlike Tialla to think any plan of Caylen's deserved merit. They were usually met with derision.

"You think it's really so simple? With that beast in their camp? If he comes for her, he could tear this fucking place apart, and us with it!"

"So, what are you thinking?" she sat forward in her seat. There was little else for it.

"We need to move camp. Now."

***

"It's been three days now, father." Said Daynar impatiently. "We must begin searching."

King Pyrus met his daughters intense stare and shook his head.

"No." he sighed. "We cannot risk searching during K'lahl. I will not allow any further bloodshed needlessly."

About him, teams had been looking in all the usual places that Brianne would normally be found. She was, at best, a private person. Normally keeping to herself.
The damn rain didn't help much, grounding the search teams as it did. Doors had been opened and slammed shut constantly

during the day, once it was obvious that she was missing.

They turned at the sound of wet footsteps behind them. Isaac trudged across the square, his wings sopping.

"Nobody has seen Lady Brianne since the last attack from the outcasts." He shifted about uncomfortably.

"What?" Pyrus pressed him.

"She was outside the gate…"

Daynar sighed heavily. "Father, we must begin…"

"I've already said, no. I will not risk it."

"That's all very well father, but for one problem." Isaac looked over his shoulder.

The colossal grey form of Loran the Daemon strode toward them, now seemingly ever-present in the Citadel. Rain bounced off his bald, grey dome, running in rivulets down the back of his gossamer black wings.

"Do you want to tell him," Smiled Daynar, "Or shall I?"

***

Ashe clicked his tongue, giving the reins a light shake, geeing the old black mare along the eastern road. Var'n Rodan loomed in the distance, its stubby round-roofed buildings like giant mushrooms across the hillside. The outer wall had a couple of bored, fat guards on the gate. They checked the occasional wain. Generally, those they didn't like the look of. Stopped the odd woman.

Generally, those they definitely *did* like the look of.

He pulled his cloak around him as a northern wind swept up suddenly, looking over his shoulder at the waxed sheet covering his load.

Damn rain, he thought. Will it never end?

Ashe pulled on the reins, and the wain drew to a stop behind a load of fish from the port at Point Mar, and two ladies returning on horseback. The guards began asking the ladies a thousand and one questions and the merchant in front mumbled something, his patience wearing thin. One guard eyed him closely, then waved the ladies through.

His fellow guard caught Ashe's eye and waved him round

as they prepared to take as much time as possible with the impatient fish merchant.

Rather you two than me, thought Ashe as he got a whiff of the wain.

He trundled lazily through the gate, past a yard on the left full of cattle. Children ran across his path, people scuttling about their daily grind without paying him any mind. He turned right and headed for the familiar yard of Rayner's.

Rayner the younger, actually, having taken up his father's salt business at the old man's passing these two moons past. Ashe jumped down from the wain and clasped Rayner's hand, the young trader laughing and running a hand through his red beard.

He unloaded his wain, passing pleasantries with Rayner and his wife, a young, dark haired girl, her belly round with their first child.

Business attended to, he took the wain over to the stables, a young stable lad taking his horses reins. Ashe tossed him a coin and headed over to Vena's tavern.

He entered, taking of his dripping cloak and hanging it on a hook on the wall.

By the gods, it was good to finally be in the dry.

"Ashe, you old scoundrel!" Vena said as he walked to the bar.

"Vena! You look younger every day." He grinned.

"Oh, get away with you." She blushed, resting her ample frame on the bar. He ordered ale and a bowl of warm broth with bread, then headed to a table where two Solaanian sailors were playing a game of bones.

Ashe looked around the warm tavern. It was slow going, but then every day was slow with the myriad restrictions on merchants thanks to queen Isiarus lately. A young man sat by the fire, wrestling a tune from an old squeeze box, two chaps at a nearby table trying to remember the words to a long-forgotten song. In the corner, a table with three cattle hands was getting louder. Rough boys, by any standards. But business was business.

"Oi!" Vena bellowed as one cattle hand made a grab for Mira, her daughter, as she scuttled past with a tray of ales. "Keep your hands to yourself, boy, unless you want a cudgel about the ear!" his two friends guffawed at his reddening face, and Mira took the drinks over to a table by the window.

The old man at the end of the bar waved his flagon at her, and Vena took it and turned her back to fill it up for the third or fourth time, Ashe judged, looking at the old man's ruddy face. Behind him, the room fell silent.
Vena stood abruptly and turned as Ashe looked up to the doorway.

Standing in the doorway was a giant of a figure. Grey skin with scales on the arms, and two short horns of black on his bald head. His black, leathery wings filled the doorframe, cutting out the light completely. Mira scurried behind the bar as it walked slowly into the tavern.

"Forgive the intrusion," said Loran, his voice deep and dark, "I mean you no harm, I assure you."

"We've nothing for you here." Said Vena. "Nothing. You get, now" she picked up a bottle by the neck from behind the bar.

"I require information only." Loran raised his hands and walked further into the bar, scanning the room.

"Information?" she said cautiously.

"I'm seeking a warband. On horse, mostly. They have a prisoner with them that I'm most intent on freeing. They were camped northwest of the Moon Forest until recently."

Very recently, in fact. Loran had stood in the middle of the camp only yesterday. Dark, burnt circles with stones where the campfires had been. Flat patches where the tents were. Horse dung scattered.

"We didn't think you were real." Said a voice in the corner. Loran turned and walked over to a table where Ashe was sitting with two dark skinned sailors.

"I am." He said simply. "I tend to stay hidden, mostly."

"No fucking wonder…" murmured someone across the

room, a chuckle spreading around the tavern.
Loran smiled thinly.

"They're heading west, towards the caves at Naren's pass. Saw them yesterday, after I left Var'n Cirnan. Can't be heading nowhere else, going that way. Nothing much else out there." He picked up his ale and took a sip.

"I'm not familiar with these caves." Loran said, looking to his two dark skinned companions.

"You're from Solaan?" He asked.

"We are." Smiled one with a toothless grin. "You're familiar with us?"

"I made the acquaintance of someone from Solaan once. He became a good friend."

"I'm Gill," he jabbed a thumb at his compatriot, "and this is my brother, Tiril." Loran nodded to them both.

"Sit, drink. Have a game of bones." Laughed Gill. "Time for warbands later, no?"

"Thank you, but no. I must find them."

"A woman?" Ashe put his ale down.
Loran turned and nodded.

"It's always a fucking woman." He chuckled, shaking his head. "Head north-west toward the coast. On the left you'll see a couple of dense woodlands. Between them is a wide path that doubles back on itself. That's the entrance to the caves. Run for miles underground, out towards the coast. Big enough to hide a warband, I'm thinking." He smiled.

"Thank you." Loran said. He took a last look around, then turned and headed out, closing the door behind him.
The room was silent a beat.

"Well," said Ashe. "...seemed like a nice chap..."
Laughter sprang up around the tavern, and the music started again.
Behind the bar, Vena breathed out at last.

EIGHTEEN

"You really think he'll turn up?" Keane shuffled nervously outside the cave's entrance, looking towards the horses and the woods beyond.

"Who knows?" Tam replied, munching on an apple. "I'm bored and cold, I know that much. Pissing rain."

A horse whinnied in the distance, and Keane flinched, mumbling a curse.

"Relax, will 'ya? You'll make me nervous soon." Tam took another bite.

Keane settled back against the cave wall, looking at the woods more often than was healthy.

"They say he drinks babies' blood." He mumbled. The thought sent a shiver up his spine.

"Shite!" said Tam. "Who told you that? Was they on the ale, by any chance?" He chuckled and shook his head.

"...could be true, you never..."

"Shite, I'm tellin' ya. Now relax," Tam interrupted, "He ain't coming anywhere near here. And if he does?" He fingered the pommel of his sword. "I've got some nice, cold steel waiting for him."

High in a treetop, overlooking the cave, Loran smiled.

***

He wrestled with plan after plan. He could just fight his way in. After all, much as steel swords and arrowheads hurt, they probably wouldn't kill him. He seemed to heal much too quickly for them to have any real effect.

That wasn't the problem.

Loran really didn't *want* to fight his way in, causing any more death. Something told him these people had suffered enough as it was.

That still left the problem of how to get Brianne out.

A rustle next to him drew his attention. A white gull had settled on a branch in the next tree. It looked at him curiously, its head tilted to one side.

Loran smiled as the gull let out a screech, then took to the air. A thought passed across his mind, something he'd heard recently.

"...Run for miles underground, out towards the coast..."

Loran looked up. He could hear the shoreline from his vantage point in the trees, could see the waves crashing against the cliff face to the right, the tumultuous Oran Sea pounding the rocks as the cliffs rose to Var'n Cirnan off to the west. To the east, the shore curved out into a gentle bay. Off in the distance, the port of Point Mar a bustle of activity as barges and galleys fought for position, wating to be unloaded.

Loran remembered something his father had told him many summers ago. About he and his brother exploring the caves as boys. Not these ones in particular, thought Loran, but still.

Might be worth a chance.

Loran stretched his own wings out and launched himself almost silently. The cave mouth dropped away beneath him, and he headed out towards the coast, the wind battering his face. The wet grasslands below gave way to sand and scree as the shoreline fell away to the sea. In front of him, the gull looked over its shoulder suspiciously, screeched and headed toward the cliff face to find a rocky crag to perch on. It landed, disappearing amongst the current residents. A gust blew in from the sea, lifting Loran in a sudden updraft. He looked down intently, his deep blue eyes searching the water.

There.

A definite line of blue as the shoreline dropped away abruptly. Loran banked over to the right and dived down toward the water. At the last moment, he folded in his wings and, taking a deep breath, plunged into the sea.

His eyes adjusted to the darkness as, above him, the

foam continued to batter the shore. He swam back towards the beach and spotted what he was looking for. In front of him, the sea floor dropped away sharply, revealing a shelf of rock, stark brown against the sand. In the face of the shelf was an opening. Long, flat and black, it sank away into the rock face. Loran swam into it.

It was only just high enough for him, and he folded his wings in as much as he could, swimming forward as the walls began to close in on him. Up ahead he could make out a dim and distant light, a beam of sun penetrating from above. The tunnel continued to close in on him as he swam, looking toward the light ahead. Loran wasn't sure how long he could hold his breath for, but now seemed a good time to find out.
Come what may, he had to reach her.

The cave closed in dramatically from both sides, and Loran stopped abruptly. His shoulders were firmly wedged as, ahead, the tunnel opened out before him into a wide cave. The beam of light seemed close now, but Loran struggled to free his overlarge frame. His lungs were burning, calling for air as he wriggled and struggled.
Damn.

He stretched out his hands and dug his claws into the rock and silt, scraping desperately. His lungs were screaming as he tore frantically at the rock, the edges of his vision darkening, panic creeping in slowly.
Loran couldn't move.

***

Caylen lead Brianne down a dark tunnel, turned left and walked into a wide opening. Brianne gasped at its sudden beauty, so out of place here in the dank darkness. Before her was a pool of water, bobbing gently up and down with the tide. A beam of light shone down from above, bursting through an opening in the cave roof. It smelt damp and briny, the tang of salt in her throat.

"Father says you can wash or bathe here. Whatever. You'll be undisturbed." He said, looking about the cave wearily.

"Thank you." She said quietly, waiting for him to leave. Only Caylen didn't move.

"You're quite pretty, for an Avian." He said, almost surprised. He looked at her silently and took a step toward her. Brianne took a step back. Men were a sore topic with her, and this man in particular made her skin crawl.

"Now, don't get prissy." He said through gritted teeth. "I'm only getting to know you." He reached out to touch her face, and she recoiled again.

"Stuck up little bitch!" he growled, reaching out and slapping her across the face, snapping her head to the right. Caylen stepped forward, putting one arm around her waist and grabbing at her breast with the other.

"Get off me!" she yelped, a hint of panic in her voice. She pushed his face away as he tried to kiss her, desperation and dread taking hold. Caylen bought his hand back again, palm open.

"Caylen!" Pehl's voice boomed from the entrance, echoing around the cave. He stepped down from the mouth of the tunnel.

"We do not treat our guests in such fashion!" He snarled. Caylen turned to leave, and Pehl grabbed his shoulder.

"If I ever find you forcing yourself on a woman again, boy, I'll kill you myself!" he growled.

Caylen opened his mouth to speak, when the water behind him bubbled and foamed, getting visibly darker.

Loran the Daemon rose from the pool, water dripping down his wings. His breath came in ragged gasps as he stepped out.

Claws bared. Teeth bared.

Loran stretched his wings out and roared.

***

Pehl and Caylen both blanched visibly as Loran stepped from the pool, water puddling at his feet. He took a step toward them.

Brianne stepped forwards and placed a hand on his chest.

"Easy, big fellow. I'm unhurt. No harm done." She looked

over her shoulder at Pehl. "You should not have come here," she said, turning back to Loran, "They will release me in time, I'm sure."

Loran snarled again. He looked down at her.

"This is quite sweet!" said Pehl from behind them. "She tries to protect you, just as you come here unarmed to rescue her." He chuckled.

"I need no armament…" To make his point, Loran reached down with a single talon and sliced through the thick rope binding Brianne's wingtips. She stretched them out, fluttering the life back into them.

"Sweet?" spluttered Caylen. "You mean…?"

"Oh, come, my boy! Surely, you've eyes to see?" Pehl put his hands on his hips. "Imagine their faces, when they discover *this* romance blossoming." He laughed, shaking his head. "Whatever they're paying you, I'd triple it to see that." His laughter echoing round the cave.

"I am not in your brother's employ." Loran folded his wings back and sheathed his talons.

"So? The truth is out at last, eh?" Pehl turned and walked back up the steps. They followed behind, the tunnel darkening in front of them. Loran's eyes adjusted easily.

"To be fair," he said over his shoulder, "I did tell you to seek me out when you knew what you were involved in."

"You did. It does not sit easily with me, and I have made that clear. But this vengeance of yours?" Loran shook his head. "It will not make you feel better, I'm sure of it."

They rounded a corner, coming to a wide opening with a table full of provisions. Jugs of ale, loaves and cold meats spread out. A trencher with vegetables in it. Pehl poured them a flagon of ale, and Caylen kept walking, disappearing round the next bend in the tunnel.

"I apologise for him," mumbled Pehl. "He's not the sharpest sword in the bunch, you understand. Means well, most of the time." He sat on a wooden seat, offering one to Brianne.

She sat sipping her ale silently. The taste was unfamiliar. Sharper than she imagined.

"It isn't about revenge." Pehl announced. "It's about getting back our birth right."

Loran drained his ale. He was getting quite used to the taste himself.

"How?" asked Brianne.

Pehl drained his own flagon.

"By stealing the Seraph."

NINETEEN

"What good would that do you?" She blurted. Pehl placed his flagon on the table and looked at her for a moment.

"The queen, Isiarus? She has promised that in return for the Seraph, she will restore our wings. We can finally claim our place in this land. And not as damn outcasts, either!" he spat.

"You cannot trust that witch." Loran said, placing his own flagon alongside Pehl's. "Do you plan on pledging your allegiance to her?"

Pehl shook his head in reply. That was most definitely not on his agenda anytime soon. These people had come to trust him, and he would rather die than betray that trust by bowing down to anyone.

"I will be bound to nobody, until I get what is rightfully mine."

"She would have nothing to gain from giving you your wings back, unless you became her... airborne army of some kind." Loran said, searching for the right words. "You cannot trust her, surely you must see that?"

Brianne furrowed her brow.

"What do you mean, rightfully yours?" she asked.

"The throne." Said Pehl. "I'm the eldest of us. The throne should be mine."

Brianne stared back, wide eyed.

"You are not aware?" he asked

She shook her head slowly.

"We knew you were brothers but were told you were younger." They were told precious little, to be fair.

"No," he growled. "I am not!" Pehl sat forward on his seat.

"When I was five, our father, old King Goral decided he

could defy the precious goddess no more, and took me to Point Mar. I'd already had my wings chopped off by now and was living with a family on the outskirts of The Citadel. At Point Mar I was cast onto a ship bound for Solaan. I spent ten years of my life in that shithole, bound to a family. More or less a house slave. They were pleasant enough to me, even though I was a foreigner. One day the old cook sent me to the port to pick up some fish from the merchant. Instead, I boarded a ship headed here and returned home. To what was rightfully mine." He sat back in his seat, remembering the sounds of that ship. The smell of stale beer and sweat. "Pyrus was twelve by then, and had already claimed the throne as his own."

He filled his flagon again, offering some to Brianne. She shook her head.

"On the trip home from Point Mar, I found three dark haired Avians living with a family in Var'n Rodan. They'd been left in the forest. This fellow found them, gave them a home. They showed me the scars. Like my own."

Loran closed his eyes against the thought.

Pehl stood suddenly.

"Come with me." He said.

***

They stood, aghast. Pehl had led them down a corridor in the rock, tunnels sprouting off in different directions. Men and women were seated everywhere. All dark haired. He checked on some as they went, asking if they'd eaten, were they well.

Had their wounds healed.

Most looked at Brianne with open hostility. Some with undisguised jealousy.

All looked at Loran in awe.

Pehl led them to a tall slender woman with long, red hair in a braid. Loran recognised her as the one who'd ended up on her backside in the mud.

"This is my daughter, Tialla. She's been in Solaan, learning new fighting skills." He clasped her on the shoulder. "Keeping safe."

Tialla nodded her greeting, helping to bind a wound on another with a short man, his dark hair greying at the temples.

"Most of these people I found in the forest as children. Left to fend for themselves. Some as babies. Left to die."

"It disgusts me…" Loran mumbled.

"Aye, us too." Said Tialla, a hint of menace in her voice.

Pehl continued walking. They passed more and more children seated on rocks. Most, explained Pehl, had been taken in by other families. Outcasts, as they were, from their own. Finally, they found themselves at the cave's entrance. Keane and Tam looked on in amazement as Loran's towering form passed them.

Brianne looked at Pehl, puzzled.

"I am not, generally, a kidnapper." He said quietly. "Go. Be well. But be warned. I will be attacking again. I must end this." Loran held his gaze a beat, then nodded. Pehl turned and walked back into the cave.

"Come." He said to Brianne. "Let's get you out of here." The rain was still incessant, and she looked at the sky miserably. Loran caught her gaze and bent to lift her.

"I'll fly you back." He said.

"No."

He stood slowly and waited.

"I don't want to go back there," She murmured. "Not yet. Is there somewhere else we can go? Somewhere secluded, that I may gather my thoughts?" There seemed such a lot to get her head around that she almost felt dizzy with it all.

Loran smiled at her.

"I know just the place."

***

They headed west. The Moon Forest loomed large beneath them all to soon, and Brianne leaned into his broad chest and braced herself for the decent to the Aleas's cabin.

Only Loran kept flying, heading west further still. The forest fell away behind them, and she looked up, puzzled. Where was he taking her?

In the distance, the sun was dropping down behind the western steppes, painting the mountain peaks in orange and pink. The rain had stopped here, grey clouds melting into blue skies. The ground below was green no more, the grass petering out, replaced by sand and rubble, the occasional bush clinging to a boulder for protection.
The Desolation.

***

An idiot?
Is that how the old fool thought of him?
An idiot?

Caylen stomped from the tunnel, knocking Keane aside as he did so. He'd been listening as his father's voice echoed up the cave. Getting angrier and angrier. They should not have to explain themselves to these entitled halfwits.

Caylen stomped out into the woods, to where the horses were tethered. He kicked a stone idly, walking in circles, as a horse snorted at him.
He should be appreciated.
Nurtured.
Not derided and ridiculed in front of that stuck up bitch and her monstrous boyfriend.

He looked to the west, as the sun was setting over the steppes. He could just make out the pinprick silhouette of them flying over the Moon Forest. To the north of them, he could barely see the twisted spire of Queen Isiarus's palace.
Maybe she'd give him the respect he was due?
Maybe he should tell her of his fathers' continual failure? His weakness in letting a perfectly good prisoner go free?
Maybe that's where he should be heading?

Caylen hefted a saddle from the forest floor and saddled a roan-coloured mare. Lifting himself into the saddle, he kicked in his heels and cantered towards the twisted spire at Var'n Arden.

***

They landed in a clearing nestled between two faces of rock, boulders scattered about in various sizes. All about was

arid scrubland, sparse bushes and nothingness. In the rockface to the left was a large opening.
Oh, good, she thought.
Another cave.

Loran settled her down gently, then began gathering dead wood and twigs from what sparse brush he could, piling them up into the makings of a fire. He crouched, searching the ground for stones, discarding them until he found whatever it was he was looking for. He struck the two dark stones together until a spark lit the kindling. Fire sprang up, crackling and spitting, shadows dancing on the rock face.

Brianne stood still as a statue, slightly numb. The events of the past few days running through her head.

"Cold?" she chuckled at last, instantly cursing herself under her breath for her constant sarcasm. It had been her weapon of defence for so long, it had almost become a habit.

"It may keep the Prairie Wolves away." He said. "Stay here, I won't be long." He turned and started to walk away.

"You're leaving me?" she said quietly.
He turned and held her gaze, smiling.

"Even Daemons need to relieve themselves occasionally," he chuckled. "I won't be far away, I promise."

She watched as he padded away into the darkness, the dancing shadows her only companion.

TWENTY

Caylen cantered up to the White Spire at Var'n Arden, entirely unsure of just how he was going to get an audience with the queen. They had met but once and, although he found her attractive, even alluring, he was almost sure she wouldn't even remember him.

In front of him was a train of wains, the last one accompanied by a man on horseback. Armed with a longsword and looking decidedly bored. Caylen cantered up to the man, said hello, and started making small talk. The weather, the work, merchants in general. The kind of nonsense he'd heard a thousand times in the past from all kinds of people he'd met over the years. He learned the man's name- Pearce- and they chatted like old friends as his horse walked alongside Pearce's chestnut gelding and through the gate. The guard payed them no mind at all, just two horse guards paid by a rich trader to watch over the load from thieves and vagabonds no doubt, and Caylen walked his horse into the courtyard, nodding to the guard like he'd done it all his life.

He could scarce believe his luck! He was in, and without causing any commotion too. He told Pearce he'd catch up with him soon and dismounted at the stables on the right. He tied his horse to a post outside and walked up to the palace keep.
This would not be quite so easy.

Outside was another wain, this one being unloaded by kitchen staff. Casks of ale, by the look of it. Caylen ducked down behind a stack of boxes next to the gate and removed his sword belt and jacket. He tucked them down behind the boxes and walked up to the wain. Picking up a cask of ale, he heaved it onto his shoulder, covering his face, and strode into the palace.

Nobody stopped him.

Caylen followed the man in front of him and put the cask next to the kitchen. He turned and made his way up a staircase to his left. Long drapes of purple hung on the wall. There were no guards here, and he climbed the stairs to the next level.

The guard on this level had his back to him and was deep in conversation with one of the maids, she laughing coyly as the guard brushed her cheek with his hand. Caylen took his chance and scurried across the passageway to the next corridor. Here the decoration was different. Rich, red and gold with an ornate motif embroidered into it draped on the wall. He walked to the end of the corridor and opened the window.

Outside was a ledge, just wide enough to get his feet onto. Below, guards walked along the outside wall, watching the woods and the town. Nobody was watching the keep.

Caylen took a deep breath, then stepped out onto the ledge.

***

Brianne sat alone for what seemed hours but was, more likely, only minutes.

She hoped, silently, that he was actually coming back.

She leaned forward to rub her hands together, warming them at the fire. The heat was welcoming, the smell biting but familiar, nonetheless. She looked around, taking in the stark desert, its sparse brush clinging to rocks and boulders.

What were they doing here? How did he know this place?

Perhaps he'd been camping here on some trek or suchlike with Aleas? She'd often asked her own father if they could do something similar. A camping trip or something like that. Perhaps in the forest?

Before all the trouble started with Pehl.

Did Daemons even go camping? He'd mentioned a few times how he'd learnt something or other from Aleas, but there was still so much she didn't know about this strange, fascinating creature she was with.

And a few things he doubtless didn't know about her.

There was a noise out on the scrubland. Soft, gentle

padding. Like footsteps, only lighter. Perhaps he was tiptoeing back, thinking she was asleep?

"Better?" she mumbled.

There was a low, menacing growl in front of her. She looked up as a Prairie Wolf walked into the firelight. It's teeth were showing, maw open in an angry snarl, it's heckles up.

So much for keeping the wolves away, she thought.

Brianne held her breath for a second. The wolf took another step toward her, a low growl coming from its throat. She could see another three pairs of eyes glinting in the darkness. This was clearly dinner time, and she was the main course.

Behind her, another growl started. This one was lower in tone. Angrier. Louder.

Brianne couldn't move.

She took a breath, turned slowly and looked over her shoulder.

Loran was crouched on a rock directly behind her, wings out. His claws were gripping the stone and he was snarling back at the wolf.

A man and a half of grey Daemon. And he didn't look happy.

The alpha wolf in front stopped and looked up at him for what seemed an eternity, weighing up its options. Finally the alpha tilted its head to one side, obviously thought the better of it, then turned and loped off into the darkness.

"You think they'll return?" she asked.

"I doubt it." He hoped down from the rock, folding in his wings. Reaching behind it, he retrieved a hare he'd caught, dropping it down in front of the fire.

"Hungry?"

**

Queen Isiarus wrinkled her nose as she entered Fian's cellar workroom, leaving Loshin outside the door. As Fian stood with his back to her, hunched over his worktable.. Bottles and potions littered the shelves and floor, and large cages stood off to one corner. In the bottom of one was a pile of matted fur and blood, the result of one of his "experiments," no doubt.

A none too successful one, from the look of it.

"Highness." He bowed as he turned to her, his painfully thin frame barely filling his robes, hooked nose and long hair giving the appearance of a crow. She looked around the room, its disarray doing little to sage her impatience.

"You assure me this will work, Mage?" she said, looking into the blood strewn cage in the corner.

"It will, Highness. All I need is the Seraph. The time is right but is fast evaporating."

"Yes, yes." she said turning to him, "I have made the importance of this clear to the outcasts, they will deliver, I have been assured."

"And, what of them afterwards?" he asked.

"They will be slaughtered." She said, raising her eyebrows. "Obviously…"

She stepped out into the corridor, Loshin falling into step behind her. Guards visibly standing straighter as she passed. They walked along the corridor to her rooms in the far corner of the tower.

"What does he get up to in that dungeon?" she asked over her shoulder.

"I find it better not to ask, Highness." Isiarus herself had heard many a tale of what went on in the night, of animals melded to other animals, to make creatures of nightmarish proportions.

She opened the door to her room and stopped abruptly. There was a strange, naked man in her bed. Long, dark, straggly hair. Tall with a handsome face. His clothing scattered about the floor.

He looked familiar.

"Highness," he said with a flourish of the hand. "I am Caylen, son of Pehl."

"Ah yes. I know you." She said, waving Loshin out. He hesitated just long enough to earn a glare from the queen.

He shut the door behind them, his voice carrying through the oak door as he set upon the guards in the corridor.

"And would you mind telling me exactly what you think

you're doing in my bedchamber?"

"Waiting for you." He said, throwing the covers back. "Obviously."

She smiled slowly.

***

She watched him, seemingly fascinated, as he skinned and gutted the hare, throwing the offal out as far as he could. It would give the wolves something to eat, he explained. Keep them busy.

She mumbled that she was all in favour of keeping them busy.

Skewering the carcass on a large stick, he propped it over the fire, turning it occasionally, the fat spitting and sizzling on the burning wood.

Loran watched the fire spitting, thinking back to the last time he had spent here.

With Hanan.

He had been in the desolation only a few moons, by his reckoning, when he had spotted the fire from the distance. Loran had spent a long while considering whether to approach this stranger and make their acquaintance, as father once said.

In the end, he decided he'd endured the silence long enough.

The man had been sitting, cooking a hare just like this one as Loran padded out of the darkness. The stranger was unlike any man he'd seen before. His skin was as black as night, wrinkled and sun-dried like leather. He had no hair, but kind eyes, and was whistling a tune.

He stopped when he spotted the Daemon.

"Vororr's teeth…" Hanan muttered.

"Forgive the intrusion," Loran said. "I mean you no harm."

"Of that I'm glad." Said the man, his eyes wide.

"I spotted the fire and wondered if I might join you?" he asked. The man nodded slowly.

"I've never seen anyone like you before." Said Loran, sitting on a rock and draping his wings over the back.

"Ha!" laughed the man. "I was just going say the same

about you!"

Loran smiled and introduced himself.

"I'm Hanan." he said. "I'm from across the sea, in Solaan." Loran nodded, pretending he knew where that was.

"I've just made a jug of hot Caraeff, and there's plenty of this hare for us both, my friend."

Friend, thought Loran.

No one has ever called me that.

Hanan cut them both some meat using a large, bone handled dagger he had tucked in a sheath at his belt. He told Loran that he was a sailor, large ships coming in from afar, from Shenabaal, from Durmak. Casks of ale, meats, fish, wine. Just about anything.

"Even bought a young man back once, returning to his home. Poor lad had been sent away as a child. Terrible business."

Loran listened intently, chewing on a slice of meat. It was warm, juicy and welcome. He, in turn, told him very little about himself.

He knew very little about himself.

"I've never met a Daemon before, if that's what you are?" said Hanan.

Loran wasn't entirely sure. He searched for an answer.

"No mind," said the old Solaanian. "We're friends now, and that's all that matters. Plus, you being here will keep the wolves away."

"It will?"

"Surely," he laughed. "Sometimes you don't have to be dangerous. Just look it, is all."

Loran laughed along with him. They ate in companionable silence for a while. Hanan invited him to stay a while, if he wished.

He did.

Loran watched as Hanan sat in front of the fire, recounting a tale from a faraway land. He reached into his bag, retrieving a pipe and a small pouch. He filled it, then, taking a glowing twig, he lit the pipe, a waft of smoke drifting skywards.

An aromatic tang wafting across the scrubland.

Hanan started coughing almost immediately.

"Is that a good idea?" Loran asked.

"Probably not," laughed the old sailor. "But, old habits, you know." He coughed again.

It was about three moons they spent in the desolation. Talking, hunting, laughing. Loran would sleep next to the fire, listening to the old man's wheezing and rattling chest.
One morning Loran awoke early.
Hanan didn't.

He dug a shallow grave, his claws scraping the barren earth, his face set in stone. He erected a cairn of rocks over his friend to keep the wolves at bay. Standing over the grave, he undid his loincloth and slipped Hanan's bone handled dagger onto his belt.

***

Brianne watched as Loran looked down at his dagger, his eyes far away, then reached out to carve himself and Brianne a slice of meat.

She took it gratefully, suddenly aware that she was starving.
They ate, staring at the fire. Without taking his eyes from it, Loran said,

"You can take it off now, if you want."

She stopped chewing and looked up at him. With a resigned sigh, she reached behind her head, undid the scarf and slipped the blonde hairpiece off to reveal a head of short cropped, dark brown hair.
She dropped the hairpiece on the sand without a word, her eyes tearing suddenly.

"How long..." she sniffled.

"The instant I met you. I could smell it. Horsehair, Am I right?"
She nodded miserably.

"Father deals with horse traders. He gets horsehair to repair and make bedding. He made me this when I came of womanhood, for that's when my hair began to darken. My friend, Kall, who you met? He keeps it short for me. He's the only other who knows."

"I must admit, I wondered why you would go to such lengths but, suddenly, it's very obvious why." He cut another slice and stuffed it into his mouth.

"You can imagine how scared I've been. It took us ages to get enough of the right colour hair. How scared my parents must have been, hoping, praying, that nobody discovered, well… this!" she pointed to her head.

"I think you're beautiful." He said quietly. "And if anyone says otherwise, they'll have me to answer to!"
She stared at him, then stared down at the hairpiece.
How long would this continue for? How much more concealing would there be from the truth?

"How do you know this place?" she asked, deliberately changing subjects.

"I spent some time here recently."
She looked around.

"Here? Why?"

"I was hiding. To keep my father safe."
From what, she thought? She let the silence hang a beat.

"A few summers ago I was bathing in the Moon Pool. The water eases the sting on my scales." He looked up at her. "Three young boys were nearby. They… raised the alarm. It didn't take long for men with weapons to find the cabin. Father hid me, persuaded them the boys were dreaming or suchlike. After that I thought it safer if I dwelt somewhere without people. People are complicated."

"In that much we agree." She mumbled.
She looked down at the hairpiece again, a sudden spark of anger flaring in her.

"You know something?" she reached down and picked it up. "I'm sick of hiding who I am."
She tossed it into the fire, the flames flaring up and devouring it, an acrid smell fanning over them.

"Good for you!" he laughed.

Brianne smiled for what genuinely felt like the first time in ages.

TWENTY ONE

Caylen was awoken by a knocking on the door. He opened one bleary eye as Queen Isiarus yelled "Enter!"

Loshin stuck his head around the door, raising his eyebrows at Caylen's presence. Caylen let a smirk spread across his face.

"Forgive the intrusion, Highness, but General Wes is awaiting your pleasure."

"Thank you, Loshin. I'll be with him shortly."

The door closed and Isiarus threw the covers back and slinked over to the window, picking up a robe. Caylen smiled at her nakedness, her jet-black hair glinting in the morning sun. Last night had been better than he imagined. He'd even managed to ignore her arm!

"Time for you to leave, my dear." She said as she slipped the robe onto her shoulders.

Caylen's face reddened.

"Do not dismiss me!" Caylen shot back at her. "I am not simply a boy, a plaything for you to use. I can be useful to you. I've demonstrated that."

And he had. She'd seemed most intrigued to learn of her father releasing a prisoner. And of the Daemon.

Especially of the Daemon.

She'd questioned him endlessly about that.

She turned, tying up the robe at the front and smiled sweetly at him.

"Get out." She purred. "Before I rip off your ball sack…"

***

Out in the corridor, a wry smile crept over the face of the guards as Caylen slunk out the door, his boots in his hands, shirt unbuttoned. He shot them a dark look, then trudged off down the corridor, dressing as he walked, and descended the nearest staircase.

It took him a few moments to realise this was not the staircase he used last night. This one was darker.
Much darker.

As he got lower down, the light seemed to disappear completely, flickering wall sconces the only source. He turned into a corridor, searching for an exit. As he walked, doors were open on either side, revealing sights his mind could not comprehend. Creatures that made no sense. None of them living.

He stopped. This was useless.
Caylen turned to find a bony, painfully thin man standing directly behind him. Dressed in a long green robe, his back as straight as a spear, he looked down his long, sharp nose at Caylen.

"Do not take heart, my boy." He droned, "She is not one for making… associations."

"Who are you?" he backed away a step.
Fian turned and walked away, beckoning over his shoulder at him. Caylen followed, although he wasn't sure why.

They stopped at the door to Fian's workroom. Caylen wasn't entirely sure he wanted to go in.

"The Daemon." Fian whispered, his eyes wide. "Alive?"
Caylen nodded slowly.

"Bring it here!" he said urgently. "Bring it here and I can give you power beyond your dreams, boy. Real power." His eyes were almost crazed.

"How? It is unfathomably strong."
Fian opened the door and stepped in. Caylen didn't, wrinkling his nose from the doorway.

"I can help with that." He said with a thin smile. "Use these."
He handed Caylen some arrowheads. They were black, with a faint blue glow to them. And they were impossibly cold.

"What are these?" he asked.

"Mallenglâs. It will tip the scales in your favour. Bring him here. To me."

Fian smiled, and Calen found himself smiling with him.

***

Brianne awoke first. Thin morning light was creeping across the scrubland, the embers of last night's fire barely glowing. She was lying on her side, in the cave, looking out at the desolation. She had her wings wrapped around her body like a blanket.

She became aware that Loran was lying behind her, his arm over her waist. His black, leathery wings were wrapped over them both like a canopy. She smiled and looked over her shoulder at him, watching him sleep.

Loran opened his eyes, suddenly conscious of where he was. He looked down at his arm, wrapped over her waist.

"I, erm…" he stammered

"It's fine" she said quietly. It had felt strangely natural, somehow.

"I didn't mean…"

Brianne turned over to face him, laying on her wings.

"It's fine." She said, looking deep into his startling blue eyes.

Loran bent forward and kissed her.

That felt natural too, somehow.

***

Loran kicked out the remains of the embers, scattering ashes and soot. They kept catching each other's eyes, smiling, or laughing for no reason other than because if felt good. He sat heavily on a rock.

"Do you feel like breakfast?" he asked.

"Not another hare?" she laughed. She needed a drink more than food. Water seemed not to bother him much.

"No," he chuckled, "Not another hare. We need to go to my father's cabin. I need answers to something."

"Ok…" she said slowly.

"You should be able to fly now, the rain seems to have eased over the forest."

"How the fuck can you see that from here?" she craned her neck, but could barely make out the silhouette of the trees on the horizon. His eyesight must be unfathomable?

"Can *you* fly?" she asked, pointing to a large gash in the membrane of his left wing.

"Oh, yes." He dismissed it with a wave of his hand. "It will heal in no time."

Of course it will, she thought.

"Come on." he stood. "Let's go and wake the old man up!"

They took off together. She flew next to him for the first time, she realised, since they had met. He seemed more graceful up here. More at ease. She had to admit, she felt more at ease too. Certainly with him next to her. She raised her hands to check her headscarf, purely out of habit, then smiled as she remembered it wasn't there anymore. Would never be there anymore.

No more hiding.

It felt so good to finally have the wind through her feathers again after K'lahl. And through her own hair. She couldn't remember the last time she'd done that. She closed her eyes briefly, enjoying the peace she felt. Opening them again, she looked across at him, his wide, black wings billowing in the wind like sheets of tanners leather.

The moon forest loomed large before them all too soon. She could have stayed here, flying next to him, for ever. But all too quickly, Loran started to drop toward the treeline. She followed, the blue of the river Uret glinting through the trees.

They landed on the flat grassland in front of the paddock, the horses snorting at the sudden intrusion. As they walked up to the cabin, she slipped her hand into his. He looked down at it and smiled.

The door opened as they approached. Aleas noted them holding hands and smiled to himself.

"Tisane's on the brew." He announced. "I'll get some food ready."

"Thank you, Papa." He said as he let go of her hand to walk through the doorway.

"Good morning, Aleas." She said, kissing him lightly on the cheek.

"Hello, m'dear." He said warmly. "You look...different."
Yes, she thought.
More like me.

**

"The man's a fool if he trusts that evil bitch. She'll kill him soon as look at him. And all of them, comes to that." Aleas sipped on his hot tisane, still full from the unleavened bread and cold meats they'd broken their fast on.

"He won't listen," said Loran, pushing his platter away. "He can see no other course." Aleas nodded. There'd been men blinded by ambition throughout the ages, whether their cause was just or not. This man was clearly no different.

"Father..."
Aleas looked up at him.

"What does this Seraph do, exactly? How will it restore his wings and make that witch into a goddess?"

"It won't." He said, sipping his tisane.
Brianne stopped eating and looked across the bench at him.

"The power of the Seraph was to be conveyed by the Gods, not man. It is born of dark energy, to be sure. But in its present form, it will simply kill any man who touches it. Only the Gods Themselves can truly weald it's power. That's how your race were born by L'Shaan in the first place." He looked over at Brianne, putting his cup down.

"The only way to cure Pehl and his band is to break it. That will release the dark energy within. It has the power to restore that which has been taken away. In this case, their wings."

"That's how you cured Isaac." She said.
Aleas nodded.

"When he was small," he nodded to Loran, "I left him here, and returned to the palace. There's an underground entrance, rarely used, if ever. I retrieved some personal items, food from the pantry, clothes, that sort of thing. In Fian's workroom I found a small ball in a case of dark wood. It is a smaller version of your Seraph. I stole it, I confess, thinking it was a gemstone of some kind." He chuckled at the memory.

"Who's Fian?" asked Loran, picking up his tisane.

"Her mage. Horrid, bony old stick insect of a man. He believes he can use the Seraph to make her something she isn't, but it doesn't work that way. Her arm was that way at birth, you cannot restore that which you never had. This idea of making her a Goddess?" he shook his head. "Ridiculous."

"So what can we do, to cure these outcasts?" Loran asked as he put his empty cup down.

"Break the Seraph." He said. "Take it up high, speak the incantation of release then drop it to the ground. It should shatter, releasing the energy."

"How do we do that," asked Brianne, "If we can't touch it?"

"He can…"

He pointed to Loran, who furrowed his ridged brow.

"That's what he was created to do. To steal the Seraph. When he was first born, the small Seraph was placed in his hands and it caused the scars on his palms, and the scales on his shoulders to harden. He was deemed a failure, and I was given orders to take him out and kill him." He looked at the floor.

Loran examined his palms, tracing the lines of white scars up his hand with a talon, till they ended at his elbow.

"What will happen to him if he touches the actual Seraph?" Brianne sat forward in her seat.

"I'm not too sure, to be honest. But you'd have to be quick. If the scars touch your heart, well." He looked up at the Daemon he'd raised as his own. "It could kill you."

Loran nodded slowly.

"I'll just have to be quick then, won't I?"

Aleas smiled.

"If you want to freshen up, Brianne, there's a room you can use there." He pointed to the corner of the cabin. "Also, I found one of Elise's old dresses. Keepsake, you know. I've altered it to fit your wings, might be of use."

She looked down at her once-cream tunic dress, now brown with mud and sand and rain, one sleeve torn at the shoulder, the red piping ordaining her role as tutor now frayed and missing in places.

"That would be lovely, thank you." As she entered the room in the corner, closing the door behind her, Aleas turned to Loran and whispered,

"What happened to her hair...?"

***

The dress was exquisite. Deep, dark red with a white trim and a wide, flowing skirt. She stepped into it, slipping her arms into the sleeves, wide three-quarter length with white embroidered detail. Aleas had cut and sewn a panel in the back, which she held up between her wing roots and buttoned to the collar at the back. She looked at herself in a small bedside mirror. It was perfect.

She washed her face and hands in the basin at the side, running her hands over her short, dark hair and fluttering the sand from her wings.

What would be said when they returned?

Somehow, with Loran at her side, she felt she had nothing to fear.

TWENTY TWO

They'd been busy.
Very busy

Pehl looked up the line of horses, now fronted by two siege ladders, two catapults and a battering ram. He nodded contently.
This was it. All or nothing.
He turned to Tialla.

"No sign?" She shook her head in reply. Caylen hadn't been seen in a week. Many thought him dead, victim of a jealous partner or someone he'd insulted in a tavern.

"We can't wait." He said.
Despite his misgivings, Caylen was still his only son. He wanted him here, by his side.
Where the fuck was he?

"If you want to attack at first light, father, we should head out now." She called across from her saddle. The sun was still an hour or more away, and they had been camped at the eastern edge of the river Uret for over a moon. It meant they risked being spotted by the Avians, now the rain had stopped but, with so much at stake and the natural lay of the land providing some cover, it was a risk Pehl felt they had to take.

Tialla had really come into her own. His pride in his daughters' achievements doubled daily. Not only had she improved the ladders and the catapults further, but she'd also designed the battering ram, to be manned by ten men, and fit to burst the gates of the Citadel in like paper.
Or so they hoped.

Behind each catapult was a wain pulled by two bull aurochs, piled high with the biggest rocks they could muster from the caves at Naren's pass. That should give the bird brained arse's a few headaches.

The river was at its narrowest point just south of the moon forest. The foliage, however, would be too dense at that point to provide cover. That meant riding out now, skirting the forest and crossing the river in the thin morning light.

He looked over and nodded.

Horns blew out, and as one they trotted forward.

They skirted the forest within the hour, crossing the river at its narrowest point, the bridge at Crennels Forde. The wooden slats creaked as the axles trundled over it, horses and aurochs trudging over it slowly. Once on the other bank, they turned south and heading for the Citadel. The battering ram was out front, the point of an arrow aiming for the heart of the Avians. A horn blew again, and they broke into a canter. Ten men breathing hard, pushing for all they were worth. Horses snorting and lathering as they headed ever onwards to the gates.

Inside the Citadel, A horn blew out as the wall guards spotted the warband cantering across the open grassland in the early mist. They were almost on top of them as Lance men came running, donning armour and grabbing lances. On the wall, archers came running, most not having had enough time to don their breastplates and grabbing weapons as they ran.

Too late.

The gates buckled inward with an almighty crash and a squeal and screech of twisting metal, the battering ram running through the archway and over the first line of lance men before a dozen or more arrows pierced the men propelling it. They fell, almost as one, and the ram came to a stop halfway across market square.

Behind it came the horses.

They galloped in through the gate two at a time. The pace was still slower than Pehl would have liked, but it was steady. He was second through the gate, Tialla refusing to let her father take the first arrow. She managed to dodge it, a second bouncing off her shield boss.

At the wall, archers and Lance men alike fought to repel the wave of warriors spilling over the ladders.

***

Lord Commander Remus came running across the square, cursing and shouting orders as he buckled his plumed helm as Josten ran up to him.

"My lord?"

Remus raised an eyebrow.

"Give me a wing of archers to command, My lord. I have a plan that may buy us some time." Josten turned as a horse run in, stepping to the side and sweeping his sword through the man's thigh. He fell with a scream, the horse cantering away.

"We don't have time for wild plans now, man. Return to your post."

"Trust me, my Lord. Just a wing. Please."

Remus paused a beat, then nodded once.

"Take the third wing. Tell Gaphel you have my command to lead."

Josten didn't need telling twice. He ran across the square to where the third wing of archers was grabbing weapons and armour.

"Leave the breastplates, grab your arrows and follow me. Lord Commander has given me this wing."

"I'm in charge here." Said Gaphel, a tall, skinny Avian with short blonde locks. Others murmured their agreement.

"Not anymore. Trust me lads, we're going to make a real difference here. With me."

He turned and headed to the corner tower, fluttering his wings and flying up the wall as the sounds of battle continued behind him.

"Where are we going? Are you touched in the head?" screamed Gaphel above the din.

"Up there." He pointed to the sky.

Others exchanged puzzled looks as Josten removed his breastplate.

"Too heavy." He explained. "Now listen in. Aim for

beyond your target by about a wains length, watch the wind as it'll be more noticeable up there. Ready?"

"Flying archers?" Gaphel scoffed. "You *are* touched." He looked around for support.

Some were smiling, others considering this crazy plan of his.

"Come on lads. We can do this." He spread his wings and took to the air, high enough to reach with some force still left in the arrow, but just out of reach of the catapult.

Wing three joined him.

"Nock." He screamed into the air. Below him, one of the catapults erupted with a huge cache of boulders and rocks, raining down on the wall they had occupied ten seconds earlier. He looked down at the wall, Gaphel's legs protruding from under a pile of rubble where the wall had collapsed.

Nothing would help him now.

"Loose."

On the ground a dozen warriors slid from their saddle as they waited for their turn to get through the gate.

"Yes!" Josten fist pumped the air. "Again!"

Josten nocked another arrow when a dark shape caught the corner of his vision.

Loren and Brianne flew over the wall, heading toward the temple.

***

They landed at the temple's huge, dark doors. Loran was carrying Aleas, his hands under the old man's armpits, lifting him easily. It bought home to Loran just how thin and frail he had grown of late. Loran would have felt far more comfortable leaving him behind, but he insisted on coming along. Perhaps the thrill of a battle was too much of a draw to man who'd buried himself in the queen's army for so long.

The temple acolytes exchanged looks and crossed their lances over the doors as Loran approached.

"You are not permitted here. King's orders."

Loran barely stopped walking, but charged in through the doors, taking the acolytes with him. They hurtled to the floor as Loran waked right over them, Brianne following with an apologetic look.

The buzzing in his brain started at once. Thousands of voices. Angry, whispering. Relentless. He walked to the dais as the temple elder blustered and raged at him from the side of the temple. Loran blocked him out. Blocked everything out.

He stood in front of the Seraph, staring at its deep blue-black glow, waves of energy pulsating over its surface.

"Concentrate." Brianne said, looking up at him. Loran looked down at her.

"What do you think you're doing, Daemon?" They turned to the voice from the doorway where King Pyrus stood, arms akimbo.

**

On the wall, Kall ran from the northwest tower behind two lance men, sword in hand. He'd managed to grab his helm and breastplate on route, then buckled his weapons belt whilst climbing the stairs. He ran onto the wall, slashing through the arm of an outcast who had just climbed over the parapet. The man screamed, clutching his bicep as Kall spun around him, blocking a sword that was aimed at his head and, in the same movement, slashed through the first outcast's throat. As he collapsed in a torrent of red, Kall sidestepped a second outcast and slashed at his torso, slicing through thin air as the tall, wiry warrior spun away. They circled each other, looking for an opening.

At that moment, the left-hand catapult erupted again as launch times got quicker and quicker. A rainstorm of rocks the size of his head showered the wall, knocking the outcast to the floor. Kall ducked, covering his head.
He stood. The outcast didn't.

Kall ran onward, watching as another outcast dispatched a fellow Avian swordsman a dozen paces from him. He ran towards the warriors back, stopping short as the warrior turned. Long, dark hair in a high ponytail. Boiled leather armour buckled tightly over her lithe form.

Sande.

Kall ran to her, dropping his sword and embracing her for all he was worth.

"Kall. Oh, my Kall. You're safe." She kissed him briefly.

"None of us are safe yet, my darling. You should try to get away." He led her over the inner parapet, away from the catapults.

"We both should." She looked around for an opening. A way out.

A miracle.

"Go back down, my love. Please." He pleaded. She shook her head before he'd finished speaking.

"I can't, I'd be noticed. This is hopeless." They looked around at the madness they were trapped in.

There had to be a way out for both of them.

***

Caylen slid from the saddle, his horse wandering off to find some vestige of food in this barren scrubland. Caylen looked around at the desolation. The cave mouth was deserted. On the ground before it was a circle of ash and soot, the last embers of a fire long gone out. The carcass of a hare off the right, long stripped of any scraps by the prairie wolves.

"Arse." He screamed.

He had worked his way along the coast from Var'n Arden, with no sign of the Daemon or his bitch of a girlfriend. There had been a couple of strange reports from trades people he had encountered, and he'd followed that trail here.

Too late, it would seem.

Where would they have gone from here? Further west, to the starklands? South, perhaps?

He looked to the east.

Surely, not back to the forest?

Caylen took a last look around, and stepped back up, into the saddle.

***

"Sire, I tried to stop them but…" the temple elder

blustered.

"Eral, please." Snapped Brianne. She stood behind Loran at the steps leading up to the dais. King Pyrus strode into the temple, walking down the aisle toward them.

"Young lady," Eral began, "I don't believe that…" he knotted his eyebrows and stared for a heartbeat.

"Lady Brianne?" he gasped. "What has happened?"

The king looked over at her, undisguised revulsion on his face at her appearance.

"Yes. Stare all you want to." She barked at him. "This is me. This is who I am, and I care not for your opinion." She put her hands on her hips, wingtips fluttering in anger.

The King stood, mouth agape, before turning to Loran.

"What goes on here?"

Loran wrenched himself away from the never-ending buzzing in his brain.

"I mean to end this chaos. Today."

King Pyrus looked from Loran to the Seraph and back. He could not. Surely, he would not be able?

"You cannot interfere in matters that do not concern you. See how you have corrupted the very fabric of our society?" He raged, pointing at Brianne. She bit back a retort.

"This ends. Now." Loran growled back.

"The scriptures of the Goddess are very clear. Only those of light hair shall inherit the divine gift of flight. It is clearly written." He ranted, pointing at the large cream and gold tapestry hanging on the back wall of the temple.

"That's not what that actually says…"

They all turned and looked at Aleas, standing in the doorway.

"Father?"

Aleas walked up the central aisle to the Seraph.

"Father?" gasped the King. "You are responsible for creating this…abomination?"

"Have a care, King! He is not of my blood, but I have raised him as my own, and will defend him likewise." He looked up at the tapestry and translated.

"It actually reads: Only those of light headedness shall be of worth to inherit the divine gift." He looked at the king. "Who translated this?"

"Our best scholars. They are…"

"…Wrong. It doesn't say light hair, as in colour. It actually says light of head. In this case, it is a lightness of the spirit. Of learning and of divinity. This symbol here?" he pointed up at the cursive script. "It means worthiness. You must be righteous enough to deserve it. I would think you should hand your wings back." He smiled.

"Enough of this." Loran snarled. He turned back to the Seraph. King Pyrus's eyes widened, and he took a step toward the Daemon.

He stopped suddenly and looked down at the sword pointed at his belly.

Aleas pressed the point in a touch further, just so there was little question. He nodded to Loran.

"Remember. Be quick."

The Daemon turned and stretched out his hands.

TWENTY THREE

The pain was immediate. It jolted up his arms like lightning, the buzzing in his mind turning to shouting turning to screaming. Loran steeled himself and heaved at the Seraph, lifting it from its floating position above the bronze column. His back and arm muscles were straining as he stepped back off the dais, his scales aching.

Loran looked down at his arms. The small, white fingers of scar tissue were inching up his inner elbow, tendrils of ice climbing towards his chest.
He didn't have long.

He turned, looking at the high, vaulted ceiling topped with its domed glass roof. Brianne stood back, looking up at him all the while.

"Come back to me." She said.
Loran nodded once then, opening his huge black wings, he launched himself into the air.

By any Gods, this thing was heavy. His wings flapped for all they were worth as he battled to get enough momentum.

Loran smashed through the dome, sending shards of glass raining down on the temple, the occupants below scurrying for cover as he broke free. His wings were screaming in agony as he struggled to gain height, the temple and the Citadel falling away below him as he climbed ever higher.
The veins of white were at his shoulders now, inching over his chest and back. He could almost feel them growing up his skin.

Loran fought to retain control as the voices screamed ever louder in his head, the pain and power of the Seraph flooding his senses.

He was about twice tree height, way above the tower of

the palace of Sh'Bal. He looked down at the chaos below him, as Avian and Outcast battled each other.

The Daemon mumbled the words of release he had memorised from Aleas, then opened his hands and let the Seraph drop, just as the fingers of white scar tissue met in the centre of his broad, grey chest. A thunderbolt of white erupted from his heart and darkness clouded the edges of his vision.

Loran gave in to the black, and fell away backwards, plummeting toward the ground. The Seraph dropped toward the Citadel, Loran following, falling, falling, falling, his black wings wrapping around him like wet blankets.

Brianne watched from the Doors of the temple, Aleas's arm around her shoulder.

"Fly, damn you. Fly…" she whispered.

Aleas couldn't watch.

The Seraph hit the ground at an alarming rate, shattering into a million pieces with a deep, thunderous blast. Loran hit the ground a second later, his body crushing the flagstones of the market square, and burying itself shin-deep in the earth.

There was nothing for a heartbeat. Then a bright blue eruption of light from the Seraph, a ring of blue energy radiating out like ripples on a pond. It swept out across the landscape, Outcast and Avian dropping to the ground as one. Brianne and Aleas were both thrown back into the temple.

In the square, Loran was still.

***

Caylen sat on a large, flat boulder at the edge of the Desolation, his horse glad to be chomping on something approximating grass at long last.

What was this fucking Daemon up to?

Caylen knew he should have been with father for the attack but, truth be told, he usually felt more in the way than anything else.

Especially now that Tialla had returned.

He had long grown in her shadow. Her swordsmanship was better, her horse riding exceptional.

His was satisfactory. Only ever satisfactory.

He had breathed a sigh of relief the day she left for Solaan, although father was inconsolable for three days, and virtually silent for seven.

The horse whinnied, becoming twitchy. Caylen looked up, shaken from his reverie. In the distance, a bright blue flash erupted on the horizon, a wave of blue energy sweeping out across the landscape.

It dissipated somewhere near the moon forest.

Long before it reached him.

***

Brianne opened her wings and tore across the square. She landed next to him, a crater the size and shape of the Daemon in the flagstones. Kneeling, Brianne touched his cheek.

"No. No no no no no…"

Aleas ran across to join her, as fast as his aging legs would allow. Brianne looked across the square at the bodies strew around.

Pehl was only a few paces from them, his horse having thrown him and now trotting away aimlessly with its brethren. Pehl threw back his head and screamed, as his boiled leather shirt tore open at the back below each shoulder blade, two white fingers of bone protruding through, growing ever outwards like long, misshapen hands. His back distorted and convulsed, muscles growing where they were never needed until now, sinew and tendon snaking out to join the new wings.

She looked across at Tialla. Her blue sable cloak had torn likewise, her wings growing ever faster out of her shoulder blades, back muscles warping and growing with them. A layer of grey, wet down covered each wing, like a fledgling's, only much larger.

Pehl's wings were grey and downy and damp now, with a black stripe over the tip of each wing where the primary feathers would grow.

All around them, outcasts where yelling in pain as hands of white tore through their clothing, growing at a startling speed. Avians were sitting up, shaking heads and clearing their thoughts. They watched, horrified, as their enemy grew wings they were not allowed to have.

"Come on," a voice rang out, "We can slaughter hundreds of these fuckers while they're fallen."

A great war cry sprang up as the Avians ran toward their dark haired brethren, swords drawn and faces angry. A tall, muscly blonde stabbed a dark haired warrior between the shoulder blades, his face contorted with rage as the warrior screamed, the life bleeding out of him. His wings, not yet formed, went limp as he fell face down on the flagstones.

Brianne looked on, aghast, as Avians slaughtered their enemy as they lay. The Avian ran to another fallen dark hair, his sword sweeping down to the warriors head.

It clanged off the blade of Tialla as she stood over him.

They regarded each other coldly, the Avian stepping back and setting his feet as he swung at the red head. Tialla bought her sword up, ready, and blocked, looking for an opening. She twirled around him, parrying, darting in and out of his defence and making the Avian look like a fledgling at practice, finally slicing his head off in one fluid movement.

"Loran…" Brianne blubbed, looking back down. "Loran. Come on, open your eyes. Please…" She needed him more than ever now. She could see no other way of ending this mayhem. Something was different.

His scales were softer, more like leather plates than scales now. His brow less ridged. Smoother, somehow.
The scar tissue that stretched across his arms was gone.

"Loran?"

***

He could hear voices. Quiet. Distant.
Pleasant.
He knew these voices. These were not the buzzing multitude he had fought to ignore before. No.
These were friends.
He couldn't move.
Why couldn't he move?

He tried to open his eyes, but nothing happened. He knew he was alive. He felt alive.

He must be alive.

How was he alive?

The voices got louder. Closer.

"Loran?"

There was darkness. Sweet, blissful darkness. He felt warm. At peace. Perhaps he would stay here, in this sweet, blissfully warm, darkness.

"Loran?"

Slowly, Loran opened his eyes. The light was blinding and painful.

Brianne was kneeling over him, crying. Her hair was a shade or two longer than he remembered.

Things came into focus slowly, and he lifted his head.

"Oh, by all the Gods, he's alive." She sobbed, bending to hug him.

Loran sat up gradually, his head swimming for a beat or two. He took in his surroundings, memories cascading back to him in flashes.

The battle. The Seraph.

The Outcasts.

He stood and took in the sight.

All around him was chaos. Avians killing outcasts as they lay, some coming to in time to put up a fight. The outcasts all had new wings now, grey and fluffy and fresh. They should have been rejoicing, laughing like children on their name day.

Instead they were fighting for their lives.

Loran looked down at his arms. The scar tissue he had lived with up to now was gone. The ever present ache he had always felt from his scales was gone. He stood and stretched his own wings out, testing their mettle, giving them an experimental flap or two.

"You well, my boy?" Aleas asked looking up at him. Loran nodded as he folded in.

"I think so, yes."

"You must have been caught in the blast from the Seraph. If you'd have hit the ground a couple of heartbeats later, you might not have been so fortunate." Aleas looked around at the havoc again.

"I'll find the King. You see if you can put a stop to this insanity."

Loran looked about the square, his eyes settling on the king, standing aghast in the temple doorway. Aleas followed his gaze, running over to the temple, the acolytes at the door too preoccupied with their new wings and sudden hair growth to stop him. He ran in to find Pyrus sitting back on a bench, head in hands.

"What have you done?" The king muttered.

***

A line of Avians ran toward a line of outcasts, some still shaking the fog from their minds as they bought their weapons to bear. Steel rang out against steel as they clashed in the centre, outcasts fighting off Avians who were trying to use the advantage to slaughter their enemy.
Loran landed amongst them.

Bodies fell about as he knocked them all aside. Talons and teeth bared, he roared at the Avian line like a Sayer-bear. They stepped back, outcasts using the brief respite to gather their breath.

"It's bad enough you gave the scum their wings back," an Avian spat, pointing an accusing sword at Loran, "Now you protect them too?"

"Aye." Shouted another voice. "Stand aside, Daemon!"
Loran stood his ground.

"End this slaughter." He snarled. "Now!"
More shouts and jeers rang out. Did he have the strength and wherewithal to fight them off?
Especially as he'd been near death a few moments ago?

***

"What's done is done." Aleas said, looking down at the sad figure of the King. "It will not be undone."

Pyrus looked up at the old mage briefly before turning his attention to the melee outside.

"It will not need to be." He spat. "The battle commences despite your meddling. My people are determined to end these outcasts."

"You could stop them..." Aleas said.

"Why would I do such a thing?" The king knitted his brows together. "Don't you understand? You've undone years and years of belief. Our very way of life." He stood slowly. "These outcasts should die."

"Why" Aleas yelled. "Do they not deserve this way of life you hold so dear? I have told you already, your precious scriptures are nonsense. Your beliefs are based on lies and half-truths. Nothing more." He waved a hand at the tapestry. "The seraph is gone, their wings restored. Anything else is nought but mindless slaughter."

"Who am I to tell my people they cannot fight their natural enemy?" Pyrus gestured to the outside.

"I thought you were their King?" The mage thundered back. "Fucking-well act like one, if only this once."

Pyrus stood and met his stare.

**

In the square, the jeers and shouts were deafening, especially to Loran's over-sensitive hearing. He stood, towering, at the centre of the two lines as if daring either side to break first.

Suddenly the hubbub fell away, blessed hush falling on his ears as the line of Avians parted, and the King strode to the centre, Aleas beside him.

"Enough." Pyrus thundered. "This hostility is now pointless. They have what they wanted. I will see no more death this day."

Jeers and outcry sprang up, Pyrus holding up his hands to silence them again.

"These... Avians.." he spat out the word. "..will leave. Now" Pyrus turned and held Pehl's gaze, his brother finally nodding.

Dark haired Avians began uneasily sheathing swords, gathering their dead as best they could and loading them on horseback. Slowly, the line of Avians, once outcasts, fell away. Pehl alone stood where he was.

"They will grow quicker than usual. Mine did." A voice said. Pehl turned to a young, curly haired, blonde Avian staring up at him.

Pehl looked over his shoulder, his wings catching him unawares.

"You'll get used to that, too. Especially as they grow." The young man said. Pehl knotted his brow. There was an air of familiarity to him that Pehl couldn't quite place.

"I'm Isaac. I'm the Kings son." He said. "Your nephew. Uncle."

"Good to meet you, young Isaac." Pehl looked about the square. "I wish it were in differing circumstances."
Isaac smiled, despite the dark look from his father.

"Why did yours grow quicker?" he asked, something clicking in his brain.

"I was clipped at birth. Given as a Temple Acolyte. I had my wings restored." He looked over to Loran and Aleas.

"…by them."

***

"Kall!" Sande ran to him, falling into his arms. "Oh, look, Kall." She said as she broke free, her eyes wet with tears. "Look at them." She turned, showing off her short, stubby wings covered in grey down.

"Beautiful." He said, kissing her deeply.
They were standing in the corner of the square, partially hidden behind the remnants of the gates. Kall had spent most of the battle worrying for her or looking for her.

"Must we be parted again?" she sobbed.

"Only for a short while, I promise." He held her tight, silently vowing a way for them to be together.
Come what may.

***

"This was all I wanted, brother." Pehl said. "I never wanted a war. It was simply the only way forward."

"You dare call me that?" The king shook his head. "You have your spoils of war, now fuck off." He growled.

Pehl walked away slowly before turning and looking back from the gates.

"We will camp in the glades at the forests' edge." He turned to Isaac. "I hope to see you again, young Isaac."

"Somehow, I feel positive that you will."

Pehl turned and left.

The king walked away, watching bodies being covered and weapons being gathered. He walked into the temple, his boots crunching on the glass that carpeted the floor, and sat down on a bench.

TWENTY FOUR

It had been three days since the breaking of the Seraph. An uneasy quiet had settling over the Citadel, with heated discussions in the feast hall equalled by hushed whispers in corridors. The dark haired clan, as some had now named them, were indeed camped on the edge of the Moon Forest and had fought off the occasional night-time skirmish from disgruntled blondes; a feature that had prompted the King to make an announcement in the town square that any Avian found guilty of such skirmishes would be expelled from the Citadel.

Loran stood in the square, people blatantly staring at him or not meeting his gaze at all. But he knew they all talked about him.
And his girlfriend.

They made little secret of their affections now. Daynar had reported to Isaac that she'd never seen her friend happier. And the hair? Well. She'd always suspected.
Not that she was a gossip. No.

"Hello."

He turned to find Brianne standing behind him. The sight of her made his breath quicken, every time. She'd refused to change her dress, instead washing and drying Aleas's gift before re-wearing it again. Her hair was now just below her ears. She'd had her share of dark looks and jaded comments these past days and had stared back or simply shouted them down. Even those that had demanded she leave.
She looked divine. As always.

He was silent, a far-away look in his eyes.
"You're leaving." She said quietly.
"I must, I'm afraid." He rumbled. "There's something I

must attend to."

He'd been putting it off for a while, only to be reminded again during their stay in the desolation. "I'll be back before nightfall, my love."

"I like hearing you call me that." she purred, walking into his embrace. "You are sure I can't help?" she said eventually, breaking away.

"Not this time. This I must do alone."

"I'll see you at nightfall, then." He bent to kiss her, then stepped back and launched himself into the air, his black wings always drawing a gasp or whisper from onlookers.

She watched him leave, the hairs on the back of her neck standing up, for some reason.

***

Caylen was camped at the outer edge of the moon forest. The rain had left the ground soft in places, the smell of honeysuckle and lemongrass around him. He'd been here two nights, trying to console himself.

He'd missed out. Again.

Tialla never missed out, oh no. There was a sure bet that she'd got her bloody wings back. But him?

A thousand different scenarios played out in his head. Ways to get revenge, ways to capture that damn monster.

Fun he could have with its girlfriend.

Caylen had to bring it before the queen. That was his only play, now. Fian could tear it into pieces for all he cared, he just wanted what was rightfully his.

Power.

That was what the old mage had promised him. Real power. Then he could take what he wanted. And kill anyone or anything that got in his way.

Including his father.

A sound above caught his attention. Caylen looked up, just in time to see a dark shape flying overhead.

The Daemon!

This was too good and opportunity to be missed. He could

follow the thing and pounce when he got the chance.

Caylen sprang to his feet and saddled the horse.

***

Brianne stood in the square, watching the swordsmen sparring. A clatter of wooden practice swords rang out continuously, amongst it a friendly banter and whooping as swordsman bettered swordsman. She walked over to where the wooden practice swords jutted out from a large crate at the side of the practice corner. Picking one up, she twirled it around in front of her. She'd not voiced her opinions, but the sight of Pehl daughter with the red hair fighting the way she had gave her cause to think. She wanted, more than ever, to be able to wield a sword in such a fashion. Where the thought came from, she'd no clue. She had not come from a long line of warriors, and women were banned from training to fight.

But things change, she thought.

"Put that down." A voice thundered. She turned to see the Lord Commander walking over to her.

"Remus, I…"

He snatched the sword from her grasp and threw it back to the crate.

"Women do not train as warriors."

She met his gaze.

"I have seen women fight. And fight well." She stared back at him. "better than you, even!"

"Aye," he chuckled, "*their* women. Not ours. Even if you do look like one of them…"

"Careful, Lord Commander. I have a powerful friend, remember?" she said through gritted teeth.

Remus bit back a retort, turning to walk back to the sparring. She swore under her breath at his back.

***

She landed in a clearing in the Moon Forest. It was late, the sun barely visible above the treeline. Crows cawed, finches chirped. The river rolled languidly past on her right as always. Aleas's cabin was a little way to the north of her, the sound of the waterfall at the Moon Pool lost to the forest. The trees were her only observer.

She reached under her skirt and pulled the wooden sword out from the lining. It still amazed her that she had managed to hide it there while everyone else was occupied by the accident. A gushing nose only this time, but she welcomed the timing, nonetheless.

She hefted it again, enjoying the feel of it in her hand. Brianne swung it in a lazy circle, raising it above her head, then chopping down at an imaginary foe.

She turned, swinging her sword, only for it to stop suddenly as it clattered against Tialla's steel one. The redhead gave a gentle shove, and Brianne fell on her backside.

"Set your feet." She said, leaning down to help her up.

"You could have just said…" Brianne mumbled. Tialla laughed.

"I didn't even hear you approach." Brianne huffed, brushing the grass off her skirt. "I watched you fight? The other day? I thought you were exceptional."

"Thank you." She replied, knitting her brows together. "I saw you land. Why are you out here, practicing alone? You could be killed."

"I've little choice. I want to learn swordcraft, and women are banned from training in the Citadel."

Tialla stood, one foot in front of the other, the back foot slightly turned out. She turned her body sideways, giving a smaller target to her opponent.

"Like this." She said. Brianne copied her stance. "Better. Now, slowly at first, yes? Block." She thrust her sword out, blocking an imaginary blow. Brianne copied again.

Tialla took her time, showing Brianne move after move. Over and over. Then she stood in front of her, nodded, and thrust her sword at Brianne's midriff.

Brianne blocked it, almost without thinking.

"Good." Tialla nodded. "Again."

***

Loran stood in front of a cairn of stones. A gentle breeze wafted over the desolation, brushes and twigs carried across the scrubland. He had been glad to see his friend's resting place had been largely undisturbed, but for a few scratch marks from the desperate Prairie Wolves.

"Sorry it's taken me so long, my friend. I've been somewhat busy." Brianne's face came to him, and he smiled. "You'd like her." He bent and brushed a few twigs away.

"I like her. A lot." Hanan would have smiled his lopsided grin at that, he was sure. He'd spoken often of his own family, back in Solaan. A wife, three children. Two girls and a boy. His adventures at sea. Loran spoke to his friends memory of the events of the past few weeks.

"Well," said Loran. "It will soon be time for me to be going, my friend. You rest easy, eh? I'll try not to leave it so long next time."

Loran felt a blinding pain in the side of his stomach. A white hot needle of agony in his abdomen.

He looked down to see an arrow protruding from his stomach. Dark red, almost black, blood flowing from the wound. He reached down to pull it free, but this hands wouldn't grip the shaft.

Another arrow imbedded itself into his chest. Loran looked down at the shaft sticking out at an angle, black-red blood seeping down his chest. He felt the ground slip away, like he was on water, his head spinning. The arrowheads seemed to burn white hot.

Loran collapsed to the ground.

Caylen came and stood over him, grinning as Loran struggled to focus.

"That's Mallenglâs. Hurts, I suspect!" He chuckled. "Now then. Time for your audience with the Queen. Mustn't keep her Highness waiting, must we?"

He heaved at Loran. "Gods, your heavy." He panted. "You wait here, I'll fetch a horse and wain. Not that you're going anywhere soon."

***

"Excellent, excellent." Said Fian, almost jumping with glee. Four castle guards strode out past Caylen to his horses, sweating and heaving to get the Daemon's colossal bulk from the wain. They carried him in, a man on each limb, his wings sweeping the floor behind them.

"So?" said Caylen impatiently. "Do I get what you promised?"

"Hmm?" Fian said, far more distracted by his new prize. "Oh yes, yes my boy. Of course. You will get the power you crave. You will become unstoppable. You will be so much more than you are now." The wizened mage crooned.
Caylen grinned at the news.

"In fact," continued Fian, "We were just discussing that, eh General?"
Caylen turned abruptly. Behind him, the short, bald, stocky form of General Wes stood, hand on his sword. Caylen looked back at Fian, nervously.

In one swift motion, General Wes unsheathed his sword and cracked the pommel into Caylen's skull, a slight grin as the young man crumpled to the floor.

"Take him in." Fian called to the guards.
They picked him up, this time only taking two of them. At least this one was lighter.

"I'll inform her Highness." General Wes nodded and turned, striding off down the corridor.

Fian walked into his chamber. Loran was suspended from the ceiling by chains of Mallenglâs, the icy cold blue-black metal glowing faintly in the dim workroom. Fian sidled over to the cages against the wall. Caylen was now lying within one, face down, his hair matted with blood. The other had a huge cave bat, clinging to the bars, its wings fluttering nervously. On the floor, a Prairie Wolf prowled back and forth.

"Now then, my boy…do I have plans for you…"

***

Tialla thrust her practice sword forward, Brianne parried, stepping sideways. She'd been caught out more than once by the red haired warrior's faint and lunge. Tialla tried it once more, smiling when Brianne anticipated and blocked. They circled each other slowly. Brianne lunged at Tialla's groin, Tialla bringing her sword down to block.

She blocked into thin air, stopping suddenly as Brianne's sword touched her throat.

They smiled at each other, stepping back. Tialla nodded, gathering her breath.

"My, you're a quick learner. Well done."

"My thanks. You're an exceptional teacher. Again?"

Tialla sheathed her sword, shaking her head.

"Not tonight. It's getting late, and I should get something to eat before sleep." She smiled at the Avian. "Tomorrow, though?"

Brianne nodded. "Thank you."

Tialla smiled back, then loped off into the forest.

Sleep?

Loran should have returned by now. She'd been so busy she hadn't even noticed the late hour. She'd not seen him fly overhead. Not that she'd been looking at much except her sword and Tialla's.

But still.

Where was he?

TWENTY FIVE

Pain.

Loran had never known pain, not like this. It burned through his skull, his wrists. Just about everywhere was screaming in pain.

He opened one eye. Barely.

No. That definitely hurt.

His head sagged to his chest. He heard voices. Dim, distant. Cold voices he didn't recognise. Not like before, when he broke the Seraph. They were familiar voices. Friendly. His father. And…what was her name…?

He opened an eye again, hoping that her face would jog his memory. His surroundings were unfamiliar. A dark, dank looking room, maybe underground. A tall, painfully thin man he had never…

…Brianne. That was it.

He wanted to see Brianne.

"Ah," chuckled the thin man, "Awake, are we? Good…"

It didn't feel good.

"I have plans for you too, my dear Daemon." He continued. "You were my greatest creation. Cast out like vermin. Unwanted. It gladdens my heart to see you here."

Loran did not share this man's gladness. Not at all. He mumbled something, lifting his head and opening both eyes.

He was chained by his wrists to the ceiling. The chains were the same blue-black metal that the youngster had used on him in the desolation. He had a collar on made of the same metal. The room was cluttered with bottles, boxes and jars of things he'd never seen.

Nor wanted to. A work bench stained with blood sat in the centre of the room. He turned his head.

Definite mistake. Waves of nausea flooded him.

In the corner were two large cages. One had two animals in it, a huge bat and a wolf. The other, the young man from the scrubland. Injured.

"Creation?" he muttered, barely audible.

"Yes, my boy. I created you, from the darkness of the otherworld. The very fabric of perdition. With a little help from Her Highness, of course. I suppose you could think of her as your mother, really." He droned, his breath foul in Loran's face.

"Highness? Mother?" He'd heard tell of the witch queen, everyone from Aleas to the children bathing in the moon pool had mentioned her. But mother? Surely not.

"Yes." She said from the door. "Mother. I had you created of my own body. And how is the Daemon I thought dead, hmmm?"

I've been decidedly better, he thought, his skull pounding. He looked up as she glided into the room, her jet black hair almost red as it caught the light from the sconces on the wall, her withered arm cradled across her stomach.

"You assure me this will work? I will tolerate no further mistakes, mage. Another failure will cost you your head, I assure you." She said, all the time looking over Loran. She ran a fingernail down his chest, then lifted his sagging chin. "You may be off use, after all, great one." She whispered. Loran watched through groggy eyes, the voices distant as she swayed over to the other side of the room.

"It will, highness. The results may be a little unpredictable, but the incantation of revival is certain." He turned to the guards. "Take him to the table" They unchained him, straining as his colossal weight sagged to the floor. Two more guards rushed in, and, between them, they dragged him to the workbench in the centre of the room.

"Now. Hold still my dear boy." He watched as the guards shackled his arms out to the side, his wings hanging limp.
He hefted a large cleaver from the shelf and bought it over to Loran's left shoulder.

***

Tialla and Brianne circled one another carefully. Swords raised, each looked for an opening in the others defence. Brianne had arrived early, retrieving her sword from its hiding place, and joining it with another for her sword mistress. She was more determined than ever, sleeping little last night, thoughts of moves, feints, lunges and blocks swirling in her mind. She was prepared to work as long as necessary on anything that Tialla said she needed to work on.

Tialla thrust her sword out towards Brianne's face. She blocked, stepping sideways as another thrust came to her gut. She turned the sword aside, sweeping her own up toward her tutors' chest. Tialla blocked and stepped back, smiling. They circled again. This time Brianne thrust out first, her sword blocked easily. Tialla turned herself around as she blocked, knocking her opponent to the ground with her wings.

"Sorry," she said, holding out her hand, "I'm not used to these yet. I need as much practice as you." Brianne stood, nodding her thanks.

"Doubtful" she mumbled. She'd already earned a handful of bruises and it was still early.

"Time to break our fast, I think." She announced. She sat on a tree stump and opened the cloth pack she'd bought along, sharing out some cold meat and cheese, and unleavened bread. Brianne thanked her and took a bite. The cheese was strong and salty, but welcome.

"You're distracted." It wasn't a question. Brianne nodded in reply. "Because your lover has not yet returned?" she said matter-of-factly as she took a bite of bread. Brianne blushed and gave her a look. They were not yet lovers, physically at least. Also, verbalising it
so made it sound so much more...petty. They'd only just given in to their feelings and already she was worrying without cause. Surely, he'd return when he was ready.

"It would help if I knew what he'd gone to do." She said as broke off another piece of cheese. Loran had been decidedly

cagey with details. Whatever it was, he said he'd be back. Although he did say before nightfall…
Relax, she thought. He is a Daemon, after all!

***

The pain had gone.
Loran was in the dark. A swirly, misty fog of black enveloped him. Touching him, cold and clammy against his grey skin. He tried to walk, but his feet were leaden, like wading through the water against the tide. Loran looked down.

His feet were huge, misshapen hoofs. His toes colossal, his talons long and cruel. His hands were the same. Long cruel talons on elongated fingers. He reached up, feeling his horns. They were gigantic.

He felt suddenly icy, his skin peppered with gooseflesh. Almost shivery. Loran looked around. Black fog was everywhere. Wherever he was, it was unrecognisable.
And yet he knew this place.

Something in the back of his mind told him he'd been here before. He knew not when, or how. But it felt oddly familiar.

The mist started to clear in front of him, parting to reveal a figure. It was tall, as tall as Loran. Dark grey, almost black skin with long legs that ended in cloven hoofed feet. It's arms were long and skinny, with elongated fingers ending in cruel, curved talons of yellow. It stared at Loren with black, unreadable eyes. Large horns sat on its head.
Loran stared back at it.

"I know you…" Loran murmured, his voice deep and course, his teeth sharp fangs.

"You do." The creature said in a grating rasp.

Loran looked around, the mists having cleared enough to see vast mountain ranges in the distance, lightning flashing against them. On the periphery of his vision, he could make out strange beasts lurking. Waiting.

"I've been here before." He said, turning back to the thing. It was standing almost nose to nose with Loran now, making the Daemon startle. There wasn't much that made him nervous.

This familiar beast made his heart pound, and he didn't know why.

"You have." It said.

"Where is this place?" he already knew the answer before he asked.

"The Otherworld." Said the creature. "You were born of here. At least, part of you."

Am I dead, he thought, stepping back?

No, said a rasping voice in his head.

At least, not yet. You hang in the balance.

Why do I look different?

This is your truest self. The image of you that exists only here. In the otherworld, you are true Daemon.

I don't want to be dead, he thought. I have much yet to do.

And that is why you are in the balance of life and death, young Daemon. Your first thought is of your life in the world. Your wants and needs.

So, he thought. How do I get back there?

Your worldly figure is mutilated. If you go back, you will need all your strength to survive. Here is easier. Here you can be a God. With me.

No.

Brianne. All he could think of was Brianne.

"Forget her!" The strange being snapped, turning and walking slowly away. Loran followed without really knowing why.

In the corner of his vision, the beasts were following also, always lurking on the edge of the black mist.

Think about it, young Daemon. Said the voice in his head. *We can rule over here together. There is much still to do. You can be all powerful. A true God amongst beasts.*

What would I do here? He thought.

Rule. Over those that have strayed from the path, and do not cross the bridge. Those that exist here, in the Otherworld.

Like those? He looked to the beasts in the mist as they walked.

They are the truest form of those that have strayed. Their inner self, if you will. Rule them with me. They must be eternally punished for their crimes in mortality.

"No." he said firmly, as much to convince himself as the stranger. It would, in all truth, be easier just to give in. To exist here, in this otherworld. He felt stronger here. Powerful. Like he belonged here.

But again, her face came to his mind.

"I must return." He said.

"Forget her!" It screeched at him again, turning, its foul breath pungent in his nostrils. "I have need of you here."

"No." Loran said firmly. "I love her."

"Foolish." It rasped.

At that moment, the pain started again.

Loran opened his eyes to find himself in a cage with barely any light. Alone.

With only one arm.

He closed his eyes against the agony, his body shivery.

***

Brianne took a swig of water from her skin, then walked over and picked up her practice sword.

Tialla didn't.

"Not this time." She said. Instead, the red haired warrior walked past the wooden swords to a roll of sable fur leaning against a tall oak tree. She unrolled it to reveal two swords of unfathomable beauty. They were long, with a gentle curve and bone handles, ornately carved and decorated.

"These were made for me by a master swordsmith from Durmak. The metal in the blade is folded for strength and cooled using an age-old process that few ever master. It will cut through anything…"

She handed one to Brianne.

"…and it is yours."

"I can't.." she began to protest.

Tialla nodded once. Brianne took the sword, her hand trembling. She noted it was only sharpened on one side, and looked up, giving her tutor a questioning look.

"If properly wielded, one side is all you will need. Today we will learn Ché."

"Ché?"

Tialla walked back to the clearing. Brianne followed.

"Ché." She said. "The dance of swords. A series of moves that will help you relax, attune to your weapon, and be mindful only of the sword, your enemy, and nothing else. Not the Lord Commander, not the Daemon. Only the sword."

She stood, legs at the ready stance, sword held high above her head pointing forward.

Brianne copied. Tialla stepped forward, sweeping her sword down slowly, through an imaginary enemy, her student copying. A series of fluid moves followed, sweeping arcs, turns and lunges. Brianne tried to memorise them.

"You're thinking too much." said Tialla, stopping. "You must concentrate only on your breath, the sword, and Ché. Nothing else."

Brianne nodded. They began again.

With only the trees, the birds and the Uret for company, the two winged warriors danced the dance of swords, their movements effortless, slow and deliberate. They mirrored each other precisely.

***

Standing on the edge of the forest, Brianne looked down again at the sword.

Her sword.

"Thank you for this." She said for the eleventh or twelfth time. Tialla simply smiled again.

"Same time tomorrow?" The sword mistress asked with a glint in her eye.

Brianne didn't answer. Her attention was drawn to a horse and wain she could just make out pulling through the arch of the citadel.

"What's wrong?" Tialla asked, following her eyeline.

"That wain is unfamiliar, that's all."

"So?"

Brianne looked back to the redhead.

"We only deal with certain traders here. Others are unwilling to deal with us, for some reason."

And unfamiliar wains were not a good sign. The hairs on the back of her neck stood on end again.

Brianne opened her wings without a word and flew to the Citadel wall. She landed, folding in, and looked over her shoulder to see Tialla running to catch up, her own wings not yet mature enough for flight.

Oh well, she thought.

Things always change eventually.

**

They entered the gate together and walked past the wain, swords sheathed across their backs, to find Josten deep in conversation with Lord Commander Remus. Something in his expression didn't sit easily with her.

Remus raised his eyebrows at their entrance, noting the swords over their backs.

"My lord," Josten was saying, "there's a trader at the gate. He demands to see someone of importance." Remus sighed heavily and walked over to where a tall, thin man was standing next to his horse. Brianne and Tialla followed.

"Name?" Remus snapped.

"Ashe." He said simply.

"...and?" Remus sighed.

"Well, see, I was heading out of Var'n Arden yesterday, having served my business when I saw a wain heading in past me to the palace, see."

"What of it?" sighed Remus, his patience thinning by the second.

"Well, I caught a glimpse of the cargo. Blowed if it wasn't your Daemon friend." He scratched his beard, looking around. "Leastways, I think he's a friend of yours. Looked dead to me."

Remus cast a look at Brianne, her eyes wide. He thanked the trader and told Ashe to get him some food for his return. As

Ashe walked away, Brianne called after him.

"I've not seen you here before, have I?"

Ashe shook his head, uncertainly. "No, can't say as you have…"

"Why not?"

"The Queen. The Alliance of traders is based in Var'n Arden. She's threatened them all with death if they continue to deal with the Citadel. Most aren't brave enough to call her bluff."

She nodded her thanks and Ashe turned to walk to the feast hall, flanked by two guards.

Brianne spun and walked away, the Lord Commander calling after her.

"I've seen that look before, my lady. What have you in mind now?"

"What do you think?" she snapped. "I'm going to Var'n Arden."

"You'll not get within a hundred leagues of it, my lady." Called Ashe. "There are archers on every rooftop between the palace and the moon forest. They'll cut you down in seconds."

"I'll not leave him there." She said firmly.

"Horses." Tialla said.

She turned to the redhead.

"Use Horses." Tialla said. "We can hide our wings under cloaks, blend in with the trader's traffic. A small party might just slip in." she smiled.

"We don't ride horses…" Brianne protested.

"I can teach you. Consider it." She replied

Brianne nodded. "I will. Thank you…"

"You mean WE will." She said. "You don't think you're going in there alone, do you?"

"I can't ask…"

"You're not," she interrupted, "I'm offering. It's settled."

"I'm coming too." Said Josten. "You could use an archer, and I'm the best here."

The ladies looked at each other, then nodded to him.

"A fight? Sounds like fun." Said a cheery voice behind them.

Josten turned to see Kall walking up to them.

"Not now, Kall. This is serious."

"I am serious. If that Daemon had not restored the wings of…" he left the sentence unsaid. "Well. If he were here, I'd want to thank him. This is the least I can do."

Josten had seen Kall volunteer for a scrap many a time. He'd never seen him this determined.

"Ok…"

Kall looked at the ladies.

"Where are we going, exactly?"

"The White Spire." Brianne said.

Kall's face blanched.

"Oh shit…"

***

They gathered in front of the open archway in the north wall, the remnants of the portcullis gate leaning against the inside wall. Tialla had introduced Brianne to a black and white mare she called Patch.

"She has a lovely disposition, and will make a good first ride, won't you Patch?" she cooed, rubbing its nose.

It didn't look lovely. It eyed her suspiciously and snorted.

"Here," she said, handing Brianne the reins. "Put one foot in the stirrup like I showed you, then bounce up and swing your legs over the saddle. Get the other foot settled before you sit down."

Brianne did as she was bid, made decidedly easier with the black trews and shirt Tialla had provided her with, adjusted quickly to accommodate her wings. She'd largely ignored the dark looks the Lord Commander had given her.

She sat in the saddle uneasily, her horse jittering and fidgeting.

"Sit still," said a man's voice behind her. "They can tell when you're nervous."

She turned in the saddle to find Aleas sitting behind her astride a dark brown gelding, wearing a black leather overshirt and trews. His broadsword hung from his weapons belt, a dagger on the opposite hip. His beard was neatly trimmed, and his long greying hair tied at the nape.

"Aleas, I can't allow you…" she started.

"He is my son." He said, giving her a look that clearly brooked no argument. She nodded with a sigh. Tialla turned her horse, the others doing likewise, trying to remember all they had briefly been told.

"The King will be displeased, my lady." Remus said.

"Fuck the king.." she snarled, kicking in her heels.
They cantered out of the arch, heading north.

TWENTY SIX

Isiarus was seated before the window, her jet black mane billowing in the breeze. There was a knock on the door, to which she called "enter."

The door was opened from the outside by a guard, who stepped to one side to let Loshin sweep into the room, closing it again behind him.

Loshin nodded his head, waiting while she stared at her knew arm. It was almost identical to the right, except that it was pale grey in colour, muscled and taut, the fingers long and cruel and topped with grey-yellow claws instead of fingernails. She sat, gazing at it. Turning it and examining it all the while. She retracted the claws, then extended them with a smile. She couldn't help but wonder what her father would make of this spectacle, had he been here to witness it.
Perhaps, now she thought on it, it was fortunate he was not.

"How is it, highness?" he asked at last.
She looked up, as if forgetting he was even there.

"I'm getting used to it. It is functional if nothing else. The colour is unfortunate, but it has other benefits I am getting used to." She said, holding up her hand, claws extended.

"Fian tells me our guest is now awake. The results of his experiment are, I have to admit, spectacular." He shuddered visibly at the memory. Loshin had been in the basement with Fian for an age examining his other work. She was keen to see that, too.

"I'll be along in a while." She said dismissing him with a wave of her hand.
Her normal one.

***

He awoke, the cage cold and dark. His head hurt. He was lying on his front, his hind legs curled underneath him.

Did he always have hind legs?

He lifted his head, his long ears flapping, standing upright and shifting to hear what he could. The cage was silent, the dungeon was silent.

He couldn't remember having long ears either.

Leaning up on the tips of his folded wings, he lifted his head…

Wings?

It was all so fuzzy. He couldn't remember who he was. No name would come to him. He looked down at the body he had, long and powerful, covered with a downy fluff of dark brown fur, his hind legs curled beneath him, his body resting on his wingtips.

He opened his maw to speak, but what came out was a long, howling shriek.

Was that him? Was that his voice?

So fuzzy. Couldn't remember anything.

Why couldn't he remember?

The doors opened and she entered.

He knew her. He definitely knew her.

She was his Queen. Wasn't she?

He shrieked again. A long, mournful howl.

"There, there, my pet." She cooed through the bars. "No need to be sad. Look how magnificent you have become?" The old man, long and thin, joined her. He remembered the old man. He didn't like the old man…

"Outstanding work, Fian. Truly outstanding." His Queen said.

"Thank you, highness." The old man replied, dipping his head. "It was a lot of work, but the results are worth it, I think. How is the arm?" he nodded to her left hand.

"I'm getting used to it, thank you. It wasn't the result I'd hoped for from this venture, but it will suffice. And now, to business." She turned back to the bars, putting a hand through and stroking him under the chin. He purred low and deep.

"You want to please me, don't you?" she looked deep into his dark eyes.

He did.

"Then, go." She hissed. "Go to the Citadel and kill them. All of them. I don't care what colour their fucking hair is, I want them all dead."

He howled again. He would do anything for her.

She was his Queen.

Wasn't she?

***

"We'll make camp here, slip in with the morning traffic tomorrow." Tialla announced as she slid from her saddle. They were just on the northern edge of the Moon Forest now.

"Thank the Goddess!" mumbled Brianne. They were so close, but her backside had gone numb some leagues back. She was seriously wondering whether her arse would make it to the Palace, let alone back to the Citadel again.

"I'll get a fire going." Kall said as he wondered off. Josten slid from his saddle, rubbing his back, then helped Brianne from hers. Between them they unsaddled and tethered the horses, Tialla feeding them from a bag of grain she'd taken with her. This was definitely a task none of the blonde Avians seemed comfortable with.

They had a fire going in no time, a pot of stew made form vegetables taken from the kitchen and a deer that Josten had killed and skinned. Tialla sipped on a hot tisane, taking a whetstone from her saddlebag and running it lightly down the curved blade of her sword. Brianne never took her eyes of her tutor, watching her edge her weapon.

"Here." The red haired Avian tossed her a spare whetstone from her bag. "Like this, see?" Brianne unsheathed her sword and copied her tutor, and lately, friend.

Josten sat on a tree stump next to Kall. The usually cocksure youngster had been quiet all journey. Very quiet. Brianne had never seen him this way, distracted like this.

"Everything ok?" Josten offered the young man a drink from his water pouch. Kall took it and sipped, handing it back with a nod. Josten nodded back and made to rise.

"Jost..."

He sat back down.

"I keep wondering. What kind of relationship would Rhyl and I have had if things had been different, you know?"

"That does you no good, and you know it, my friend. What's done is done. No ifs or buts or maybes. It is what it is." Kall nodded. He knew his friend was right but still, this niggle in the back of his mind wouldn't let go. If only they'd had more time.

"Did you say goodbye to her?" Josten asked, taking a sip.

"So, you've found us out, eh?" Kall smiled. He must have known he would not keep the secret for ever. And maybe, when they returned, Kall could think of a way for them both to be together at last?

"I did." He said quietly. "We will be together now, Jost. Soon. Nobody can stop us."

I'd like to see them try, Brianne thought.

Tialla looked across at her pupil, nodding approvingly.

"What happened to your brother?" Brianne asked as she polished. Tialla's whetstone paused a beat, before continuing.

"Nobody really knows. He often goes off in a huff like this for days at a time. He's a spoilt brat, really. Thinks the world owes him something, you know? Doesn't realise you've to go out there and make life happen for you."

"He's missed on his opportunity this time though, surely? He won't have got his wings unless he was in range when the Seraph broke."

Tialla shook her head.

"Nothing I, or anybody else, can do about that now." She picked up a cloth from the saddlebag, tossing one to Brianne, and polished the blade to a final shine down its length. Nodding, she sheathed her own sword and inspected Brianne's.

"Perfect. You're a quick learner, Bri."

Brianne chuckled.

"What?" Tialla looked at her sideways, narrowing her eyes.

"Oh, nothing. It's just that the only person that calls me Bri is my Pa."

Tialla apologised.

"It's ok. I like it." She smiled back, sheathing her own weapon. "Did you go to Durmak to get these?"

Tialla shook her head.

"I picked them up in Solaan." She said "I spent two summers there, learning, fighting. Having fun!" she smiled, winking. She shifted her weight to get comfortable. "Gods, these things take getting used to." The others laughed, Kall and Josten getting quickly accustomed to her company. Wings weren't a problem when you were born with them. Hers were still downy and immature, but growing at an alarming rate.

"They're exquisite." Aleas said, nodding to the swords as he sat alongside them. "How are you planning on getting through the gates at Var'n Arden? They'll be checking traders, especially now, with a rescue attempt expected?"

"I'm not really sure, yet…" Tialla seemed lost in thought for a moment.

"I may have an answer." He said quietly. "There's a gate on the eastern wall that is barely used, if ever. Last time I used it, Loran was but a babe. It was overgrown and neglected then. It leads into the rear of the stables. Might be our best hope." He smiled.

This plan seemed to meet with her approval.

"Let us hope it is still neglected, eh?" she smiled back. Kall handed them a bowl of stew each, and they ate in grateful silence for a while, each thinking on their outcome.

Except Brianne.

All she could think of was Loran.

***

Alden and Kady ran across the throughfare, a horse whinnying as they passed in front of it. It was late and Mama had

been calling for a while, but Kady wanted to see the piglets one more time as they were just SO cute and squiggly. Her brother said they were smelly, but what did he know?
Boys were stupid.

Alden held her hand nonetheless as they ran into the front yard of their squat, mushroom topped home in Var'n Rodan. As they ran through the low picket gate, Kady dropped her knitted dolly on the floor.

"Mahri!" she called. Breaking free of her brothers hand she ran back to the gate to fetch it. Her mother called again from the doorway, just as a loud thump came from behind her. She had to fetch Mahri. Mama had spent such a time knitting it just right. From the end of the throughfare, people screamed, and Kady looked up toward the end of the wide lane.

At the end of the row of homes opposite was Rayner's horse yard. In the paddock was a horse lying on its side with a huge animal, like something from a bad dream, standing over it, tearing a chunk of flesh from the horse's neck.

It was half wolf, half bat. Its huge, grey body covered in downy fur. It stood tall, resting its weight on its wingtips where it's front legs should be, blood dripping from its large maw. As it bent down and tore away another chunk, Rayner the younger came out of the house brandishing a pitchfork. The beast lifted its wingtip and swung it sideways, knocking Rayner from his feet. The pitchfork clattered against the corral fence as the beast bent down and bit through Rayners neck, a spray of blood gurgling, his wife screaming.

The beast opened its large, brown wings and took to the air. Kady was swept up in her mother's arms as the thing flew overhead, landing at the opposite end of the throughfare. Here it found cattle, and held one down with its hind leg while it feasted on its intestines. It looked up as people ran across the wide lane into houses and buildings.

It lifted its head and howled into the air.
Kady screamed.

***

The fire was burning bright, painting an orange glow over the forest. Everyone was quiet. Aleas was sat with his back to the fire, watching the two ladies.

They stood in identical poses, swords held aloft. In unison, they moved swiftly through the movements that were fast becoming second nature to Brianne. Slow, deliberate and fluid, they swept, blocked, lunged and chopped through an army of imaginary foes. At the end of the chê, they turned to face each other, and gave a polite nod.

"You're ready." Tialla said quietly as they walked back to the fire.

"You think?" Brianne stopped, and they faced each other.

"I do." She nodded. "You remind me of me." She sheathed her sword.

"Is that good?" Brianne asked as they started walking again.

"I think so, yes. You're determined, and a quick learner. You won't be dissuaded once your mind is set. You'll make a fierce warrior."

"Not bad for a teacher of fledglings." She chuckled.

"You are what you wish to become, not what others have made you. I would have been but a dutiful sister and daughter, had I not persisted in my quest to learn swordcraft and weaponry. Perhaps you and I are not as different as I first thought. I never had a sister, only my fool of a brother." She turned to Brianne. "I would like to consider you such."

"And I you." She held her hand out, and Tialla took it in a warrior grip. A sister was something she had not considered either. Even friends were few in her life. Loneliness had been her companion for a long time, solitude her only true friend. Now, she and this assorted band were about to go into the bears mouth together.
For him.
Gods, how she missed him.

***

"And you let them leave?" Thundered King Pyrus.

Lord Commander Remus shifted uncomfortably, but stood tall and proud nonetheless, staring straight ahead, his helm under his arm. The forum members were silent, having had their discussion on the recent events and their new brethren intruded upon.

"With respect, Sire. I couldn't very well stop them." He said through gritted teeth.

Not that he'd tried that hard, the king was willing to wager.

"My daughter can be quite stubborn," came a voice from the door. "Can't imagine where she gets it from!" Pehl strode into the dim forum chamber, standing before the oval table next to Remus.

"You have no right of audience in here. Get out." Pyrus rose, his face turning puce.

"Come, come, brother. Will you not accept what your eyes tell you? What you know to be true" he fluttered his still-immature wings, down fluttering to the floor. They were
growing quicker than a fledgling's would normally, as Isaac had said. Still, they were nowhere near ready for flight yet.
Pyrus hoped that they never would be.

"Do not call me that. That beast from the otherworld may have given you back your wings, but that will never make you one of us." A murmur went round the table, not all of it agreeable. Pyrus eyes the forum members silently. He had to tread carefully if things were to return to some form of normality. He had to have the members on side. Isaac had already suggested the idea of blending both factions.
The thought sent a shudder down his spine. That boy always was quite gullible. Nothing like Meryl.
He had to have the members on side if he was to rid them of these dark hairs once and for all.

"You cannot simply cover your ears against the noise of progress."

"Progress?" the king scoffed back. This was anything but progress. Years of work undone.

"Yes, progress." Pehl raged back. "We are all that remains

of the first Avians, all but wiped out in the Century Wars. The Gods would have us dead, given their way. And you still cling to this misbegotten belief that one of them grants you a gift? To be protected?" He shook his head.

"That is a belief we have had for a long time." Said an elder form his seat. "Change takes time. Time to acclimatise, time to adjust. Time to become accustomed to a new way of life. Give us that time."

Pehl nodded slowly. Time.
That, he said he could give them, as he turned and strode from the room.
Time was good, though Pyrus. Time to formulate a plan that would put things back as they should be.

TWENTY SEVEN

A long line of wains and horses sat on the road to Var'n Arden. The raft of checks made on all entrants to the city had ground the route to a stop. Horses snorted, and drivers huffed, as they crept forward towards the gate. The driver of a wain full of Durmak White Wine slid from his bench and put a pail of water down in front of his faithful old horse. The horse drank greedily as the old man wiped the sweat from his brow, the downpour of the past month having done little to dampen down the heat of summer.

Five horses trotted past him, down the line towards the gate.

"Wait your turn, you whoresons." He bellowed after them as they trotted onwards. They slowed to a walk at a hundred paces or so from the wall, peeling off to the right and walking around the wall. Their hoods up, they pulled up near a clump of trees nestling against the wall, the breeze from the ocean rustling the leaves, brine filling the air.

Aleas slid from the saddle, dropped his hood and looked carefully around the wall towards the ocean.

Sitting a score or so paces from him was a gate in the wall, wide enough only for a foot soldier.
Standing in front of it was a guard.

Aleas swore under his breath. This was exactly what he'd feared. Clearly, somebody was taking no chances with Loran as their guest. The dozen or so archers they spotted on various rooftops and barns was a testament to that.

"Now what?" whispered Kall in his ear, peeking over his shoulder at the gangly looking guard, his breast plate and greaves freshly buffed, his sword new. The sigil of the queen newly stitched onto his claret surcoat in gold thread.

"Wait here." He hissed as he stepped confidently out around the wall.

The young guard looked at him uneasily. Clearly expecting an easy, boring duty watch.

"Halt." He said, his voice cracking. He made a grab for the pommel of his sword as Aleas raised his hands.

"Fear not, friend. I am but a lost traveller." Said Aleas, walking up to him slowly. "How goes things?" he nodded to the palace.

"Not good. Not good at all." He said quietly, sliding his sword back into its sheath. "Best keep clear of this place. All kinds of…"

Aleas placed a finger on the young man's forehead and whispered.

"*Nadir Lách Gavaal…*"

The guard's eyes glazed over white, his hands slipping to the sides. Aleas steered the man by his shoulders out of the way of the gate and beckoned the others.

"I'm glad you're on *our* side." Whispered Brianne as they passed the guard. The young man stood staring out into nothing with eyes of pure white as Aleas reached down and retrieved a set of keys from the guards belt, turned and unlocked the gate. It creaked agonisingly loud as he pulled it open.

They slipped inside, Josten closing the gate after them and bringing up the rear. They were in a long, dark tunnel, lit only from open grills above their heads every ten paces or so. It was obvious this hadn't been used in some time, judging from the cobwebs in the corners and green moss on the floor. They walked in single file behind Aleas. There would be little chance of escape in here. Water trickled down the stonework as noises drifted in from ahead.

The corridor turned sharp right, a large archway marking its end. Light came through from the back of the stables, the familiar smell of horses wafting in. Josten watched the rear gate constantly, his bow nocked and taut as they rounded the bend.

Small beads of sweat ran down Kall's face.

They emerged behind the stables, young lads just visible running back and forth through the breaks in the wood. The noises and bustle of the morning drifted in from the courtyard beyond.

"I'm not one to worry," whispered Kall, "But once we find this Daemon, how the fuck do we get him out of here?"

"I'm working on that one." Aleas mumbled. He'd dreamt up and silently rejected, a dozen or more plans since last night. They reached the end of the stables, and Aleas glanced in.
It looked deserted.

He crept in and snuck a look in the first stable. Standing in it was a small piebald mare, not yet broken in, he guessed, judging from the size.

"Aleas," hissed Brianne, "What are you up to...?"
He undid the stable gate and slipped in. The horse shied away as much as it could.
Aleas slapped it resoundingly on the flank.

The horse whinnied and bolted out, running across the yard and out into the square outside the palace doors. Shouts and commotion could be heard as it ran across the square.
Kall risked a glance out into the square and smiled as three guards ran from their position against the wall to chase the horse down.

They slipped out and crept across the square, trying to look as nonchalant as possible. In the wall of the palace was a door. Aleas tried it.
It opened.

***

Queen Isiarus sat staring at her left arm, as she had done almost daily since the procedure. The large hall was all but deserted, a couple of serving girls chattering in the corner.

Now, at last, everything was working out in her favour. She was disappointed that plans had had to change, of course she was. Fian's assurances that her powers would be unstoppable had come to nought. But here she was, sporting a

new arm that was as strong as it was deadly. And she had a new pet to do her bidding to boot. Not too bad of an outcome.
One had to adapt to the situation, after all.

The large doors opened and Loshin swept into the room, his long cloak of black and purple sweeping out as he walked. He stopped at the Dais and bowed.

"General Wes to see you, Your Highness."

About time. She had been waiting on the generals report for a few days now, but other matters had always gotten in the way.

"Send him in."

Loshin bowed again, and swept from the room as the equally bald, stocky form of General Wes strode in to take his place. He nodded curtly, his hand on his pommel.

"Ah, General. What news of my army?"

"Returning, Highness. The uprising in Durmak is all but quashed. I've left a century to maintain order, and the rest are returning as we speak. They should be here in a moon or so."

"Excellent news, General. I may have a new task for them."

General Wes furrowed his brow, no doubt expecting some down time. A couple of weeks at least.

"Highness?"

"This creation of Fian's. He assures me he can repeat it. I want an army of those things. I want no further mistakes or delays. I will maintain order here in my lands at all costs and I cannot do that with a Daemon and a host of winged freaks on the loose. I remain
unconvinced that young Caylen has the wherewithal to beat all of them. Even in his current state"

"As you wish, highness." He nodded. "What would you have your men do?"

"Gather livestock. Cave bats and Prairie Wolves. As many as you can. At least a dozen of each. I want these beasts to be unbeatable."

General gave a broad grin and nodded again. He strode from the room, and Loshin returned.

"What of our other guest?" she asked whilst pouring a goblet of wine.

"He is not expected to last the day, Highness. Fian is convinced the loss of the limb will kill him."

She looked up and took a sip.

"Excellent."

***

They slipped into the barracks room, closing the door behind them. Three guards slept in low beds against the wall, the rest of the barrack thankfully empty. They crept down the central aisle, stopping dead when a door banged outside in the corridor, two guards walking past the closed door at the end of the barracks. They waited as the footsteps retreated and Kall let out a hefty sigh, the others giving him a dark look as one sleeping soldier stirred. They waited till he was still again.

Aleas opened the door and stuck his head out. The corridor was clear. Wall sconces lit the way. They crept along the corridor, Josten keeping a close watch to the rear all the while. About fifty paces along they came to a set of stairs down. Aleas went first, the others following in single file.

Down here it was dark. Uncomfortably dark. Flickering sconces were dotted along the wall, but the light seemed to evaporate at once. There was a long corridor off to the right that housed the cells. Ahead, another long corridor with a dark door at the end. Aleas remembered it from the cobwebs of his memory.

Fian's workroom.

Aleas opened it quietly. It was deserted. He closed the door and shook his head at the others.

***

Outside in the courtyard, Tialla waited until the horse was bought back to the stable, then rounded the palace, walking as casually as possible around the large doors. She hoped against hope that her undeveloped wings would not be noticed under her cloak. On the other side of the doors was another small door, hidden by a low wall. She took the key that Aleas had given her and opened it.

Inside were casks of ale, stores of dried meats and fruit. Assorted vegetables.

And three large drums of fat, used for cooking.

Tialla smiled.

***

To the left of Fian's workroom was a set of double doors. Brianne waited, he patience almost at breaking point whilst he opened the door and stepped in. she pushed her way in behind him.

Inside were two large cages. One was empty.

The other wasn't.

Loran lay on his back, his wings folded beneath him. Aleas turned his attention to the lock on the gate.

"*Ollod Gatellen*" he whispered. The lock pinged, and he swung the gate open.

Brianne rushed past him and knelt on the dusty floor by Loran's side, cradling his head. His skin was pale, almost ashen, a dark black-red gaping wound where his arm should be.

"Loren, oh my Loren. What have they done to you?" she brushed her hand over his cheek.

It was cold. Very cold.

"Does he live?" Kall asked from the doors, watching the corridor.

"Only just." Said Aleas. "This wound should have killed him. It would any normal person, I'm sure. Bastards."

"What are these shackles made of?" Brianne touched them briefly, tugging her hand away at their coldness.

"That's Mallenglâs. It's keeping him subdued." Aleas bent down and whispered a spell. The collar around his neck opened and Aleas flung it across the cage with a clatter, the shackles following.

"Let's get him out of here." Brianne stood, nodding to the two warriors at the door. Kall took his Legs, Josten his trunk. They struggled to lift him easily, with only one arm to grab under.

"Arse, this man's heavy." Kall panted. They half lifted, half dragged him to the door. The corridor was still deserted. Aleas closed the door behind them, Brianne took the lead and Aleas lifted Loran from the waist, holding his wings off the dusty floor as best he could.

"I can't let you do that, I'm afraid."
Brianne looked up into the face of a bony, painfully thin man in a long green robe with lank hair and a hooked nose, standing at the end of the corridor.

"Fian!" Aleas recognised him at once. The years had done little to enhance his skeletal form.

Fian furrowed his eyebrows.

"I know you..." he said, recognition on his face. "I'm afraid that the Beast must remain here. Her Highness is quite determined to watch it die." He droned.

"Her highness can kiss my arse." growled Brianne, a chuckle from Kall.

"Stand aside, old man," said Aleas, coming to stand in front of Brianne. The other two put Loran's body on the floor and unsheathed their swords. Brianne hissed her gleaming, freshly sharpened sword from its curved scabbard.

"Weapons? Really?" Fian chuckled, holding his hands in front of him, making sacred signs with his fingers.
Aleas did the same.

"You cannot think to be a match for me, you pitiful Mage?" Fian and Aleas eyed each other warily.

"*Lasaar*" Fian shouted, flinging his hand out in front of him. Bright blue streaks of light came from his hand.

"*Relont.*" Aleas said, a barrier of red light forming in front of him. Fian's blue streaks crackled off it harmlessly. Aleas mumbled something and flung his hands out wide, a great rush of air knocking Fian back.
The bony old mage grinned.

A clatter from the stairs drew the attention of Kall and Josten. They ran into the cell corridor, turning to face a half dozen of the queens guards as they rounded the corner. They engaged at once, Kall blocking and parrying with a tall, broad swordsman, ducking inside the man's guard to slice an opening on his leg. The guard stepped back, and Kall opened his throat. Josten took on a second guard who sliced open a wound on the archers forearm, blood trailing to his hand. Josten stepped back as a sword whistled past his neck, then rushed in to plunge his own into the man's groin. The guard fell with a groan, and two more took his place. The cell corridor was, luckily, not wide enough for more than two abreast.

A tall, muscular guard walked past the two mages to where Brianne was standing, sword ready.

He stepped in, chopping towards her neck. She lifted her blade quickly, the impact jarring through her shoulder. She took a step back and swung wildly for his torso, but he jumped out of reach, then swung for her head. Brianne ducked just in time. He chopped at her viciously, a ferocious series of blows knocking her back, almost off balance.

He grinned broadly and readied his blade again.

"Smile at me, you bastard, and I'll open your guts!" she snarled.

"Give it up, girl," The guard laughed, "Put that thing down, 'fore you hurt someone!"

Brianne turned sideways and raised her curved blade above her head, left hand forward.

The first position of Ché.

She closed her eyes briefly.

She opened them as the guard stepped in quickly, lunging toward her abdomen.

Suddenly, the world seemed to slow down. The sounds of fighting from the cells diminished, the crackles of magic from the mages almost silent. Her breathing the only sound.

She stepped forward, sweeping down to knock his blade aside. He stepped away, surprised as she swept in, lunging at his stomach. He managed to block, moving in to stab at her neck.

His blade stabbed into thin air as she slid sideways, slicing

through his bicep. He clutched the top of his arm, a stream of red flowing between the fingers. Brianne ran through a fluid series of movements, knocking him back all the while, then stepped sideways, cutting through his thigh. He fell back, his eyes wide.
She opened her wings slightly, using them to balance as she spun on her tiptoes, and swept her blade in a wide arc, separating his neck from his body. His head tumbled sideways, his torso crumpling to the floor, sword clattering off the flagstones.

Behind her, another guard rushed at her back. Without looking, she spun and chopped his arm off at the elbow. The man screamed, falling back as she opened his abdomen, entrails tumbling.

TWENTY EIGHT

Tialla strode across the square as smoke billowed out from the storeroom behind her. Shouts of alarm pealed out as she approached the wain driver waiting at the stable. She handed him his bag of coin as agreed, then climbed up onto the bench.

She looked around the palace square. Guards were running in all directions. Some toward the storeroom.
But not all. Some were running into the main gate of the palace, orders shouted. Weapons raised.

This didn't look good. Aleas had warned her to look for signs that they'd been spotted. This definitely looked like they'd been spotted.
She swore under her breath.

Time for plan number two. She clicked her tongue, giving the reins a little whip. The black mare ambled out of the gates behind a couple of horses as the wain driver headed for the tavern across the square.

She rounded the side of the palace, looking ahead for a tell-tale slope downwards in the ground.
There it was.

Tialla bought the wain to a stop and waited.

***

The two mages stood trading blows of light and energy, each using more and more drastic spells to try and out-do the other.
Aleas could feel the advantage slipping. It had been a long time, after all.

Fian mumbled a spell and bright white light crackled across the floor, his hands twisting in shapes.

Aleas lost his footing and stumbled back, almost falling across the body of a slain guard.

"Old fool," laughed the gaunt mage. "You may have been a mage once, but your powers have faded. Your strength is minimal." He snarled.

Aleas turned back to face Fian from the floor, the dead guard behind him.

"Once a mage…" he flung his wrist out, the guard's dagger flying through the air into Fian's gut.

"…but always a soldier."

The stick thin mage fell back, blood seeping down his robe, and propped himself up against the wall, his breath coming in ragged gasps.

"We need to get out of here, Aleas." Brianne said as she helped him up, the acrid tang of spellcasting almost catching in her throat.

"Quickly," he said to Kall and Josten as they dispatched the last of the guards, "Let's get him back in here." The clatter of footsteps could be heard in the stairwell above.

They wouldn't be getting out that way anytime soon.

They carried the Daemon's limp body back into the room. Kall dragged a cabinet across the doorway. At the end of the room were two large double doors, locked.

Aleas cast a spell, and they pinged open.

"What now?" Kall's eyes were wide with fear, his heart pounding.

"We can hope."

They half carried, half dragged Loran up the slope to ground level.

Sitting at the top of the ramp was a wain, Tialla at the reins.

"We'll never make it. There're archers everywhere!" Brianne hissed.

***

Josten looked around him, his mind made up. Perhaps he could buy them some time.

"Get ready. I'll join you soon" he said, casting off his robe and shrugging his bow from his shoulder.

"Jost, no!" Kall hissed.

The archer took off without another word

He flew up the wall, the white spire climbing away above him. He kept close to the stonework before darting up next to a startled guard.

The guard reached for his sword as Josten's arrow pierced his neck and he crumbled to the parapet. Three more arrows found their mark before the alarm was raised.

He looked down briefly, smiling as the wain took off south, four horses, one riderless, following.

Josten flew high over the wall, two arrows hissing past him. He fired off two more of his own, one in the belly of a sentry on the door, the other at the guard on the opposite wall, who fell and crashed through the stable roof.

White hot pain shot through his leg as an arrow embedded itself in his thigh. Jost looked around for the archer, spotting him at a battlement on the wall, next to the palace tower. He fired off an arrow which clattered harmlessly off the wall next to the guard.

Josten's vision narrowed as an arrow thudded into his back between the wing roots. He spun, looking for the archer and another hit him in the stomach.

Darkness clouded his sight as he landed in the square with a thud, guards surrounding him. Josten dropped his bow and reached for his sword.

A dozen arrows thudded into him at various points, and he dropped to one knee. He looked up in time to see a thick set guardsman bring a sword down through his neck.

**

On the south road, Kall looked over his shoulder briefly.

"Best not to, lad." Mumbled Aleas.

Kall turned his face back to the south again.

**

Sande left the food tent with Willard. She hadn't spent much time with the youngster, only having joined Pehl around a summer ago. They'd found him working the dockside at Point Mar. She'd spotted him first, working, as he had been in high summer with no shirt on, the wounds on his back were an instant tell. He'd proven to be a good warrior, older than his years in some respects, but still innocent enough to learn and eager enough to want to.

They'd eaten in relative quiet, her thoughts of Kall. He'd left suddenly, all very secretive. She couldn't help but be concerned. And Willard's company was a pleasant enough distraction from such worries.

Plus, food was getting scarce. Something else to worry about.

Both their wings were filling out nicely, having dried out soon enough and the down now falling to make way for the primary and secondary feathers.

Kall had taught her the names, laying in each other's arms one night. laughing every time she forgot one. She smiled at the memory, her smile evaporating as two blonde Avians blocked their path between the tents.

She stepped back and raised an eyebrow.

"Had a nice meal, have we?" the tall, gangly blonde on the left spat on the ground at her feet. "Eh, outcast?"

His compatriot chuckled, and she could feel Willard's hand sliding towards his sword.

Sande caught his eye and shook her head.

This was exactly what they wanted. Trouble. A chance to say it was self-defence. To kill without fear of rebuke.

She took a deep breath and silently vowed not to give them that pleasure.

"Go on, youngster," gangly goaded, "I fucking dare you. Let me give you a swordcraft lesson. Right here and now."

'Chuckles' chuckled again, and Sande hoped one day she'd get the opportunity to remove his tongue.

"Move." She said quietly. "You must return to the Citadel." They both bristled and stood taller, all mirth gone.

"Giving orders now, is it, outcast? Eh?" he leaned in close. "You giving me orders?"

"You should not be here." Said a voice behind them. They spun on their heels to find Isaac standing behind them. Once a temple novice, the young prince had taken to keeping watch over the makeshift tent city on their doorstep. And keeping the peace seemed to be a day-to-day occurrence.

"My lord, um. I, that is we…" gangly stammered. They stood aside to let Sande and Willard pass. She nodded her thanks and headed off into the relative safety of the night.

Isaac held their gaze a beat.

"I expected better from my own kind. Return to the Citadel at once." He stood aside and they walked ahead.

"Arse…" Gangly mumbled under his breath.

***

They skirted the edge of the Moon Forest, the wain making it almost impossible to edge their way through the trees. The forest path was far too dangerous. They'd spotted several more archers on rooftops on the road out of Var'n Arden, mostly watching the sky. Some eyed them suspiciously, but otherwise paid them little heed. Loran was safely covered in a black tarp in the back.

Brianne rode at his side constantly.

Aleas watched her a while, his own dark brown gelding plodding ever onwards. It had felt good to be back in the saddle again, however dangerous their task. Good to be doing something positive.

It had even felt good to be trading magic with that bony arsed old fart!

Fian was a strong one, though, of that there could be little doubt. Aleas had no misgivings that his dagger would wound him only for a short while. His own spells had left him bone weary.

He doubted they'd seen the last of him.

Kall was understandably quiet on the return, having lost a man who, by his own admission, had been more like an uncle to him. The young swordsman sat at the back of the group, his brow furrowed, his mood dark. The youngster was a tremendous fighter, though. Good to have in a scrap, no mistake.

As was Brianne. Her skills with that curved blade were improving daily. She'd dispatched with those guards in little time. There was no qualm that she was coming into her own. No doubt, either, that she loved Loran.

"Aleas!" Tialla called from the wain's bench. He looked up, stirred from his reverie.

Ahead was a multitude of people. Some walking, some on horseback, some in wains, with bairns crying. Cattle or horse tied to the back. All loaded to bursting.

"Wait here." He kicked in his heels, the old brown gelding cantering away. Tialla bought her wain to a stop, her hand straying toward the hilt of her sword

Aleas cantered to the head of the group. They were all heading south, toward the river Uret. He pulled alongside the lead horseman, a grey haired man in a white top.

It was covered in blood spatters. He eyed Aleas through thin eyes.

"Trouble?" the old mage said.

The man nodded gravely.

"There's a lot of you." The man looked at Aleas again and nodded. He turned his head back to the path.

"We're from Var'n Rodan. Or at least, we used to be." He said monotonously.

"Used to be? All of you?" Aleas looked back at the column of people behind him. "What happened, friend?"

"All gone." He spat. "The village, the cattle, the buildings. Most of the people. Gone."

"How?"

"Monster. A beast unlike any such I've seen before, that's how. A huge thing, the stuff of nightmares. Half bat, half wolf. Landed in the village and killed just about anything that moved. Including my children."

"I'm sorry for your loss, truly." Aleas had known loss. This would hit the fellow hard, that was for sure.

"Where are you headed for now?"

"Not too certain, really." The man murmured. "The beast took off for the forest, and we thought it best to move on before it returned. Not much left to stay for now, anyway."

"Cross the Uret and head for the Citadel of the Avians. You can seek refuge there."

"Hah! Those stuck up bastards don't help anybody. Besides, it would incur the wrath of the queen to be anywhere near there." The man shook his head in disgust.

"Isiarus is the least of your problems. Head there. Ask for Isaac. Tell him I sent you all."

The man looked at Aleas a long while, then nodded. They needed refuge. Desperately.

Aleas cantered back to the others.

"Well?" Tialla let her hand slip from the hilt.

"We've got another problem. And I suspect it's coming our way."

TWENTY NINE

Loran stood in the Otherworld, the thin black mist ever-present. The stench of decay and death cloying.

"Still you resist me!" Came a screech from behind him. He spun around to find the creature standing not a handspan behind him.

"Why have you bought me back to this place?" he demanded.

"I have need of you, boy." It rasped, the creature's breath rancid in Loran's face. "You must, will gladly, rule the Otherworld with me."

"I'm happy to disappoint you." Loran growled. He looked about him, the beasts still lurking in the periphery of his vision. Watching. Waiting.

"Be sensible. Your earthly body is mutilated, your strength gone. What have you left to go back to?" It flung it's arms wide. "Stay with me, here, and rule as a God!"

"Never. I have more to live for now than you know." Strange that both his arms were present here in the otherworld. The creature sneered at Loran, his black eyes unreadable.

"Her?" It laughed, "Ach. She is fickle, worthless. Useless. She will not accept you now. She has no more love for you than an insect." It waved it's hand dismissively.

"Obviously, you don't know her." Loran smiled at the memory of her, clearer now than before.

"Stay. You must stay. I am all powerful, all knowing."

"Then why have you need of me?" Loran furrowed his ridged forehead. The creature took a step back.

"You have no more power here than them." Loran realised, pointing a long talon at the beasts in the mist. They were waiting and watching, but not for him. For this creature before him. Waiting, perhaps, to take its place.

"I can give you a gift, in exchange for your assistance." It hissed, circling the Daemon.

"Gift?" Loran turned, keeping the creature in view. Beasts from the periphery closed in all the while, snarling.

"I can allow you control of your lost limb. For a short while only."

"What use have I, to control a limb no longer attached to me?" Loran laughed, the insanity of this place making his head swim.

"Ahh," it sighed, "What use indeed. I have foreseen your fates. You may yet thank me. Assist me in keeping these creatures at bay. They grow ever more daring. Ever more powerful."

"And then you'll return me? For good?" he growled.

The creature nodded.

"What is my fate?"

It smiled.

"Nothing is certain. There are many paths for you to tread, Daemon. I have seen but one."

Loran looked to the beasts closing in. He started toward them, then stopped.

"Am I truly a Daemon?" He asked over his shoulder.

"Here, yes. In the world? You are a mixture of Daemon and Man. Unique"

A four legged beast snarled at him, huge maw dripping saliva. It rushed towards him, and Loran opened his wings, flapping hard as he flew to meet it. They collided in a crash of fur and teeth, the creature opening a gash on Loran's chest.

It healed immediately.

Loran grinned.

The beast came at him again, and Loran reached out, slapping its head away, and reaching around its muscular neck. The beast flailed and thrashed in panic as Loran squeezed ever tighter.

It stopped thrashing and he let it sink to the ground, the mist enveloping it.

Loran turned as another beast, standing on its hind legs, came at him, claws raking for his eyes. He cuffed the hands away and headbutted it viciously between the eyes. The beast fell back, it's vision clouded. It opened its eyes in time to see Loran impale it through the neck with his overlarge claws.

Another two beasts came at him. Loran clawed one across the neck, his talons huge and yellowing in the Otherworld. It fell away in a gargle of red as he grabbed the other either side of its head and twisted. There was a crack, like a twig snapping, and the beast crumpled to the floor.

The mist enveloped them also.
He turned to see the rest running toward the distant mountains, black rain and lightning pounding the peaks.

"I don't think they'll be back for a while." He said as the creature came to stand before him again, it's breath fetid.

"You have done well." It rasped. "Your gift will be yours when you return. Use it wisely, for it will only work but once. That may be all you need…"

Loran nodded and pointed an accusing talon at the creature.

"Then know this," He snarled, "If you drag me here again, I will tear you asunder with my bare hands and feed you to them in pieces. Now, return me."

"As you wish…"

***

They headed east. Aleas and Tialla left the wain hidden in a copse of large cedars with Brianne and Kall guarding Loran. Like he could have torn her away from him, he mused.

He insisted on seeing first hand exactly what they were now dealing with. And that meant only one thing.
Going to Var'n Rodan.

The stench of death hit them both before they got a hundred spans from the gates. The constant buzz of flies, the cawing of carrion crows. Aleas knew before he got to the gates, hanging limp on their hinges, what to expect. Tialla threw back her sable edged blue cloak, now adjusted for her wings, and drew her sword.

"Not sure you'll need that, my dear." Aleas mumbled as they pulled up outside the gates and slid from the saddles. Tialla tethered them to the gates as Aleas walked in.

Bodies littered the street. Most recognisable, some not. Some had great gaping rends in their abdomen, guts ripped out and littering their clothing. Some were missing limbs, some heads. The crows were feasting on eyeballs and offal, cawing in protest as he crept in, flying off only to land again as he passed. He walked up the main thoroughfare, horses lying in a paddock to one side, all similarly mutilated. He trod on something and stopped to look down. It was a small, knitted dolly with red hair. The word MAHRI embroidered on its small white dress. From the corner of his eye, he spotted a small child's body lying in the paddock. It was missing its legs.

"What has hit this place?" Tialla came to stand beside him. The wounds in the bodies were vast. Far too big for Prairie wolves. Bigger, even, than Sayer-bears. If they even ventured this far north.

"Whatever it is, I'm not sure this was its intended target."

"What makes you say that?" she looked sideways at the old mage, turned soldier.

"There's no pattern. It just wild, wilful killing. Like a child testing out a new plaything. This is feasting and murder, nothing more." He dropped the dolly on the floor. "I've seen all I need to. Come on." He turned on his heels. Tialla looked a beat longer, then followed.

***

Brianne sat on the wain's side panel, her feet near his head, her wings draped over the sides. Kall sat off under a tree, lost in thought and remorse. Best to leave him with his feelings for a while. She looked down at the still, barely breathing, form of Loran.

How her world had been turned topsy turvy since he

arrived in it? How things had changed, evolved into this new vista they were looking at? The Avians and Outcasts were now on an even footing. The war with Pehl seemed at an end. Her path had veered dramatically from the one she thought to tread a few weeks ago. She still felt like a tutor of fledglings, inside. But something had shifted. She no longer wanted to teach them the same, tired old doctrine they'd been spoon fed since birth.

She wanted to tell them the truth. The real story of how things came to be as they were. She wanted to give her fledglings as much knowledge and free thinking as was possible and see them make their own minds up about how things. How to live their lives.

And about him. She watched his chest rising and falling, slowly and steadily. She picked up a water skin from the wain floor and dribbled some onto his ashen lips.
Loren swallowed silently.

"Live, my darling, live." She whispered. He had to live. She couldn't lose him now. There was so much they had to learn about each other. And yet, she felt she'd known him forever. He seemed to look right into her with those startling blue eyes. To know her very being.

She looked down at his left shoulder and furrowed her eyebrows. Where there was once an ugly, gaping wound of dark red, almost black, blood and tissue, was no longer a wound.
It was a mound. The beginnings of a small stump seemed to have pushed its way out of the scarring and scabbing.

"Was it always like that?" Kall asked over her shoulder, startling her.

"No. I need to speak to Aleas, but I think something's happening." She stared at the mound protruding from his shoulder. "How are you doing? She turned to Kall. His eyes were sunken and bloodshot in grief.

"I've been better…" he mumbled. She swung her legs over and hopped down. They walked back to the tree Kall had been sitting under and stood beneath its canopy, leaning their wings on the bark.

She was silent a while, letting the empty air sit between them. Hoping he would fill it when he was ready.

"I like your hair." He murmured at last.

"Thanks." She's almost forgotten her new look. She brushed a hand through her newly grown brunette locks, wondering if she'd have had the nerve to expose them at all without Loran.

"What made you finally pluck up the courage?" He asked, as if reading her mind.

She nodded to the wain.

"Him." Was all she whispered.

"He's quite something. I hope he makes it through, truly." He will. He has to.

"He was a real pal, you know? Jost?" He mumbled, looking at the floor. "A real pal."

"I know. We will avenge him, I'm sure."

She could recall him taking the youngster under his watchful gaze when Kall had first joined up, what seemed a lifetime ago now. Ever present, ever steering him in the right direction. Ever a kindly word.

The sound of hooves, gentle at first, drifted to them as Aleas and Tialla cantered back towards them.

***

"So, what do we think it is?" Kall asked, taking a great gulp from the water pouch and handing it to Tialla.

"Whatever it is, it's big." She said, taking it from him.

"This could be the work of a Meldling." They turned to look at Aleas.

"A what...?" Kall had never heard the word before. So much of this world of magic and mages was strange to them all.

"A Meldling. A very dark art, forbidden in every seat in the land. It involves using dark spells to fuse together animals to make a kind of hybrid creature. If Fian is dabbling in this, he truly has lost the path." He shook his head, remembering back to his time at the seat in Var'n Cirnan. The long lecture on forbidden practices, on the dark days of long ago. The Century wars, when Gods and man fought over the power of magic, of creation itself.

"Whatever this thing is, Fian has created it for one purpose, and one alone. Revenge."

They were silent a beat.

"We need to get back to the Citadel. Now." Said Brianne. They all nodded and started packing things way.

Aleas looked at the shoulder of the Daemon.

"What of that?" she asked him. Kall and Tialla stopped and turned to him.

"It's possible that his arm may regenerate."

"Re… You mean grow back?" Kall spluttered. "Can Daemons do such things?"

"Possibly. When he was but a bairn he picked up my wood chisel, while I wasn't looking, and dropped it on his toe. Cut the damn thing clean off." He could still picture the dark red-black blood spurting from a tiny grey foot.

"God's love him, he never made a murmur. I packed it and dressed it as best I could. A week later I took the dressing off to check the wound and it had grown back. Completely. Brand new toe, complete with claw, like nothing ever happened."

"But an arm, Aleas, is a lot different to a toe, surely?" Brianne said, staring at Loran's shoulder.

"It is, admittedly. And he had youth on his side then. But, in truth, there is so much about him that I really know little of. All we can do is watch and wait."

They cantered out of the copse a short while later, headed southwest and crossed the River Uret at Crenels Forde.

Just as the sun hit high noon, the Citadel loomed large on the horizon.

Outside the walls was a makeshift camp, not of dark winged Avians, but refugees from Var'n Rodan. Tents and wains littered the grasslands north of the Citadel walls. Children ran, chasing each other, mothers scolding as the smell of cookpots and fires drifted across the grasslands. As they neared the walls, all noise and commotion stopped. The village elder that Aleas had spoken to earlier stood at the front of a large group of people. He caught Aleas's eye and gave him a nod. Aleas returned it.

They entered the archway to the Citadel, the gates having been abandoned, and pulled up sharply.

In the market square was a multitude of Avians, dark and light haired alike, forming a wall of people leading to the medical building. All were staring at them.

It would seem that Loran had made friends as well as adversaries here.

On the steps of the Forum, King Pyrus looked on, his face stone.

***

It awoke around midday, nestled beneath a clump of tall, broad trees that blocked out most of the sunlight. It was thirsty, so plodded a dozen or so steps to the water's edge to drink. The water was cool and refreshing, and it lay its head forward, lapping at the stream for a while. The river was still here, away from the pool and the waterfall. The ripples on the surface subsided, leaving him looking at his reflection.

It wasn't a reflection he recognised. He looked a while at the head staring back at him. The long ears, large eyes and dripping maw with long teeth.

Was this really him?

He felt a heat building in his head, a rage bubbling to the surface.

Damn them. They had done this to him. This was their fault. They'd pushed him into this situation, like they pushed him all the time. His father, his sister. The Avians.

The Daemon.

Oh, how he wanted to kill the Daemon. To taste his flesh, to crunch his bones with his powerful jaws. How he longed to hear them lament as he feasted on the Daemon.

He lifted his head and howled in frustration.

Time to kill again.

THIRTY

"Here!" said Malaner, pointing to an overlarge cot bed in the corner. "Biggest we could find."

It took six of them to heft the Daemon's huge frame onto the bed. One by one they filed out, leaving Aleas alone with the balding, grey haired healer. They were both silent a while as Malaner looked over the wound. Finally he raised his head and looked at Aleas.

"I'm not entirely sure what you expect me to do with him. I know nothing of his physical makeup, or his healing abilities." Me neither, thought the old man.

"Just make him comfortable." Came a woman's voice from the door. They turned to look at Brianne, looking little like the teacher he had met a few weeks back. Dressed in black, a curved sword jutting up from between her wings, her dark brunette hair swept back from her face with a black band. She looked formidable.

"How, exactly?"

"Keep him fed and watered. Check the wound…"

"Ah yes, the wound." He bent to inspect it more closely. "You say its regrowing?" He shook his head. "Fascinating." The arm had grown to mid bicep, grey skin inching its way behind the dark red scabbed wound.

"Aleas, you should rest. I'll sit with him a while."
The old mage, turned soldier, raised his hands in defence.

"No, my dear. You need rest too. I'm fine for a while. Go. Eat, drink, sleep. Come back in a few hours."

She nodded wearily, the events of the past few days catching up with her. Aleas dragged a chair over to the bed and fell into it, dropping his weapons belt on the floor at his feet as she closed the door behind her.

***

Outside the medical building was a multitude of people. Avians and humans alike all staring at Brianne expectantly.

"What news of the great Daemon, my lady?" someone shouted from the crowd.

"He lives." She said loudly. "His recovery will take time." She looked about the crowd in amazement. What effect this Daemon had taken on people? Where once they would be fearful of him, and each other, now they stood in awe like believers awaiting news of their God.

From Daemon to Deity, she mused.

Things really do change.

***

Aleas felt his eyelids drooping and shook his head to wake himself up.

"Here." The healer handed him a flagon of ale. Aleas drained it gratefully.

"You think he'll recover fully?" Malaner asked as he sat in a chair opposite, draping his wings over the back and sipping from his own flagon.

Aleas shrugged.

"I know as much about him as you, really. Next to nothing. I do know his healing abilities are beyond any I've seen. He could grow that arm back in less than a week. Or not at all. Who knows?"

Aleas reached into a pocket and took out his pipe.

"Ah, I'd rather you didn't in here, if you don't mind?" The healer said. Aleas nodded and put it away.

"Quite right…" mumbled Loran from the bed. "… filthy habit anyway."

Aleas grinned

"Loran, my boy. You had me worried there for a while …" the old healer stood and held a beaker of water to Loran's lips, which he drained noisily. He nodded his thanks and looked around the room.

"She's just left. Quite taken with you, that one. You should have seen her fight. Remarkable." He shook his head at the memory.

He was silent a beat.

"They've taken your arm, my boy." He said quietly, letting the words sit between them both.

"I know, Papa." He said. "I know." He remembered the room, the grinning mage. The Queen watching from the doorway.

The Otherworld.

The door opened and Pehl strode in, his grey dappled wings looking dishevelled as they shed their down and grew the primaries and secondaries.

"I heard you were back. You've quite a following out here, you know."

Loran smiled and nodded.

"How have things been since we left?" Aleas asked.

Pehl and Malaner exchanged looks.

"That bad, eh?" he shook his head. "That was to be expected, really. The barriers that once divided your clan have been torn down, your differences stripped away. That's bound to cause friction. Some people won't understand. And people always fear what they don't understand."

"Indeed. There's been much infighting and squabbling. I'm almost sure the King is behind some of it, too."

"My daughter has been telling me of your adventures." He continued "They will be told around campfires for some time, I'm sure."

"She's performed admirably. A credit to you." Aleas took another sip of ale.

"What of these refugees from the village? They arrived asking for Isaac, of all people. That ruffled the Kings plumage, I can tell you?" Aleas help but grin at the thought of the King's bluster as Isaac no doubt took charge of the situation, allotting clothes, food, water, and supplies.

"The tales they tell, though?" he shook his head. "They

make little sense."

"The Queen's mage has been creating a Meldling."

"A what?"

Aleas explained it to him, Pehl's eyes widening further as he listened.

"What makes little sense to me though, is how she's able to give it commands? Generally, Meldlings are feral creatures. Uncontrollable. Not this one, by all accounts."

"She's blended the creatures with a human." Loran mumbled from the bed, weariness catching up with him.

"A human? By the Gods. There isn't a seat in the land that would teach that. Has he lost his mind?" The old mage was a wild one, that was for sure. But this?
This was something else entirely. This hadn't been done since the Century wars.

He'd heard tales in the great seat of mages asking questions on forbidden spells and practices. He'd always thought it only hearsay.

"What human?" Pehl asked.

"Your Son." Loran met his gaze. "I'm sorry, but the Meldling is Caylen."

***

Isiarus descended the stairs, guards coming to attention as she passed. She wafted downwards, her gold and red cloak billowing out behind her, a guard either side of her.

She hated having to come down here. It was dark, and dank. And smelly. But Fian had been locked away in his rooms almost continually, despite her sending for him several times. Damn that mage.

She stepped off the last stair and rounded he corridor to the end, the cells on the right now virtually deserted. Executions were always necessary to keep the people on their toes somewhat. Her father had taught her that. The old man would have been proud of her accomplishments, she was sure. Of her resolve and her merciless nature.

The guards went on ahead and opened the door, and she

entered the room without waiting.

A queen waits for nobody.

Fian was bent over his bench, the tabletop littered with books opened at various pages. He muttered and cursed, flittering from one book to another and flicking back a page or two to check on something.

"This is what has kept you?" she yelled. Fian looked up, startled, unaware of her entry.

"Highness. Forgive me, but I'm loath to waste our recently acquired resources. I must check and double check the ancient Dermal scripts. The books from the Great Seat have nothing on the kinds of incantations required for this to work."

"But you've performed this ritual before on that young pup? Did it not work then?"

"It did, highness. But I fear something is amiss in his nature. I must be sure."

She looked about the room, the cages in the corner filled with cave bats and prairie wolves. The wolves had been given a sleeping draft to avoid them killing each other before the ritual could even begin.

"Perhaps the fault is not with the procedure, but the candidate." She bought her gaze back to him, his green robe looking dank and stained dark where the blood had seeped into it.

"Perhaps. I have been reading up on that very fact. Caylen was an intelligent boy, but not a natural killer. Also, he's immature, which may leave him open to distraction."

"If it's natural killers you require, then look no further. There's an army of them out there to pick from." She nodded to the outer wall.

Fian straightened, smoothing down his dank robe.

"Highness, you cannot mean to convert your own army into these Meldlings?"

"Why not?" she put her hands on her hips. "A dozen of these things, melded with trained soldiers, is worth two dozen mere humans."

It made perfect sense to her. A dozen soldiers converted into these monsters? Able to take orders, trained to kill and obey? What was there to consider?

She turned to the guard on her left.

"Find General Wes. Tell him I want him to pick twelve guardsmen. Ones he doesn't mind losing."

The guard nodded and strode from the room.

"Good enough?" she swept a lock of hair back from her face with her left arm.

"Yes highness. A wise plan." He nodded low.

Isiarus swept out into the corridor without another word. As she stepped onto the stairs, a strange feeling came over her.

She stood still and looked down at her left arm, grey and powerful, its hand topped with cruel black talons.

"Highness?" the remaining guard had stopped a few steps in front of her, looking back.

"It's nothing. It's just…" She rubbed her shoulder and bicep with her right hand.

"For a moment, it felt as if it belonged to somebody else…"

***

"It will need to be stopped. You understand that?" Aleas put his empty flagon down.

Pehl nodded slowly.

"I do. And it sounds as if there's only one way to do that. This… Meldling? It must surely be killed." He closed his eyes briefly, all thoughts, hopes, and plans for his son evaporating before his eyes.

"I understand this is hard to take. You need not be present, I'm sure…"

Pehl held his hand up.

"Please. I need no sparing. If this thing has committed the atrocities you claim, then all trace of the man my son was, is unquestionably gone." He met Aleas's gaze. "It must die."

"Very well," Aleas nodded, "then we'd best start making plans to deal with this thing." He met Pehl's gaze. "We will need everybody."

Pehl nodded, knowing full well it was not he that would need convincing.

"I suggest we move the refugees inside the walls, at least? That will afford them some protection?" Aleas continued. "Along with your clan?"

"I'll see to it." Pehl turned and strode from the room without another word.

Loran pushed himself up on one elbow, wincing as he fell to one side, forgetting briefly that the other elbow was missing.

"And where, exactly, do you think you're going?" Malaner sauntered over and pushed the Daemon back onto the bedsheet. He put up little fight, his eyelids as heavy as boulders.

"We can deal with this, my boy." Aleas smiled down at him. "Rest up. I'll keep you posted." Loran nodded weakly as his father walked to the door. It had been some time since the old man was stronger than he.

Loran closed his eyes and drifted off to sleep.

Outside, Aleas glanced about the square to see where Pehl had headed and smiled as he realised he had sought the help of the one person he could rely on to organise things.

Isaac.

***

Isaac stood almost nose to nose with King Pyrus, his jaw set. The King, arms akimbo, was ranting and bellowing, as he had been for an age, now.

"I don't have time for this, father." Isaac countered, trying to shout the King down. He still had much to do. The women and children had been ensconced in the main hall, crammed and crowded as it now was, with people of all sorts. He had given orders for both camps to remain outside for now in hopes they may serve as some kind of distraction from whatever it was they were facing.

He had been working closely with his uncle.

And it was abundantly clear that his father didn't like it.

"You take up with that wolfs head, without so much as a word from your King?" Pyrus raged, spittle flying.

"It was necessary. There wasn't time..." Isaac started. The king ranted on over the top of him, deaf to his protests. In point of fact, his time with Pehl, although grave in nature, was surprisingly pleasant. They'd chatted and talked amiably. He found his uncle easy to talk to and get along with. Easy to discuss his time as a Novice, his hopes and fears, his friendship with the Daemon.
None of which he could bring up in present company.
The sound of a horn from the wall bought them both to a stop.

***

The Meldling flew in low across the grasslands, wings flapping lazily. It landed on a wain first, squashing it flat, shards and splinters of timber exploding outwards. The horse tried unsuccessfully to bolt, tethered as it was to the remains of the wain, and a timber the length of an arm embedded into its flank. The beast stepped forward and crunched its dripping maw through the horses neck, the horse screaming and frothing in pink from the mouth before falling silent.

It opened its wings then, and flew over to the tents, landing on one, stamping on its flat remnants and tearing at the fabric before moving on to another. It was similarly empty.
It lifted its head and howled in frustration.

An arrow the length of a man thudded into the ground next to it. The beast lifted its eyeline to the wall, a flicker of recognition sparking in his brain.

"Go to the Citadel and kill them. All of them. I don't care what colour their fucking hair is, I want them all dead."

He spread his gossamer brown wings and lifted off, heading for the wall. A dozen arrows whizzed past him, one hitting him in the leg. Another huge arrow sliced through his left wing, doing little to slow him down. He landed on the wall, arrows whizzing at him, most harmlessly, some embedding into him. He bit down and tore them out before stomping forward, his weight on his wingtips.

An Avian with a sword ran at him, and he batted the blade

aside with his wing before biting through the man's shoulder. The Avian screamed and fell away in a torrent of red as another two ran at him. One opened a wound on his right wing limb, and he bit through the Avian's neck opening a great, gaping gash, blood running in a deluge down the Avian's

breastplate. The other sword he batted aside and stepped on the Avian with his powerful hind legs, a bone splintering crunch from the Avian's chest as he plodded onwards.

He had instructions to kill them all.

But he *wanted* to kill the Daemon. He wanted it badly. Could almost taste his flesh, his black blood. He screeched in anger, taking off as another volley of arrows clattered off the stonework. The archer teams on the corner turrets tried to swing their giant crossbows round to bear, but they were never designed to aim at the Citadel itself, only the outside grounds. They thudded against the stops on their pivots.

He landed in the square and bit through a swordsman's dark-haired head. The Avian, his grey dappled wings barely half feathered, crumpled to the floor, blood and brain running down his chest.

The Meldling sniffed the air. A scent lingered, one he recognised, and he followed it, turning his head toward the medical block.

Daemon!

He licked his lips and plodded towards the squat building. Two females blocked his path, both dressed in black with long, curved swords in their hands.

One with white wings, one with grey.

"Not today, my ugly friend." Brianne snarled. As one, they set their feet and adopted the first position of Ché. As the beast plodded towards them, they swung their blades down together, turning and spinning, their weapons a blur of steel and death.

The beast stepped back, anger bubbling to the surface. He snarled, maw dripping, and roared as an arrow thudded into this side. The beast bit down and tore it out, blood seeping from the wound.

Pehl ran forward, joining them, setting his feet and drawing his longsword. He glanced to his right and raised an eyebrow as King Pyrus flew toward them, sword drawn. The King landed with a thud in the stonework, his breath coming in gasps.

The beast opened his wings wide, settling his weight back on his hind legs, and roared, its breath rancid and reeking of death. The Archers had gathered on both sides now, arrows whizzing at the beast in waves. He snarled as they hit home, but they only seemed to make the thing angrier. It folded in and plodded forward, pulling its head back to avoid Brianne and Tialla's swords at the last minute. In a rage, the beast lunged toward them, giving them little time to bring their blades to bear.

They were both knocked to the ground, the beast trampling over them as if they weren't there. Tialla covered her head with her free hand, blindly stabbing upwards with the other as she spat out dust and scree. Brianne cursed, rolling to one side to avoid a hind foot.

Another volley of arrows whizzed at the beast from the right, and it growled, lunging over to grab one archer that had gotten a little too close. The Avian screamed as the beast shook him from side to side, finally tossing him afar and turning back to the medical building.

The beast lumbered to the steps, growling at the door. Pehl ran over, lunging his sword at the beast's throat. It fell back quickly, snarling at the swordsman. Pehl pressed his advantage, lunging forward to stab at the beast's jugular. The irate creature bought his wing up and knocked Pehl to the ground. Maw drooling, the creature lunged forward, it's jaws snapping towards Pehl neck.

A sword pierced the creature in the shoulder, and it reared up in pain, wrenching the longsword from the hands of its owner and stumbling back a few paces. Pehl looked up to find King Pyrus standing over his brother, a smile on his face. The king looked down, seeing

the boy he knew before he'd been sent away all those years ago. Seeing his brother, as if for the first time.

The Meldling plodded forward and crunched his jaws down over King Pyrus's head, bone and brain squelching out the sides of his teeth. The King slid to the ground as Pehl roared in anguish and torment.

Another volley of arrows thrummed home, most hitting it on the flanks and side. The beast roared again, making for the doors and Pehl in front of them. Tialla and Brianne picked themselves up behind it, readying their swords to attack is from behind.

The beast reared up on its hind legs again as Pehl got to his feet, it's maw open, teeth dripping with blood and gore. As it sank down, a sword struck it in the throat, coming out the other side, blood sheeting down the beast's neck. It's eyes rolled back into its head.

Isaac ripped the sword free, fresh blood running in torrents, and the creature spluttered and gasped for air, it's throat in ruins.

Isaac bought the sword up, slicing it cleanly through the monster's neck and separated the head from the body. The head tumbled to the ground, and the body collapsed.

Pehl crumpled to his knees beside his brother's maimed figure, tears streaming down his face, his breath coming in great gulps.

THIRTY ONE

Isaac stared down at the body of his father, the head in ruins, and turned away.

"I'm sorry, young Isaac." Mumbled Pehl. "He... he saved my life. Why would he do that?" He cuffed the tears away with the back of his hand.

"They say blood is thicker than water." Brianne muttered. She clasped Isaac on the shoulder. "I think we have some clearing up to do...Sire."

Isaac met her gaze slowly.

"No." He shook his head. "I don't think we need a king. Not again. Not a ruler. A dictator. We need a leader of men and women, certainly. Of Avians of all kinds. One the people have chosen as their own."

"A vote?" Pehl sheathed his sword. "Really?"

Isaac stood tall.

"Yes. A vote. The people should decide on their leader." He looked about at them all.

"All the people."

This was the way forward for the Citadel, he felt sure. Then the forum could be put to best use. Deciding by majority, not appeasing a King at every turn.

This was what he wanted.

Aleas walked up to them, nodding his greeting to Pehl.

"You hear this?" the leader of the once-outcast warriors chuckled, "We're to become a democratic people."

"You do not approve, father?" Tialla asked, standing next to Brianne.

"On the contrary. I think it's a most excellent notion." Pehl did not feel the conviction of fighting for the throne as he once had. That seemed unimportant now. And in any case, certainly a decision they could leave for another time.

Aleas looked over the body of the beast, it's head, face down, a little way away.

"Good job you decapitated the thing. We might never have beaten it." He mumbled.

"They're called Wraiths. That is the only way to kill them for certain."

Isaac was suddenly very aware that they were all staring at him.

"It is written in the Dermal scriptures of the Century Wars. The texts are in the temple's basement vaults." He looked around at the faces turned toward him.

"I assumed you all knew?"

***

General Wes strode across the courtyard and mounted his horse, the reins handed to him by a stable lad. Wes nodded and looked about him.

The courtyard was full to bursting with horses. His cavalry were waiting patiently, swords sheathed, cuirasses polished, helms gleaming in the mid-morning sun. Outside the gates were three centuries of men on foot, their scarlet cloaks billowing.

Beyond them stood the Wraiths.

Wes shuddered at the thought of them. Over two dozen of his men had been sacrificed in total, none of them particularly quietly, either! Nor would he have gone quietly, once it was apparent what their new mission was to be. He'd not dared to enter the basement after that. Loshin's daily reports were quite enough.

And now he had two score or more of those… things! His, by all accounts, to command, such was Fian's confidence in this new method he had established. They waited, staring at him with blank eyes. Jittering about eagerly, they flapped and yipped occasionally, hopping about like impatient gulls.

He had considered just letting them get on with it. Send them in, then follow on behind to mop up what remained.

Which wouldn't be much, by all accounts.
But she didn't want that.

He looked to his right. Queen Isiarus was mounted on a pure white gelding, it's tack threaded with gold. She was dressed for battle in a shining gold cuirass and a gold trimmed cloak of claret. A helmet of gold sat on her head, her jet black hair flowing from beneath it.

"You're certain you wish to ride with us, highness?" he asked for the umpteenth time.
She shot him a look that brooked no argument. Wes nodded.

"Very well, your Highness. If you're ready?" she nodded back at him, looking around the courtyard.

He lifted his hand and bought it down.
The Wraiths plodded forwards, some howling at the sky. Foot soldiers followed at a distance, none wanting to get too close to those things! After what seemed an age, the cavalry kicked in their heels and the horses, whinnying and snorting, moved out.

It would take the best part of two days to get to the Citadel at the usual rate of a warband, he ventured. Her highness had not been best pleased at that, but to drive the horses any quicker would render them useless when they arrived.
Or worse still, dead before they got there.

He had suggested that they let the Wraiths go off and feed tonight, then keep them hungry on the morrow for battle.
She liked that idea.

As she seemed to like a great many ideas. Like ridding the skies over this land of those damn feather brains once and for all. She still had ranted continually for days about the attack on the white spire, or the audacity they showed to take the body of the Daemon.
No doubt they had buried it in some shallow, unremarkable grave, she'd ventured?
Somehow, Wes wasn't so sure.

***

Isiarus looked about her as the warband moved out, General Wes to her side, his face stone. She was looking forward to this, relishing the idea of taking revenge.

How dare they raid her home? Her White Spire? How dare they make off like common thieves with the body of that Daemon? She'd wanted so much to watch it's last dying moments. To see the last vestiges of life fading from its eyes. Maybe this would set her on the road to her final purpose?

Since scrutinising the dermal scriptures with her scholars and discovering about her past self, she had been more determined than ever to finish what she could not complete in bygone times. She could, finally, complete her destiny. Maybe even appease the Gods enough to earn back her position?

Learning about that had bought her a great many pleasures. A great many nights of fantasy and imagination.

She kicked her heels in, her white gelding snorting and plodding forward. Her mind was filled with possibilities. With ideas and outcomes.

With the death of the Avians.

***

Brianne cast her vote, along with the rest of the Citadel, at the forum building. Her name was taken at the door, marked against the tally sheet, and she was issued with a piece of parchment no bigger than her hand. This she took into the forum itself and took an empty place at the table, each position separated with a barrier to afford some privacy. Outside, she'd been accosted by protestors and supporters in equal measure. Some bandying words in scorn of the mixing of the clans, as it was largely being referred to. Some in support of forum members or Pehl himself. Protests had been heated, and palace guards now stood around the square, ready to keep the peace.

Afterwards, she wandered across the square, the hubbub of the forum falling away behind her. The sun was disappearing behind the Palace of Sh'Bal, the sky turning a shade of purple like a giant bruise across the firmament. She'd looked in on Loran before voting. He was better. Much better. His arm was down to the wrist now.

Remarkable. That's what Malaner called it, and he was

right. It was truly remarkable that a being like Loran even existed, never mind his healing abilities. Even Aleas had admitted several times that he had little to no knowledge of exactly what Loran was capable of.

She'd torn herself away from him at his insistence. News of the vote had reached him fast. She'd even half joked that he should put his name forward among the list of candidates to vote for.

She had tried to hide her dismay when he reminded her that he did not live in the Citadel. Neither was he one of them.
He felt like one of them to her.

She reached the training corner to find Tialla waiting for her. Without a word, they stood next to each other and drew their swords from between their wings.

Brianne looked across the square to find Kall walking towards them. He said nothing, his face unreadable. The young swordsman came to stand next to them and drew his sword. It was not curved like theirs, but was a standard short sword, the hilt jade green, interwoven with silver. A small, silver hand at the pommel held a pure white crystal.
It had been a gift from Josten.

Tialla caught his eye and nodded once. Giving the first command, they all adopted the first position of Ché. She called out the manoeuvres, Brianne learning them along with Kall. Up until now, she'd only learnt the positions.

They ran through the manoeuvres slowly, letting Kall catch up with them both. It was soon apparent that, like Brianne, he was a quick learner. He adapted to the unfamiliar moves in no time.

Soon they were joined by others. Slowly at first, a couple joining after the first set, the Lord Commander looking on, his face unreadable. Then more.

Now, she stood at the head of nearly two dozen warriors, Avians all. She called out moves by name, louder now, so that her voice would carry.
Behind her, two dozen warriors moved as one.

**

Malaner looked over it again and again, fascinated by the sight of it. It shouldn't be possible, he kept mumbling. At all. Let alone in such a short space of time.

Loran turned his left hand over, examining the palm for white fingers of scar tissue.

There were none.

With a faint hiss he extended the claws, black as night, long and shiny new. They were perfect. He'd been afraid they would turn out long and yellow, like his claws of the Otherworld. He'd breathed a sigh of relief when he first tried them.

Malaner shook his head at the sight.

"Remarkable." He said again. Loran smiled and swung his legs over the side, the huge bed squealing in protest as he sat on the edge. He stood, giving his wings a gentle flutter.

"You're sure I cannot persuade you to remain with me another day? Just in case."

"In case, what?" Loran smiled. "It falls off…?" he clasped the Medic on the shoulder.

"Thank you, Malaner."

The doctor dipped his head in reply, although he remarked that he'd done very little, and Loran ducked his head and headed out the door. He looked over to the right of the square, anxious to see what all the hubbub had been about after the vote. He found Tialla at the head of two dozen or more warriors, all preforming a practice routine.

He smiled at the sight of Brianne, standing beside her. The routine ended, and Tialla turned, nodding to her new followers, and the practice broke up.

Brianne sheathed her sword and turned, stopping in her tracks when she spotted him. People were passing by, most gawping at him. Some stopping to mumble a greeting. Or simply stare, like a God had come amongst them.

He resisted the urge to fly across. His head was still a little woozy, although he dare not admit that to Malaner. In any case, that would seem a little over keen, even for him.

They met somewhere in the middle ground, people milling around them. Staring. Pointing.

They were both oblivious to it. They simply smiled at each other.

"It's fully grown?" she said after a while.

"Yes." He flexed his hand, extending and retracting his claws.

He took a deep breath.

"I've been thinking..." She started.

"Me too." He cut her off. "And if there is to be more fighting, more battles, I think it would be wise if you were to remain with your fledglings. To protect them, you understand?"

"No," she said, furrowing her eyebrows, "I'm not sure I do."

He took another deep breath. He was afraid of this.

"Please. I only want to keep you safe."

"And what makes you think I need keeping safe?" she put her arms on her hips, wingtips fluttering. Loran tried to interject, but she spoke over the top of him.

"Why would I need protecting? Am I not capable of protecting myself? What is the point of learning swordcraft, only to sit in a room full of fledglings, hiding away while my brethren are slaughtered?" her face was puce.

Loran held his hands up.

"I only meant to..."

"I know full well what you meant to do. Keep me safe, protected, hidden. Do you not think I've heard that my entire life?" she ranted. "The whole point of everything we've gained together is NOT to stay safe. To live life to the fullest. As others do." She turned and walked away. Loran followed.

"I don't mean to..."

She turned

"I need to be alone a moment, please."

Brianne opened her wings and took to the air. Loran watched her go.

***

She landed in the moon forest, in a clearing between two

broad oak trees. Their leaves were turning a pale golden in the early autumn, some crunching beneath her feet as she paced back and forth.

How could he be like the others?

Surely he understood? Surely he thought of her as more than just a tutor? She expected this lack of respect and belittling from others.

From her parents.

But never from him.

She couldn't blame her mother and father really, not for wanting to keep their only child safe. Her sister had died at birth when Brianne was but three. She had little memory of it now. Only stories, half-truths and painful recollections, hastily brushed away with a glib comment or a change of subject.

But him? He knew how desperate she was to prove her worth. How far she had come.

Didn't he?

She didn't hear him approach, his wings nearly silent. But she heard him land behind her. It was difficult not to.

She couldn't turn around.

Her eyes were wet, and she couldn't turn around.

"I'm sorry." He murmured.

"I thought you understood…" she said, desperate to hold back the tears.

"I thought *you* understood? I'd give my arm all over again just to make sure nothing happens to you."

She turned then, wiping a lone tear away.

"A fine promise, when you can grow the fucking thing back again."

"That's not the point, and you know it." He walked toward her slowly. "I'd rather do anything than see you come to harm. Even if it means upsetting you."

He took a deep breath.

"I love you."

She looked up at this giant of a being. A Daemon in name and

looks, she'd seen him tear a man asunder.
She'd seen him laugh at the water on his feet.
"I love you too, you big fool." She chuckled, falling into his embrace.
They kissed each other. Finally breaking free, she stepped away, turning to face him.
"I must fight for what I believe to be right. I must be who I am."
He nodded. He said he understood.
She looked down at the trews she'd had made for him.
"How are you getting on with those?"
"Fine, actually." He said. She met his gaze with a slight smile.
"What?"
"Take them off..." she breathed.

***

Their first time together was hurried. Desperate. Passion and lust boiling over and consuming them both in the moment.
The second time was better. Slower. She sat astride him, her wings spreading wide at the moment of release, before collapsing on his chest, breathless and sweaty. She lay there a while, listening to his impossibly slow heartbeat. The sky was dark now, the sun having set some time ago.
She hadn't noticed.
"You're cold." He whispered, rubbing the gooseflesh on her arms. "I'll light a fire." She nodded, and clambered off him to get dressed, retrieving her clothes from the branch she'd slung them over. He stood and collected some dry wood and brush, watching her shrug into her black outfit from the corner of his eyes, a little disappointment on his face as her nakedness disappeared.
They fell asleep in each other's arms, her head on his broad, grey chest. The fire light dancing across the woodland.
She awoke a while later.
Alone.
The fire had gone down, the embers barely glowing. She

squinted, letting her eyes adjust to the dark.

Loran was standing a way away from her. Listening. His claws were out.

"What is it?" she whispered, creeping to stand alongside him. She could neither see nor hear anything.

"Horses." He whispered. "I can smell Horses."

"You're sure?"

He looked down at her.

Of course he was.

"I'll go and look." He whispered. "I think you'd better..?" she raised her eyebrows.

"...never mind." He mumbled.

***

They flew over the forest canopy, the treetops hurtling past beneath them. She could see almost nothing.

Perhaps he's been mistaken? Perhaps the events of the past few days had left him a little... unsettled? Nervous?

Did Daemons even get nervous?

Loran suddenly veered off to the left and dove down into the treetops. He landed in the top of a tall Cedar, claws gripping the bark. She followed cautiously, unsure how she would negotiate landing in a tree, but desperate not to prove unworthy of him after all the fuss she'd made. Finally, she folded in her white wings and landed on a broad bough a way beneath him. She looked up, the spiky leaves tickling at her face, the tree dancing with her weight.

She could barely make him out above her, in the darkness.

She followed his eyeline, out, past the forest to the glades beyond. There, she could just make out pinpricks of firelight. Tents dotted the landscape, like tiny white anthills. All except for the one in the centre.

That one was gold and crimson.

***

Isaac, Aleas, Tialla and Pehl sat around a large table in the basement vaults of the temple. Isaac had not even bothered to ask permission this time, and simply ignored old Eral's blustering as they descended.

It was a good idea that Aleas had bought to them in the feast hall. To go and take a look at these 'Wraiths' in the Dermal Texts and see exactly what is was they were up against.

Isaac had entered the gated area at the back and retrieved the huge tome. He had sat it down with a loud thump, flicking through page after page until he found it.

"Here," he said excitedly, "You see? The method for creating Wraiths. Half wolf, half bat, like a meldling, but with human addition."

"It's sickening." Said Tialla, wrinkling her nose.

"It's all here in the texts of The Century Wars." He said, flicking through the pages.

Pehl bent forward.

"What are those?"

Isaac studied the page intently.

"The ancient Gods. They're all here, Look." He said, flicking through pages and reciting ancient Dermal.

"Vororr The Supreme, Rotaldir, Blaise." He flicked another page. "Myla. Betris. Torna. Even old L'Shaan herself."

Pehl snatched the book and swivelled it around to face him.

"Show me that…" he said, staring at the page in disbelief.

"What?" Isaac looked at his uncle's uneasy face.

Pehl turned the book back around.

"See for yourself."

Tialla leaned over Isaac's shoulder and stared at the page. An ancient, cursive script flowed across the parchment. At its centre was a depiction of the Goddess herself.

Tall, beautiful, and lithe.

With long, flowing, dark hair, a sharp nose.

And a withered left arm.

THIRTY TWO

The Century Wars
Year Ninety Seven.
The Holy City of Lianna
Durmak.

Goral stood in front of L'Shaan's lavish throne, his hands held out in appeal. Behind her, the large, white-blue orb, known to all as the Seraph, floated above its pedestal. An almost imperceptible hum of energy came from it constantly, crackles of light flowing over its surface, showing the lines of grief and worry etched on Goral's face.

"Please, My Lady, I beg of you. I am losing more and more warriors every day."

"I am losing warriors, you are simply leading them." She said flatly.

Goral stiffened, his rage bubbling over.

"You are not the one who has to explain to a hundred widows that their husbands and sons died in vain! In the pursuit of a foolish and impossible…"

"Watch your tone, mortal." She bellowed, standing abruptly "You are addressing a Goddess. You are lucky not to be losing your head as well as your temperament."

Goral took a deep breath.

"I meant no Insult, My Lady," He sighed, "simply that I feel we are gaining no ground. I cannot see a way forward with this plan." That was the reason he had dismissed it all those years previously. He kept that thought to himself.

She sat, regaining her composure, and Goral breathed a sigh of relief. This long, hard fought war with the Dark Gods, as they were now know, seemed endless. And yet Vororr was insistent that L'Shaan use her Avian army for this specific task. The loss seemed immaterial to him. It was almost as if..?

No. he put it from his mind completely. They were her personal creation, made using the energy from the Seraph, and she had overseen their birth every step of the way. Vororr knew only too well how important they were to the Goddess of flight.
Surely Vororr would not use them, simply to dispose of them? Would he?

***

Hayden stood at the opening of the tent.
"Please, Sir. You need sleep. Just take it for one night. We can cope, I swear to you."
The young, blond haired warrior had been his Shield Man for only two moons or so but was already fitting into the role quite nicely. Easton would have been proud of him.
He could still see Easton's ashen face looking up at him, great gaping bite marks in his torso.
"Don't move," Goral had insisted, "You're losing blood."
A lot of blood.
He'd taken his friends hand then. Cold and clammy and listless.
"Just hold on…"
Easton's hand had slipped from his, as the life had slipped from his body.
Damn this stupid war. Damn the Gods and their fool creatures. Damn all of it.
"Sir?"
He looked up into Hayden's face, the youngster's once-white wings now covered in sand. He held out the sleeping draught that their healer, Quinn, had drawn up for him.
Goral took it, examining the vial closely.
Something struck him then. An idea Easton would have been proud of, he was sure.
"Go and ask Quinn if he can make more of this stuff. Lots more." *He said excitedly.*
Hayden furrowed his brow.

"Sir?"

"Quickly, now." Hayden shrugged and slipped out, and Goral called for his captains. Both flights would be needed for this.

They assembled two hours or so later, just as the sun slipped below the dunes to the west, turning the River of Light a pale orange. He gave his orders to Hawksley and Scarrow, his flight captains. They nodded. All seemed in order.

He patted the tan leather satchel bag over his left shoulder that contained vials and vials of Quinn's sleeping draught. The healer had, by all accounts, been sure that Goral had lost his mind. Nevertheless, he had spent the next two hours mixing and preparing the potion as requested.

They would only get one shot at this.

Half of flight one attacked Blaise's castle, as they had hundreds of times before, drawing the creatures out into the air as the rest slept in the dungeons below. Only this time, rather than creeping in and trying to kill as many as possible before they awoke, the remainder of flight one and all of flight two crept into the dungeons and searched for the piles of meat, rotting and pallid, that these vile creature ate.

They spent the night taking each fly-infested slab of flesh and dousing it with a vial of sleeping draught instead.

Just as the sun began to peer above the eastern horizon, they flew back to their camp. The first half of flight one would never join them.

Now they waited.

That morning, two young lads from Blaise's castle used a couple of pitchforks to pick up each maggot-speckled slab of meat and hurl it into the mouth of a wraith. They fought amongst themselves, snarling and tearing each slab between them. Afterwards, the lads opened the two large gates leading from the dungeon out onto the dunes. The Wraiths howled and roared, taking to the air.

As dawn broke proper, the whole of L'Shaan's Avian army assembled in the sky, leaning back into their wings, and flapping lazily to hover in place.

At their head was Goral.

"You should be leading us from the dunes, Sir." Hayden yelled across at his leader.

Goral shook his head slowly.

"No. This was my fool plan, and mine alone. I will lead us into whatever comes…" He trailed off.

Goral craned his neck forward, shielding his eyes against the morning sun with his hand.

In the distance, the ever familiar sight of a flock of wraiths headed towards them made his heart sink.

"Oh well…" he mumbled. It was worth a try, at least. Right now, he would try just about anything.

Hayden started yelling orders.

"Wait!" Goral held up a hand.

The lead wraith was flapping ever slower, until finally, it sunk to the sand, landing with a heavy thump and folding it's wings in to lean on the wingtips. It's head swayed from side to side, until finally, with a snarl, it sunk to the ground.

Behind it, wraiths were landing everywhere.

"Attack them in two's. No time to lose, men."

The avian army fell on the Wraiths like a rainstorm.

***

L'Shaan stood before her supreme, the snivelling Torna standing to his left. Since his arrival yesterday, he had been at Vororr's ear almost constantly. Preening and simpering and currying favour. Claiming to have been working for the supreme all the time. She wanted to scream.

"Torna tells me that your Avians are making progress, at last." He said, his voice low.

"Yes, My lord." She'd had word of Gorals plan and thought it brave. She almost wished she'd dreamt it up herself.

"After this has ended, I mean to make right this land, and it's people."

What did that mean? She had a bad feeling about this.

"Lord?"

"I will make repatriation and punishment as I see fit. Those *that have transgressed will be dealt with most severely."*

"I see."

Vororr sat forward. Torna was trying hard to disguise a grin.

"I want your Avians brought here. As soon as this is at an end."

"To what avail, My Lord?" They were her army to command. What use did the supreme have of them?

"They will be…" he waved a hand. "…disposed of."

"What?" she almost screamed.

Torna grinned at last.

"They do not belong in this world, or this land. I must make right this transgression. The army of Wraiths was only created to depose your army of Avians."

"I will not!"

Vororr stood slowly.

"You would defy the Supreme?" he said at last.

"They are my army, my creation."

She would not, could not, give them up to be slaughtered.

"Think carefully on this, L'Shaan. Carefully, mind." Torna snivelled at last.

"Oh, shut up, turncoat. Were I supreme, I would take your head."

"But you're not!" Vororr sat again. "You will deliver them to me. At once."

She took a breath.

Perhaps this was the best course of action. If this would bring peace to these lands…

"Very well, My Lord"

Betris, listening outside the door, shook his head. He turned and headed to the tower to find the raven keeper.

Writing a quick note, he gave it to the keeper, and a raven was dispatched to Myla's castle on the dunes.

***

Ten minutes later, Goral opened the note and stared at it in disbelief.

They had dispatched every Wraith that lived. Heads taken, the

beasts sat rotting in the sun.
And yet he was betrayed.
By that dark haired bitch.
He gritted his teeth and crumpled the note.
"Sir?"
Goral turned to Hayden.
"We are betrayed." He said at last. "We must leave. Now. At once."
"Yes sir." Hayden turned to leave.
"Hayden?"
The youngster turned and waited.
Goral had decided. He wanted nothing that reminded him of her or her betrayal ever again.
Also, it would prove useful to have somebody else to blame.
"We are betrayed by our dark haired brethren." He said flatly. "Slaughter them."
Hayden paused a beat.
"Yes sir." He turned and left.
Goral began gathering what he could, looking around at the things he was leaving behind. His eyes fell on a book of dermal texts, only a few years old.
He grabbed them and headed out.
Outside, screams and blood littered the land, dark haired bodies strewn about the dunes. Goral felt nothing as he looked around. His eyes settled on his wife, carrying their blond new-born.
His oldest son, Pehl stood at his mother's side, dark hair billowing in the desert breeze.
Goral strode over.
"Put a cap on him, or something, Nadya. Cover his hair. We'll deal with this when we get there." He would steel himself to be reminded by his son. He could deal with anything else another time.
"Where? She said, rooting around her bags for a hat.
"Far away from this land. Across the Oran sea, to Murrecia."
Nadya turned and walked towards the shore. "This would be a long flight," She said gravely, "and the children will need to be carried."
"The children will be fine." He turned away, Nadya calling

after him.

"I'll join you." He said. "There's something I must do first."

"Goral?" she looked up at him.

"I'll join you, I promise." He took her hands and kissed her. He watched them leave, then returned to Hayden and the dozen men he had gathered.

All blonde.

"With me." He said, and took off, heading for Lianna Palace.

***

"Why?" Goral growled. She stood in front of the Seraph, humming away on its pedestal. He stared at her, eyes full of hate, his men standing along the back wall.

"I had little choice, Goral. Besides, A Goddess need not justify herself to a mortal." She stuck her nose up slightly.

Goral found her infuriating.

"You do when you order the mass murder of my entire army." He snarled through gritted teeth.

"MY army!" she corrected him.

Goral turned away, trying to gain control of his temper.

"Do not turn your back on me." She yelled. "I will dismiss you when I see fit."

"Dismiss this." He snarled, turning and shoving her squarely in the chest.

L'Shaan stumbled back, putting out a hand to steady herself, and placed it on the Seraph.

The Goddess of flight screamed as crackles of white energy travelled up her arm, the skin wrinkling, the muscles shrivelling. She pulled her hand off, watching in horror as her left arm withered like as dying rose. The pain was all-encompassing.

The world went dark, and she collapsed.

Goral looked down at her. Without a word, he opened his wings and walked to the window, when a thought struck him. Turning, he looked at the Avians watching him.

He would not leave the Seraph behind to be used for further creation. He alone would guard it now.

"Get two long poles and bring that with us. Don't touch it."

He said, pointing at the Seraph. They struggled, carrying the great orb to the window, and managed to heave it out between them. "We never discuss what went on here this day, men. Never."
They all nodded silently.
He would need to allow his Avians to follow their Goddess. Many would not be dissuaded from that. Plus, a little distraction from the mundane was never a bad thing.
He decided he would rewrite the dermal scriptures himself. The truth would be his to show people.
Or not.

***

Vororr looked down on them from his throne. Before him stood Blaise and Rotaldir. The unconscious form of L'Shaan lay next to them.

"Blaise." he said at last. She stiffened slightly. "You have shown much short sightedness in your pursuit of power and the hunt for glory. For that, you will see no more."
Blaise screamed as her eyesight disappeared and two black holes took the place of her eyes.

"Rotaldir."
The God of the Otherworld stared back at him defiantly.

"You have tried to end my life. My reign. To send me to the Otherworld. For that, you will be banished to the Otherworld for ever, to fight off those that cannot cross the bridge."

"As you wish." He hissed.
Rotaldir disappeared.

"As for you, L'Shaan? You have defied me in the loss of the Avians to a foreign land. You will be made mortal, to live as one without power." He said to her unconscious form.

"What of her wound, my Lord?" Betris said, standing next to the throne, thankful that Vororr had not mentioned the message he'd sent to Goral. Either he deemed it of little impotence, or did not yet know of it at all!

"She will keep it."
L'Shaan disappeared also.

***

A few hours later, high in the twisted White Spire at Var'n Arden, a new-born baby was delivered by the Queen. The King looked down at his daughter as his wife held her, trying to hide his disappointment.

"*We will call her Isiarus,*" *She said.*
The king nodded but said nothing. Simply stared at her left arm.

THIRTY THREE

The newly formed council sat in the forum chamber, around the familiar oval table. Hushed whispers crept around the room as Pehl stood, the whispers subsiding.

"Ladies and Gentlemen." He began, a nod to Tialla and Brianne, the first female Avians allowed to sit at the council table. "This session should be bought to order. It seems we have a most pressing problem facing us. As Loran and Brianne have said, the Queen's Army is on the other side of the forest, under a day's march. If they have set out this morning, as we broke fast, they will most likely reach our walls at sundown."

Another whisper crept round the room, more urgent. Loran stood at the back wall, Almost in shadow, next to a marble bust of some previous elder. He and Brianne had rushed back in the early hours to raise the alarm. The council was alerted at first light, and Loran seemed to watch the proceedings with a bemused fascination.

"Lord Commander," Pehl said, addressing Remus, "What preparations need to be made?"

Finally. Something that made sense.

"Well, with the number of foot soldiers and cavalry she has, I need a master of swords to lead the ground force. I'll lead the lance men myself."

"Do you have somebody in mind?" Pehl looked around the room, catching Kall's expectant face.

"I do," Remus said casually. "Tialla."

The murmurs started in earnest. Kall looked crestfallen at having been overlooked.

"A lady?" one of the elders seated opposite him spluttered. "Really?"

Remus rounded on him.

"Have you seen her fight? Or train, for that matter? I have. She's the master of swords for me, no question."

Pehl smiled and nodded his approval. "And what of our sky-archers?"

With Josten gone, the fate of the twenty third airborne archers seemed doomed. It had been his idea, his project.

Ended all too soon, it seemed.

"For that we need somebody of quick mind, cunning, and daring. Are you up for the task, young man?"

Kall looked up to realise that the Lord Commander was talking to him.

"Me?" he gasped. "You're not serious? I can't shoot an arrow anywhere near as well as some of those archers."

"You don't need to be the best to be a leader, my boy." Said Aleas. "You just need to inspire those around you. You're more than equal to the task. What say our new Premier?"

All eyes turned to Isaac, seated at the head of the table, his fingers steepled. He was deep in thought, as he had been almost constantly since his appointment yesterday. As much as surprise to him as it was to anyone else. Especially as he didn't remember entering his name to the candidate list. He had his own personal suspicions as to the culprit, but it was immaterial now.

They had much more important things to deal with.

Pehl's Avian clan had just about finished growing their new primary feathers. Most of the feathers had come through a dappled grey colour. Some, with red hair like Tialla, growing brown instead. They were ready for flight. Given time and patience they would soon be adept in the air.

Commodities they had little of, it seemed.

"Those appointments all sound fine, as long as the Lord Commander is happy?"

Remus nodded.

"Very well. I think our new brothers and sisters had better get some airtime in while they can. As for the rest of us?" Isaac looked around the room. "Swords sharpened, feathers preened, and armour donned, I think. Let us prepare for war."

"Where do you want us?" Aleas asked.

Isaac shuffled some papers and stood, lost again in thought. Aleas repeated the question.

"Hmm? Oh, Aleas we can't expect you to stand with us. This is not your fight."

"Are you touched in the head? That crazy witch needs to be stopped. That's everyone's fight. Where else would we be?"

Isaac rounded the table, clasped him on the shoulder and nodded.

"Very well. Join the swords, please. As for you…?" He looked up at Loran.

"I'll just kill anything that gets in the way of me and that woman." The Daemon growled.

"Now that sounds like a plan." Chuckled Pehl.

***

A Short while later, they stood around a hastily drawn up map of the glades surrounding the moon forest. The main throne room at the palace had been made into a makeshift barracks for the Var'n Rodan refugees. Bedding had been piled in intervals along the walls, bags of belongings and piles of clothing scattering the floor.

Not that Isaac felt particularly comfortable in there anyway.

Instead, they now occupied a corner of the feast hall, the map spread out on a large, dark table.

Isaac studied it intently, suddenly wishing somebody else had won the vote.

"It seems to me, that an army of her size would struggle to navigate the forest path effectively." Aleas mumbled, thinking aloud.

"Indeed," Pehl nodded, "I've struggled to squeeze a small attack force through there myself. It isn't an easy task."

Not that long ago, to be fair.

"Surely, her best bet is to skirt around it?" Aleas studied the map himself. Navigating around a forest was hardly a difficult task.

Crossing the river, however, might be.

"Our best play is to destroy the bridge at Crennels Forde." Aleas said, tapping the map. "That will, at least, slow down the ground force enough to let us contend with the Wraiths."

"Destroy it how?" Pehl looked up at the old man.

"I have a spell that may work." Aleas looked up briefly.

"Very well." Said Isaac. "We'll leave that in your hands. I think the lancers should be here..." he tapped the map once. "And the airborne archers waiting in the square until signalled by us."

Heads around the table nodded in agreement. Kall gave some ideas to Isaac about waiting for the right moment to launch the airborne, the new premier listening to the advice of others before reaching a decision.

Brianne turned her head, searching the feast hall for Loran. The point at the back wall where he'd been standing was now empty.

***

Brianne excused herself and ventured outside to find him standing alone, being watched by an awestruck fledgling. The bright eyed boy, his wings barely covered in fluffy down, was looking up at the towering Daemon. Loran looked back uneasily, shifting his weight and trying to look unbothered.

She wandered over and shooed the boy away. He trudged off unhappily, looking back over his shoulder.

"Don't pay them too much attention," she chuckled, "They're still curious. You can't really blame them."

"I don't get on with children very well." He mumbled darkly.

"They're harmless enough." She said, looking deep into his startling blue eyes.

"Brianne." A voice from the steps caught her unawares, and she turned to see Hayden walking toward her.

"Loran, this is Hayden, forum member and maker of beddings," she said. "My Father..."

"A pleasure to finally meet…" Loran started.

"Are you returning to teaching the fledglings, now that all our hard earned work to conceal things is for nothing?" he snapped, interrupting him.

"No." she said defiantly. "I have other things to attend to."

"This new venture of yours." he sneered. "And you've taken up with this…creature."

Brianne started protesting, Hayden holding up a hand to silence her.

"I'm not sure what hold you have over my daughter, but it should surely end." He hissed to the Daemon.

Loran simply glared at him. He turned to Brianne.

"I am not a monster, Brianne, far from it. I would simply want the best for my child, my own fledgling."

As he walked away, Pehl came down the steps and fall into step with him.

"Fledglings aren't the problem…" Brianne said.

"It isn't the fledglings I don't trust." He turned to walk away. Brianne reached out and took his arm.

"This is about that incident in the forest, isn't it? When you left for the Desolation?"

He nodded slowly.

"What happened? What really happened?"

"It's not important."

He couldn't tell her. She'd hate him, even view him as others had.

"Clearly it is." She reached down and took his hands in hers. They were huge, like great grey shovels, her hands lost amongst his grey fingers.

"I panicked… I.." he shook his head. "I didn't mean to hurt the child. I panicked."

"It's ok." She said quietly. "You've been isolated from people your whole life. We all have to learn how to deal with things."

"You don't understand." He closed his eyes.

Brianne waited patiently.

"I killed him."

***

"I know you." Pehl said, "But I know not where from."

Hayden smiled thinly.

"The last time I saw you, you were but a young fledgling yourself. Newly clipped and crying. Being hurried onto a boat, bound for Solaan." The old forum member replied.

Pehl's searched his memories. He remembered the boat, the dock at Point Mar, his mother crying, his father...

He looked up. The picture in his mind was not of old King Goral, but the man standing before him.

"You?"

"Aye," Hayden nodded. "Me. You father wanted you slain. I was his shield man, persuaded him to cast you out to Solaan instead."

"I'm not sure I should be grateful or resentful." Pehl quipped.

"Neither am I." Hayden mumbled.

***

It was a risk. That much he had told her repeatedly. A risk to the horses, more than anything else. It was true, skirting the forest in the darkness was much less risky than riding through it. No roots or fallen branches for the animals to trip over.

But it was still a risk. And one General Wes would prefer not to have taken. The animals could still trip or fall on wet grass and soft ground. A dozen lame horses would be of use to nobody. It seemed Her Highness cared little for horses. Or anybody else, for that matter.

The moon was high, the late autumn night nearly cloudless.

That was something in their favour, at least.

The Wraiths had flown into the forest as the sun set. It seemed they liked the darkness less than he did.

Strange, soulless creatures. All teeth and dead eyes. He shivered at the thought of them. But they would prove deadly, he hoped, when the battle began. It was difficult to see how the Avians could deal with these creatures of death. Especially since their Daemon had almost certainly perished.

He highness had been unapproachable that day. Screeching in rage, thundering at the guards. She'd killed one with her new claws just for stammering an answer back to her. He was a good lad, too.

Shame.

But what was done was done. She would have to contend herself with Fian's assurance that the Daemon had most likely died as a result of his wound.

Wes thought it strange, nonetheless. He'd seen more than one soldier lose an arm in battle.

He was almost sure they bled more than that.

No matter. He shook the thought from his head and checked his surroundings. The forest loomed large and dark and impenetrable on his right. He couldn't help but find it unnerving, despite his years as a soldier.

Ahead of him, he could just make out the River Uret, flowing sluggishly toward the forest. A broad bridge of large, old, wooden slats ran over the river where it was at its narrowest and shallowest.

Crennels Forde.

***

Remus walked along the line of Lance men, their helms and cuirasses gleaming in the morning sun. He nodded to some, adjusted cuirass straps on others. Behind them stood a wall of swords. Men and women, blond and dark.

Avians all.

At their head stood Tialla.

She was dressed head to toe in black, her blue sable-edged cloak over the top. Her wings of brown protruding from the back.

Beside her stood Brianne. The once-timid tutor of fledglings stood tall and proud, clad similarly in black, her white wings preened and fresh-looking behind her. A curved sword jutting up between them, her dark hair pulled back from her face in a short ponytail.

She searched around for Loran. She'd spoken to him little after last night. She'd tried to understand. Things undoubtedly had not been easy for him, that much she got.
But killing a child?

Then she remembered that, if Aleas was correct, Loran was little more than a child himself at the time. His growth rate was near impossible to convert to theirs as a comparison. She shook her head. Now was not the time to deal with this. They would have time to discuss it later if things went to plan.

But where was he?
She's said last night that she needed to think, to be alone a while. Loran had simply nodded and took off, carving a path through the dark haired Avians hastily learning to fly.

Isaac had taken to his role as Premier and flight instructor better than she'd hoped. She had little regret in putting his name forward while nobody was watching. He was more than equal to the task. And people had picked him overwhelmingly. That was even more than she had hoped for.

At the front of the lancers, Remus raised his hand, and brought it down. They marched out of the front arch, the archers on the wall watching them. Their brethren in the square waiting for instructions to launch from their new leader, Kall.

His appointment had not gone well with everyone. Some pointed out Kall's lack of prowess with a bow, some his age, some his leadership skills. Kall had fronted them all down. Now they stood, patiently waiting for the order to launch from him. The time was not yet upon them, and some were getting twitchy.

At the head of the lancers, Remus walked alongside Pehl and Aleas, the morning fresh as they walked onwards The old soldier and mage had insisted he would join the fight, and Remus, for one, said he was glad to have him. Experience in a battle was something no gold could pay for, he said. And Aleas had in it spades. Plus, if all went well, he would dispatch the bridge long before Queen Isiarus and her army could cross it. By her reckoning, they would be less than half a day yet. Time was against them, but she felt sure that…

The Avians came to a halt as they crested the rise of a gentle slope, the Moon forest looming on the horizon, the river splashing lazily past on their right. A dark, uninterested observer.

Between them and the moon forest, stood the army of the Witch Queen.

How could they have gotten here so fast?

"They must have travelled in the dark." Mumbled Pehl.

"Risky."

Aleas grunted in agreement, reaching for his sword.

"Nothing for it now." Said the old mage. "Only two ways this is going to end."

THIRTY FOUR

At the head of the cavalry, General Wes let a wide grin spread across his face.
Perfect.
They had managed to cross the bridge at Crennels Forde long before the bird brained fuckers had gotten here. Now, everything was in their favour. Soon, the wraiths would join them.
But for now, he was content to let the cavalry loose on their lancers.
He looked across at the Queen, sat atop her pure white gelding, her dark hair billowing from beneath her gold helm. She glanced over and nodded once.
"You should take position on the high ground, near the forest, your highness." He yelled.
Isiarus shot him a dark look.
"A Queen should be seen to lead," he insisted, holding up a hand. "Not lead the charge herself. That's what generals are for."
Isiarus took a deep breath, then nodded and kicked her heels in, cantering across the line to the forest's edge. General Wes waited until she'd taken her position, then nodded to a slight-built cavalry man to his left.
The Cavalry rider raised a long horn on a golden chain to his lips and blew out a low, mournful note.
As one, the cavalry kicked in their heels. Horses broke into a canter, then a gallop.
Wes grinned at the head of his riders. The feeling of the horse beneath him, panting and sweating. The wind in his face, his men around him.
There was no feeling like it. He felt alive for the first time in

an age as he reached for his sword, hissing the steel from its scabbard.

The Queens Cavalry thundered toward the line of Avians, horses snorting and riders whooping. Behind them, on the grasslands, the swordsmen waited for instruction.

**

Brianne took a deep breath, her heart threatening to pound its way through her chest. She could feel the thrum of horses through the ground beneath her, could hear the whooping of cavalry war cries.
She tried in vain to control the tiny quivers as her body prepared for fight.

At the head of them, she heard Lord Commander Remus give the order for the Lancers. Over a hundred Avians in Cuirass and helm ran forward, took a crouching position, and aimed their lances at an angle.

The cavalry hit them like a hammer. Horses screamed as they fell.
Avians screamed as they fell.

The first two rows of horsemen collapsed onto the lancers, crushing them beneath horse and rider. Lancers bowed like reeds on the tide. More followed, riders cutting a swathe through the lancers as the Avian line began to buckle.
The cavalry cut a great, gaping wound through the Avian line, splitting into two divisions and circling round behind them.

Brianne looked over her shoulder as a swordsman picked up a bow and nocked an arrow. His colleague lit the end of it, then he fired it into the air.
She watched it arc skyward.
At that precise moment, a series of long, mournful howls rang out from the forest.

**

Kall watched the arrow tilt in the air, then looked around at the two companies of archers. He nodded.

"Time." He said loudly.

Two companies of Avians took to the air. Kall had been

given the twenty third and twenty forth company, assigning them their own commanders. They launched, commanders at their heads and bows nocked, ready.

Kall flew between the companies, leading from the front. Josten would have approved of that.

They cleared the walls, heading high. Lines of Avian swordsmen now below them, the enemy cavalry just ahead.
They were not where Kall expected them to be.

They swooped down lower, arrows nocked, aimed just ahead of the riders to allow for drop and wind, then loosed and peeled away to regroup.
A barrage of arrows fell toward the cavalry.

Kall looked over his shoulder in time to see a dozen horsemen slip from the saddle. He allowed himself a small smile as his two divisions circled and regrouped.
His two divisions.

He could scarce believe he was here, flying at the head of Josten's brainwave. He would do his friend proud, he had vowed to himself countless times last night, before sleep finally claimed him.

From the corner of his eye, Kall spotted a dark cloud emerging from the Moon Forest. This cloud twisted, split, formed into coherent shapes. Large bodies, elongated ears atop an overlarge head with sharp teeth in its massive jaws. Dark wings flapping slowly.
Wraiths.

Kall peeled off to the left, climbing above his cohort of archers.

"To me!" he screamed above the wind.
The airborne peeled left, nocking and loosing at the wraiths furiously. A volley of arrows arced towards the wraiths, piercing holes in their diaphanous wings or sailing past, taken by the wind. A few managed to hit home, thrumming into flanks and chests.

None seemed to have much effect. The wraiths howled and screeched in anger, teeth dripping with saliva as they bore down on the airborne.

Kall cursed.

"Swords." He yelled, clipping his bow to his weapons belt. He slid his sword from the scabbard, strangely at ease to have its familiar feel in his hand.

The wraiths hit them head on, Avians screaming as teeth found their mark. Kall flapped furiously, gaining a little height before dropping down on a wraith and slicing his sword through the beasts neck. The head toppled down, the body sailing on a few paces before dropping.

He looked about him quickly, A wraith was shaking its head from side to side few paces from him, its huge jaws clamped around a female's midriff. Her helm toppled away to reveal a long, blond braid.

Kall breathed a sigh of relief. He'd seen little of Sande these last few days, with everything that had happened. He knew without looking that she'd be here, with the swords. He'd last seen her on the practice corner, twirling and spinning in the dance of Ché. Looking beautiful.

Stay safe, my love.

He looked up in time to see a wraith, not an arm's length from his wingtip. He folded in quickly. Dropped down a way, then spread again, soaring forward.

The wraith peeled off and followed.

A wraith's head sailed past him, followed by an Avians wing, bloodstained and tattered. He flapped hard now, gaining some air between them. The wraith growled, flapping harder still. Jaws snapping at the air, a hairs breath from his feet.

Kall landed on the soft, blood-slickened grasslands. He folded in, rolling, and stood.

The wraith landed in front of him. It snarled, plodding forward on its folded wingtips. Kall set his feet, raised his arm into the first position without realising it.

From the corner of his eye, Kall saw a fast, dark smudge careen across the sky toward him. He watched as the smudge of dark sped downwards. It landed in the centre of the Wraiths neck with a bone-splintering crunch.

The beast flattened, wings flapping, head lolling.

Loran stood up slowly on the back of the wraith, reached forward with both hands, and grabbed a hold of the beasts upper jaw. He wrenched and, with a loud squelching rip, tore off the entire upper portion of its head. Brain and blood sheeting, it collapsed under him.

Kall nodded his thanks.
Loran said nothing. He nodded back, his face dark, and tossed the remnants aside, then spread and took off again.

***

Brianne set her feet, strangely calm in spite of the chaos surrounding her. She felt comforted to have Tialla, her friend and Sword-mistress, ahead of her. Sande to her left. She'd grown fond of the dark haired beauty.
Kall's lover.

They had talked a little on the short journey here that morning, and Brianne found her surprisingly easy to get along with. She would look forward to talking to her more.
If they got through this day alive!

The smell of blood and horses assaulted her senses. She watched, aghast, as the enemy's cavalry circled around behind the Lance line. Lancers, panicking now, were hastily changing position. Lances clashed together as they turned, clattering against their neighbour in haste. The cavalry thundered down toward the Avians.

Brianne looked skyward. The Airborne archers were occupied with the multitude of wraiths that were intent on tearing her brethren to pieces. She watched briefly as huge maws clinched into Avians both blonde and dark. Blood rained down on the grasslands as screams filled the air.

She spotted a dark shape zip across the sky.
A crow?
No. Too fast.

She felt a change in the air around her. A shift in mood. knuckles whitening on hilts. Feet shifting.

A shout rang out from the line.
Remus.

The Lord Commander was knee deep in broken lances and the dead, the grass slick and red. Once-white feathers littered the ground, blood-soaked and threadbare. He drew his sword and gestured to the line.
The swords ran, war cries screaming, toward the mayhem.

Brianne ran with them, the wind in her wings and dark brunette hair. Her heart pounded now, through excitement more than fear. Tialla, two paces in front of her, sidestepped a cavalryman baring down on her and sliced calmly through his thigh. As he slid to the floor Brianne felt a calmness overtake her. A stillness she had not believed possible in the midst of battle. Her breathing slowed. Her mind cleared.

A cavalryman, horse snorting, bared down on her as she ran toward the lancers. She took up position without thinking. He carved his curved sabre toward her head, slicing through the air as she spread her wings, leaping up, bringing her sword cleanly through his neck. She flipped in the air, headfirst, and landed without looking back, hearing the horse slow, and a head tumble to the mud.

The queen's swords were running now as more of her own swordmen, and women, were using their wings to gain advantage over the cavalry. She folded in and ran toward the nearest foot soldier, a tall, musclebound youth with a lopsided grin. He set his feet, twirled his sword and smirked. That was his first mistake.
He assumed that a woman would be an easy kill.
That was his last.

He bought his sword up, a dark broadsword, and swiped lazily at her blade to knock it away. Brianne was in first position almost before his blade had moved. Lopsided swiped at the air, Brianne blocking as he turned his blade and sliced back, angrier now. She twirled, head low, blade low, slicing through thigh.

Lopsided yelped and stepped back, blood flowing down his leg, confusion on his face. He took up a double hand hold, stabbing in at the chest. Brianne stepped into second position, turning his blade and his shoulders away. She brought the blade back again quickly, spiralling toward him, and sliced through his arm.

Lopsided's eyes widened as the grip disappeared from his hand, and his sword slid to the ground.

Brianne thrust her sword through his chest, ripping it away in a spray of red as lopsided collapsed like a felled tree.

Above her, the wraiths were entangled with two companies of airborne archers. The airborne had all but given up trying to cut the cavalry down and were occupied with a score of more of wings and teeth and menace. Screams rang out in the air as huge maws bit into soft flesh, and blood rained down as wraith after wraith lost its head.

Bodies fell to the ground in even numbers.

THIRTY FIVE

Loran cursed himself for waiting as long as he had. He'd been lost in thought, the cool river running over his splayed feet, when the roars rang out from the woodland. He had taken off at once, flapping hard to catch up. Now battle was upon them all too soon.

He turned sharply, folding in, and landed on the back of another wraith. The beast roared, wings flapping, body twisting in the air as it tried to free itself. Loran's claws dug into the soft brown fur. He wrapped his arms around the neck and squeezed, pulling backwards. Pushed out with both feet, claws in the beasts back. The wraith almost flipped mid-air as Loran tore off its head.

He released the carcass and head, not caring where they landed, and spread his wings again.

Something hit him, hard, from behind. He tumbled forward, wings folding, losing height. Looking back, he saw another wraith flapping furiously, teeth bared. Loran regained his composure and dropped toward the ground to gain speed. Folding at the last minute, he landed heavily, turning as the wraith landed behind him on the slick grasslands. It roared in fury, plodding forward.

Kall landed to the side of its head, his sword separating it from the body.

Loran smiled and nodded again as the head rolled away, the body crumpling. Kall dipped his head in reply.

"Good to see you, Loran." Kall said, as he took off. Loran spread his black, sheer wings, and followed.

"I see the archery didn't last long?" Loran quipped as he took position next to Kall. The young swordsman looked down at his empty weapons belt, realising that the short recurve bow he had clipped to it had been lost in the mayhem. He simply shrugged.

"You're a little late to the feast." Kall said without looking over.

Loran nodded.

"Apologies. I got…distracted." He said, looking down at the myriad of swordsmen and women clashing steel on the grass.

"She was ok when last I saw her," Kall shouted over, following the Daemons eyeline. "At the front of the line."

Where else.

He looked across and nodded his thanks to the youngster.

"Attack them from behind and above," The Daemon yelled as he turned, "they've a natural blind spot just behind their head." He peeled away to the right.

"Thanks." Kall shouted after him.

***

Aleas pushed onward, cutting down swordsmen as he came upon them. In truth, he paid them little mind. His attention was fixed on one goal, and one alone.

The bridge.

If he could cut off their retreat, they may just pay the price or risk escape through the forest. Either option was not the ideal.

Aleas blocked a sword as he stepped in, spinning and cutting the youth down without looking back. He stabbed into another's side as the swordsman was busy engaging an Avian. The winged sword nodded his thanks, and Aleas pushed on.

Two tall, muscly swordsmen blocked his path, and Aleas set his jaw and set his feet, his sword up. They attacked together, the older mage being pushed back. He blocked one, parried with the other and swiped at the head of the first.

His feet slipped on the wet, slick grass, and Aleas tried to regain his stance quickly. The second sword thrust at his chest, Aleas turning the blade away. The first saw his opening, swiping at the mage's abdomen.

Tialla's sword blocked it as she stepped in.
Aleas thrust his sword firmly through the soldier's chest, wrenching it free as he stood tall. The second swordsman was already slicing his blade toward Tialla's head, cutting through the air as she ducked, blocking the blade on its return.
Aleas attacked from the side, cutting the man deep on the bicep as he turned away.

Tialla opened her wings, flapped hard and sprang up, her boots at head height. She kicked him squarely in the jaw, the soldier staggering back. He regained his footing, blood flowing down his face.

Aleas stepped in and stabbed him in the throat, sending a river of red flowing down his chest. He fell to his knees, then face down in the grass.

"Quickly," Aleas yelled, "let's get to the bridge."

They ran on, Tialla cutting down another soldier who spotted her too late, the stocky swordsman crumbling as he tried to hold in his intestines. Beyond him, the bridge at Crennels Forde loomed in the mist.

"Do what you must." Tialla said, clasping him on the shoulder. "I'll keep your back."
Aleas nodded and strode away to the bridge. The river Uret ran sluggishly underneath it, a thin mist across its surface.
Aleas held out his hands.

"I'm afraid I can't let you do that." Said a thin, reedy voice. Fain's bony frame walked across the bridge to the riverbank.

"You." Aleas growled.

Fian stood on the bank, the river behind him, and held his hands up, fingers twisting into shapes, white light flowing across the palms.

"I'd have thought our last encounter would convince you? You're no match for my powers, old fool."
Fian whispered a spell and cast his hands out, fingers of white energy knocking Aleas back.

"You were old when I was but a young soldier." Aleas said, twisting his own hands in front of him. Blue sparks shot across the air, Fian being knocked similarly backwards.

"Pitiful." The bony mage sneered. He clapped his hands hard, a blast of air knocking Aleas off balance.

They circled each other warily.

"Whatever did she see in you?" Fian scoffed.

Aleas furrowed his brow.

"Elise? What is she to you, that you…" He trailed off, memories dancing in this mind.

"A timid, talentless girl," Fian sneered, "promised to an equally timid and talentless apprentice. I recognised your face at once, although the years have not been kind to you. I would never have allowed her to bind herself to a dolt like you. Not even a full mage?" He smirked. "Embarrassing."

"You were the uncle she was awaiting at Point Mar?" Aleas held his gaze. "Was her death really an accident?"

"Let us say it was a very well-devised accident." The old mage smiled. "A fortunate turn of events."

Aleas chanted a spell and blasted dark red streaks of light from his hands. Fian concocted a barrier spell, the blast from Aleas knocking him off balance.

***

On the Citadel wall, an archer strained his eyes, squinting into the distance.

He'd decided he was bored ages ago.

All very well, being a back stop in case they got pushed back to the Citadel walls, but this was boring the arse off him. He'd been straining his eyes for an age, desperate to see if there was any progress.

Good or bad.

He turned to get a drink of water from an earthenware jug on the back wall and stopped abruptly.

Standing in front of him were a dozen or so men. Refugees all, from Var'n Rodan. A pair of stocky, dark skinned Solaanians stood in front, the one of the right flashing him a lopsided toothless grin.

"What the fuck do you lot want?" the young archer rumbled.

"Those horses, in the field outside?" the Solaanian "Who's are they?"

Typical. Here we are in the midst of war and these arse's want to sell the outcast's horses.

You couldn't make it up.

"What's it to you?" the archer sneered, stepping in.

"They belong to Pehl's outcast..." A voice behind started, pulling himself up short. The crowd turned to the new voice, an older archer, holding a wooden mug of something steaming.

"Pehl's dark hairs." He corrected himself. "Why?"

Gill flashed him another toothless grin.

"Well, they won't be needing them, now they have their wings. So we can use them. To help."

"Help?" the older archer eyed him suspiciously, convinced there was some foul play at work here, and he was about to be the butt of it.

"Aye." Said another voice. They turned to look at Ashe, the salt trader. "Help."

"How? What is it you think..."

Ashe held up a hand.

"These people have lost their homes. Their families, loved ones, belongings. You've shown them more kindness in the last few days than many of us have seen these last few years. Your Premier? Isaac?" Ashe smiled. "He's quite a man."

"Aye," agreed the archer, "that, he is."

He, for one, certainly didn't regret voting him in.

"We would repay that kindness." The Solaanian said. "We can ride horse, with weapons. We can help."

The archers gave each other a look. Finally, the older of the two shrugged and nodded.

"Ok. Take what weapons you need from store or the training corner. Lam here will show you." He nodded to the younger.

The Solaanian nodded and turned away.

"Head for the moon forest." He yelled after them. "You'll have to ride quickly if there's to be any poor bastard alive to save. And may the Gods be at your back."

***

Brianne moved from second to third position, slicing through a short soldiers arm. He dropped his sword, stepping back, and she spun on her heels, wings out for balance and removed the head at the neck.

Two more ran in, and from the corner of her eye she could see a cavalry horse turning towards her. She stepped in, blocking one, parrying with the second. The first rushed in and thrust at her chest, which she blocked. He leant forwards and headbutted her. She turned away at the last moment, the head colliding with her own at the side.

Pain erupted across her temple, spots of white blurring her vision for a beat. She recovered to see the second bring his sword up, slicing across her bicep. She stepped back, blood flowing down her black-clad arm. The first, seeing his opening, grinned and sliced towards her neck.

Brianne brought her curved blade up in time to block it and stepped in to knee the man in the groin. He collapsed in a crumpled heap, groaning.

The second swordsman faltered.

Just a beat too long.

He fell to the side, blood flowing from his stomach.

There was a thump behind her. She turned to see a wraith a dozen paces from her, snarling like a trapped hound, its breath foul and foetid. She raised her sword, free hand forward.

Loran landed behind the wraith, folded in and stood with his claws out.

And waited.

Brianne was suddenly aware that her pulse had quickened. She could feel it throbbing at the side of her head. She took a deep breath, held it for a few beats, then let it out slowly.

The wraith plodded towards her, unaware of the Daemon standing behind him. Watching.

Waiting.

It roared, snapping its jaws at her head. Teeth snapped a handspan from her face as she rocked back, bringing her sword down at its neck.

The wraith raised a wingtip and knocked her sideways, her curved blade clattering harmlessly off its head. She regained her footing quickly, suddenly chiding herself for being so short with Loran.

She could almost hear him clenching his jaw, resisting the urge to rip the beast's head off. The muscles in his arms and legs were knotted, tense and ready. A coiled viper waiting to pounce. But this meant a lot to her. So it clearly meant a lot to him.

So Loran watched and waited to see if things got out of hand.

Then he would probably rip it's head off.

***

Behind her, on the grasslands, the Avian lancers had been almost entirely overrun by the Cavalry of the witch queen. Lances lay broken and abandoned in the slick grass. Bodies lay tattered and still.

The Cavalry horses regrouped, turning to charge at the last vestige of the Avian line.

Remus stood, helm lost in the fray, cuirass bloodstained and dented.

"Swords, with me." He screamed as the horse line turned.

The Avians set their feet and waited.

The horses pulled up abruptly, an arrowhead formation, the stocky form of General Wes front and centre.

Remus stared at them.

"What the fuck are they waiting for?"

***

"Bastard." Aleas growled. "That girl was everything to me."

Fian shot white-blue bolts of lightning from his fingers, throwing Aleas to the floor.

He raised himself and gritted his teeth.

Both mages stood, feet set, trading bolts of energy and

magic. Each getting more exhausted from the exertion.
Each more determined that the other to stand his ground.

Aleas found the tiredness creeping up on him quicker than he expected. As a bolt of blue energy hit his chest, Aleas was thrown to the ground a second time, mud on his face and clothes.

Fian came to stand over him.

"I told you once, fool, that you are no match for me."

"And I told you, Fian. Once a mage," he pushed himself up, "but always a soldier."

"What of it?" growled the mage.

"Being a soldier means entrusting your life to your comrades."

Fian's eyes widened as Tialla's sword erupted through his chest, blood and ribs exploding outward. Fingers of white energy danced across his torso, and Tialla ripped her curved blade free, the bony, stick-thin frame of Fian falling sideways.

Aleas stood and spat on it.

Tialla nodded at him. She set her feet and fell into first position, the bridge behind her.

Aleas turned to the water. He cast out his hands, closed his eyes.

And started to chant.

Long, almost incoherent strings of sounds tumbled from his mouth. His hands shook.

The bridge at Crennels Forde stated to vibrate.

***

General Wes grinned as the Avians regrouped in front of him.

Fine.

Gather together.

Saves time hunting the fuckers down.

They might even decide to fall back. A rout now could slay almost as many as the fight so far.

Now, we wait.

***

All too soon, it became apparent exactly what they were waiting for, as a dark cloud of wings and teeth swooped low over the river, landing between the cavalry and the Avians. For all their efforts, there were still over a dozen of these dead-eyed, soulless creatures left to contend with.

Remus sighed as they army of the wraiths howled and screeched, then plodded forwards.

Damn.

"We need to fall back." He announced to nobody in particular. Around him, swordsmen and women, tired and panting, stood waiting. Wings dirty and cuirasses bloodstained.

He turned to a young Avian at his side.

"Sound the retreat." He said, disappointment etched on his face.

The archers on the roof were their only reserve now. They were forced to take to the air and risk death from the Wraiths mid-flight.

The Wraith at the front of the pack roared, trudging onward.

The youngster lifted a long, golden horn to his lips and blew a loud, high pitched series of mournful notes.

It stopped abruptly, rocked back on its hind legs and clamped its wingtips over its large ears, howling. Behind it, several of its brethren did the same.

"What are they doing?" Remus muttered. The wraith seemed to recover its senses, dropping down on its wingtips again.

Remus looked from the wraith to the trumpeter and back.

"Blow that again." He said.

The trumpeter shrugged, but blew the retreat again, nonetheless.

It had the same effect.

"Louder." Remus yelled.

The trumpeter blew as hard as his lungs would allow. All the wraiths covered their ears against the sound.

"Cave bats…." The young trumpeter muttered.

Remus raised his eyebrows.

"They're bred with cave bats, by the looks of it, Sir." The trumpeter explained. "Very sensitive ears, I shouldn't wonder."

A smile spread across the Lord Commanders face, and he turned to the nearest swordman.

"Fly back to the Citadel and gather every trumpeter and hornsman you can find." The Avian shot him a quizzical look. "Quickly, lad. You two go with him. Make sure he gets there alive."

They took off, heading south.

THIRTY SIX

"What are those fucking things doing?" General we screamed. He stood tall in the stirrups, rage and spittle flying. The Wraiths were hesitant, rocking back and covering their ears as the trumpeter blew again.

He should have known better than to trust these damn creations of hers! Damn fool idea, not that anybody had asked his opinion. Oh no. A veteran of countless campaigns and battles for the queen and her father before her. There are some things in life you just can't leave to chance.
And these... things were a huge gamble, to his mind.

"Attack, damn you. Attack." He yelled, sitting back in the saddle. His horse snorted and jittered under him.

The wraiths plodded forward. As they did, Wes looked skywards to see score or more of Avians flying low overhead, loosing a volley of arrows at the beast's neck and heads.
His horse jittered again. Wes could hear a thundering in the distance, the ground vibrating to a tune he was only too aware of.
Cavalry.

He stood tall again, straining to see over the wraiths and Avians.
In the distance a score or so horses were charging towards them.

"Where did this come from?" He yelled.

They never used horses. He'd been assured of that. Not even for tending the land. Certainly not for travel. Pointless using horses when you had bloody wings!
So exactly who was it thundering across the wet grasslands at that precise moment, bearing down on his men?
General Wes looked about him for answers, only to be met by

blank expressions.

Behind them, the bridge at Crennels Forde exploded into dust.

***

Gill and Tiril galloped at the head of the men of Var'n Rodan, whooping and yipping like children. Long, curved cutlasses held aloft, their eyes were bright and alive. Beside them, Ashe was less enthusiastic by a long margin. He felt less like he was leading the band of horses behind him, more like he was being pushed along by it. But he'd given his word, along with the rest of the village, that they would join this battle. A vain attempt to turn the tide before these monsters ran roughshod across the whole of Murrecia.

That, he would not stand by and see.

Ashe held the short sword he'd picked up from the pile in the training corner, the piebald mare under him snorting and lathering as she ran on. He looked up to see three Avians flying overhead, heading back to the Citadel.

The first of many?

He surely hoped not.

Behind him, a score of horses thundered across the grasslands, men holding various weapons and shields, and garbed in a loose assortment of helms and leather overshirts. Ashe had been unlucky to have missed out. He was just glad he'd gotten a sword that was in relatively good order.

In front of them, the monsters were gnashing and tearing into Avians, who fought back with every sword cut and slice they could. Brianne and Loran landed in the middle of the fray, She, slicing at the beast's heads, the Daemon simply ripping them off in disgust.

The riders of Var'n Rodan split into two, hurtling either side of the swords to hit the Queen's Cavalry like a hammer blow. Horse careered into horse, sword clashed with sword and rider after rider slid from the saddle. Ashe lifted his sword to block a Cavalry sabre, the shock jarring his arm. He cut down into the rider's trunk, his sword clanging off the riders cuirass. The cavalry man raised a foot to try and unseat him, but Ashe swung his horse away a pace or two before coming back in and stabbing the man in the neck. He watched in slow motion as the man slid from the saddle, landing with a wet thud on the grass. Turning his horse, he kicked in his heels and rode at the back of another cavalry soldier who was engaged with Gill, the Solaanian trading blows, clanging his curved cutlass against the Cavalryman's sabre.

Ashe cantered past and swept his own short sword at the man's neck, cutting into the flesh, but not quite enough to separate head from body.

It was enough to stop the cavalryman in his tracks, however, and Gill grinned as the rider slid sideways.

Ashe nodded, cantering on.

A crash from the side knocked him and his horse into the mud, the horse screaming from a broken leg. Its screams didn't last long, as a Wraith bit down on the horses neck, blood spurting, rending away a great chuck of flesh. Ashe tried desperately to free himself from beneath the horse, but his leg was firmly trapped.

He looked up, as the wraiths eyes fell on him. Ashe waited for the inevitable, turning his head away just as Loran landed on the beast's back and grabbed it's head, wrenching it sideways with a loud crack. He watched as the Daemon ripped off its head and tossed it aside, then flew over to his side of the horse, lifting it easily to free him.

"My thanks. Thought I was a goner there." He mumbled, standing.

"You're welcome." The daemon rumbled. "You may need another mount."

"I'll manage without." He said, looking at the mayhem that was all around him, as the horsemen of Var'n Rodan clashed with the cavalry of Isiarus, Avian swords fought human swords, and Wraiths were landing indiscriminately, tearing chunks of any Avian they came across.

He genuinely couldn't tell if they were winning or losing.

A noise behind him caught his attention, and he spun

to see a handful of Avians flying in, all blowing on horns and trumpets. The din was colossal, and Ashe watched in fascination as the Wraiths reared up, howling and roaring at the sky.

As one, they all took off and headed for the forest.

A great cheer went up from the Avians before Lord Commander Remus screamed at them to get after them. Avians took off in large numbers, chasing the beasts down. Kall, Loran's advice still fresh in his mind, yelling for them to attack them from the rear, just behind the head.

One by one, the wraiths fell.

***

General Wes looked on aghast as the Wraiths flew overhead, dropping in huge numbers. He kicked in his heels and trotted over to Isiarus.

"Highness. I fear the day may be lost for now. We should…"

"NO!" she screamed. "I will not be denied again. They must perish."

Wes tried in vain to protest, then looked about the grasslands of Murrecia as she raved on, his eyes settling on Isiarus again. He'd fought countless battles in her name. Slain countless people in countless foreign lands. And for her father before her. And for what?

He was tired. He was tired of fighting. He was tired of being given orders.

Bone tired.

He found himself picturing Bekina's beautiful, oval, face. Her hair, dark as molasses, her eyes like black opals. Suddenly he missed her touch more than air itself. Her sweet, perfumed home on the banks of the River of Light. He missed the bustle of the streets of Durmak. The market vendors, the smell of the street cooks. She'd begged him not to go back.

Begged.

Now he wished he'd listened.

Enough.

"Kill them your-fucking-self, then." He spat, dropping his

sword at her horse's feet.
Wes turned, kicked in his heels, and cantered away towards the Moon Forest.

***

She looked down upon the battleground, watching as the last of her cavalry were cut down. Her swordsmen were losing ground and losing numbers.
Isiarus screamed.
How could this have happened? It all had seemed so perfect, so right. She should, must, be reinstated by the Gods as her true self. Only through destroying L'Shaan's army could she atone for her previous sins.
L'Shaan's previous sins.
Surely then, the great Gods would bestow upon her the power she deserved?
Surely?
Her father had promised her she was destined for greatness. She pictured the old man's lined face as she bemoaned her withered arm.
She turned her horse and kicked her heels in.
The horse reared up as Loran the Daemon landed in front of her. He folded his wings in and stared at her.
"Leaving so soon?" He snarled.
She glared at him, her face unreadable. Her horse jittered about under her, snorting in the late morning air.
"I thought you dead." she spat. "My greatest failure. Had you been half the Daemon I was promised by that fool of a mage, I would be a Goddess by now."
"No." he said coldly. "You would not."
Loran took a step toward her, bringing fresh panic from her horse. "You would be nothing but the bitter, spiteful woman you are now."
"I deserve to be a Goddess." She raged. "I deserve it. I have lived in the shadow of my father and his wishes, of my useless arm, of his disapproval and disappointment, all my life."
"And you think slaughtering an entire race of people is

going to undo all that?" he shook his head. "How misguided are you?"

"Your day will come, Daemon. I am not finished with any of you yet." She sneered, turning her horse and trotting away.

Loran closed his eyes and concentrated, all sound from the battle diminishing.

She pulled up abruptly, her horse jittering again. Isiarus stared down at her left arm, grey and muscular, as it bent at the elbow, the hand facing her.

She stared at it.

Willing it to stop.

Her eyes widened as the claws slid out, great yellow talons curving cruelly from her fingertips, facing her. She tried to scream as the hand came up and clamped around her throat, choking the sound from her. Her eyes bulged, her lungs screaming for air as the hand tightened, grey muscles knotting in her arm.

The talons gripped tighter and tighter, five lines of blood flowing down her neck as they pierced the skin, blood running over the gold cuirass she was clad in. Her vision started to darken.

With a great squelching rip, her hand pulled away, tearing out her own throat.

Isiarus, the witch queen, slid from the saddle, her neck in shreds.

Loran opened his eyes, feeling control of the arm slipping from him. The thing from the underworld had been right after all.

Once was enough.

***

Tialla stumbled back to the line, supporting Aleas's weight, his arm over her shoulder. Fighting with Fian and destroying the bridge had obviously left him weary, his eyelids heavy. She'd cajoled and swore and bullied him into moving. Despite his protests, she'd managed to get him to his feet.

And, she could see, his efforts had not been in vain.

Some of the Queens cavalry, now unmounted, had made

for the river, only to find it uncrossable, especially in cavalry armour. Caught against the banks, they had all but perished, some taking a chance in the water and being carried away. Her swordsmen suffered a similar fate, some taking their chances in the woodlands of the Moon Forest. Tialla made for the line to find her father in conversation with Remus, the lord Commander seemingly aged a tenfold in the last few days. Brianne she spotted talking to Loran, both staring down at the mutilated body of that evil bitch.
She would get that story in time, she felt sure.
She'd expected a great cheer, a wave of relief or outpouring of joy. But all she felt was numb. Numb and still and slightly empty.

She looked around at the empty, numb faces of her comrades, a couple shielding their hand as they looked to the sky. She turned to see what they were staring at.

The earth trembled as two great beings dropped from the clouds to land before them. One was olive skinned with brown, curly hair, a drooping moustache, and a long, spiralling tattoo down one leg. The other, black as the night, and bald. Both had muscles most men could only dream of. Both were taller than the Daemon, and twice as wide.
The olive skinned one spoke, the trees shaking at the sound of his voice.

"On your knees, mortals." He bellowed.

"For before you stands the Supreme God Vororr!"

THIRTY SEVEN

As one, the Avians sunk to one knee, the riders of Var'n Rodan doing the same. Vororr studied them, all before him on one knee.

All except for a tall, muscular, grey Daemon.

Vororr stared at the Daemon, and the Daemon stared right back at him, a slight smirk across his face.

Vororr decided he would deal with this insolent creature last.

"Army of L'Shaan." He bellowed. "You do not belong in these lands. Or any lands. Your creation was a violation against the ways of nature. And that must be set right."

Avians began exchanging glances, Humans looking about them, puzzled.

"You must now perish…"

"I hate to interrupt…" Loran yelled. All eyes turned to him as he strode forwards amongst his kneeling comrades. "But by what right do you judge these beings?"

"I am Vororr, God of honour. I am the Supreme. It is my place to judge all things."

"And yet you allowed this war to wage unattested. Why?" Vororr shifted uncomfortably. He was not used to being questioned. By anybody or anything!

"I do not interfere with the free will of men. It is not the way of things."

Loran came to stand before the Gods, his head level with Vororr's chest.

"But you have decided to interfere with these people's lives by deciding their fate. Their very existence."

"You would do well not to question the Supreme." Bellowed his companion.

"I question all things when it threatens the people I have come to know and respect. And I stand between you and them." Vororr threw his head back and laughed.

"Wretched little Daemon. You dare to oppose me?"

"I do." He said simply.

"Then you shall perish first, for you belong in the Otherworld with the rest of the beasts."

"NO!" Brianne stood, walking to stand between Vororr and Loran. The Daemon tried to protest, but to deaf ears.

"Why would you protect this creature?" Vororr asked her, his hands on his hips.

"Because he is one of us now." A new voice said.

Isaac strode out from the crowd. He'd been watching the battle unfold from a distance, at Remus' insistence. He was the first to admit, he was not much of a fighting man. Since then, he'd been helping Malaner with the wounded and calming the horses when the Gods had arrived.
Now he, too, stood next to Loran, staring the Gods down.

"We will not stand by and see him perish. He has given much for us. And he is now our brethren."

"Aye." said a voice, Aleas and Tialla standing from the kneeling crowd.

"Aye." said another.
And another. More stood, lending their voices until all were standing, a ring of people around Loran.

Vororr stared at them, shaking his head. This, he had not expected. He was lead to believe that these Avians were a cowardly, callous horde. But this outpouring had taken him aback, it had to be said. He had wrestled long with his conscience, watching this war from afar. He had not interfered with the ways of man before, even during the conflict with Rotaldir and Blaise those long years ago.
But even he had to admit to himself, the conduct of these Avians was surprising.

"Are you not the God of Honour?" Isaac pressed, seeing an opportunity.

"I am." Vororr said quietly.

"And is there not much honour you have seen here this day? Men and women, humans and Avians, fighting alongside one another for the common good? Surely The Supreme God Vororr finds that honourable?"

Vororr looked about the field, carcasses of dead wraiths strewn about the grass, carrion crows devouring dead eyes and viscera. Tattered white wings and horses were spread around.

"Aye," he rumbled at last. "There is much honour on this field this day, I am forced to admit."

"Then will the great God Vororr not grant us a stay of execution? For we have done nothing except try to live our lives." Isaac threw his arms open wide, his eyes pleading.

There was a long silence, a gentle wind blowing across the grass, the smell of death and blood and the river.

"Very well." Vororr said at last. "But know this, Avians. I will be watching your conduct carefully. Betris and I will be back if your honour fails you."

He looked down at Loran.

"Be well Daemon. For I may have need of you in the future."

With a great leap, they both disappeared into the clouds.

Then the cheer came.

***

She opened her eyes.

There was darkness all around. A wet, sticky black that seemed to touch her. Cling to her. She longed to evade it, to see sunlight. To be free.

In the distance were huge mountains of dark rock, lit by flashes of lightning. On the edges of her vision, she could just make out the occasional beast circling.

Watching.

Waiting.

There was a noise behind her, and she spun on her heels. The mist and black seemed to part to reveal a tall, grey creature. Long horns sat on its head. It had hands of long, misshapen fingers topped with yellow curved talons. It's smell was rotten. She took a step back, her memory filled with images from the Dermal scripts.

"Rotaldir…" she breathed.

"L'Shaan." It hissed back. "Long I have awaited your presence here."

She turned and ran, only to find Rotaldir standing before her.

"I…I am L'Shaan only in image." She stuttered.

"And yet you used the darkest magic to make your Daemon. From your own body, and from my realm. You longed to return to your true self."

Damn that mage.

You should not think on him. Said a rasping voice in her head. *His time will come.*

"What do you want with me?" she snapped, stepping back again.

"Your suffering shall be legendary…" Rotaldir hissed as a beast ran towards her from the side, launching at her neck.

Isiarus screamed.

***

Brianne walked the length of the temple aisle. Everything had been prepared accordingly. A moon or more had passed since the battle at Crennels Forde, and much clearing up and repair had taken place.

The gates on the north wall had been made good, except they now opened inwards instead of the portcullis of old. The machinists of Var'n Rodan had helped immensely with that, and many other projects.

The south wall had now been extended to make way for new dwellings. Homes for the new Avians, and some of the people of Var'n Rodan who decided to stay. Many, though, had said their goodbyes and returned to their village to make it a home again. The temple roof had been replaced, and a ceremonial altar now stood where the Seraph once hovered.

She met the gaze of old Eral, the temple elder who had managed to keep his position, somehow, and now led the daily prayers of thanks to the Great God Vororr. Brianne gave him a pleasant smile and a nod, which he returned. The temple seemed... lighter, somehow. Brighter.

"Bri!" said a woman's voice behind her. She spun to find Tialla walking towards her. Her friend and sword mistress looked simply beautiful, with a long, flowing, jade coloured gown replacing her ever-present black outfit. Her red hair had been pulled up and was flowing down the back of her head, her brown wings preened and spotless.

"You look gorgeous." Brianne said, kissing her friend on the cheek.

"I was going to say the same to you." She replied, stepping back to admire her. Brianne was dressed in the same gown that Aleas had given her all those weeks ago, the claret and cream material now repaired and impeccably clean, the palace seamstresses having threaded the edges with gold for the occasion.

This day had surely kept them busy.

Her hair, now shoulder length, was pulled up similar to Tialla's, and her wings had been washed and preened to within an inch of their life.

As was befitting her place this day.

"I'll see you at the feast." Tialla said, and turned to take a seat next to Pehl.

Isaac sat on the other side of the aisle alongside Daynar. The former princess of the palace had made herself invaluable at the hospital of late. It had taken everyone aback, not least of all Brianne herself, as her friend had never even mentioned an interest in healing before. Daynar was looking over her shoulder and smiling. A shy smile. Brianne followed her gaze to a young lady with wings of beige, skin the colour of a dark tisane and long flowing hair of brown. Brianne recognised her as one of Pehl's warriors. She smiled back, equally shyly.

I didn't see that coming.

She stepped up to the altar, Eral fussing with the book for today's binding ceremony. The bottle had been prepared, a small,

blue, empty vial, that the newly bound couple would break to signify the end of their old life, and the start of a new one. Together.
And what an old life it had been.

"Thank you for being my maiden today."
She turned to the voice behind her.

Sande looked exquisite, her dark hair in a long braid, threaded with gold. Her white dress equally trimmed in gold thread and her wings preened to perfection.
Kall was a lucky man indeed, to be bound to one of such beauty.

"No thanks are needed. It is an honour, truly." She stood back and admired her. "Are you ready?"
She took a breath and nodded, beaming.

They took their place at the altar, the pews filling. Before long, Kall entered the temple, his parents either side of him, and they walked slowly towards his intended. His tunic and trews of white almost shone in the sun that gleamed through the newly built domed roof.

The ceremony was a beautiful one, some parts having been hastily rewritten to include Vororr at the exclusion of L'Shaan. Together, they made their promises. Eral took a length of golden cord from around his neck, and bound their hands together, proclaiming them "As one." They then took the bottle with their free hands and smashed it on the floor, and a great cheer and applause rang out around the temple.

Loran stood at the back, alone, slightly bemused by it all.

***

The feast was a sumptuous one, with long tables groaning under the weight of food, flasks of ale and goblets of wine flowing continuously. Five musicians sat at one end of the market square, reels and jigs and dances playing out across the quadrangle, echoing off the low, squat buildings. Laughter and dancing flowing in equal measure.

Brianne broke off from a conversation to sidle over to Daynar who was nursing a goblet of Solaanian red.

"Just go and talk to her." She said.

Daynar looked up.

"Hmm?"

Brianne looked over to the young lady from the temple. She looked away quickly, suddenly consumed with interest at a plate of salad vegetables.

"Her name is Virnia. She is Caris's sister. She's single." Daynar stopped drinking and stared at Brianne. "And she clearly likes you, too. So go and talk to her." She insisted.

"Oh, Bri. Do you think so? What would father say? What will Isaac think?" Daynar jabbered, voicing the questions she had asked herself almost continually since catching the young lady's eye at the feast hall a ten night ago. She could scarcely believe it was the same beautiful young lady she had been watching from the forest months ago, bathing in the moon pool. Before crashing into a tree, only to be rescued by a Daemon!

"Well, your father isn't here anymore," Brianne said, "and Isaac can be happy or not."

"And what do you think?" she asked, a lump in her throat.

"I think you should love who you want to love…" she said quietly, suddenly looking around the square.

Loran should have been easy to spot, towering over everyone as he did. She'd not seen him since the ceremony, now she thought on it.

"He's gone." Daynar said quietly.

Brianne met her gaze.

"When?"

"Just before the feast began. Took off without a word."

Why? She knew he was unfamiliar with the ceremony and its meaning, maybe even made uncomfortable by it. But they'd spoken little in the days after the battle. And spent almost no time alone together.

She missed him.

"Well," Daynar hissed, "don't just stand there, you fool, go after him!"

***

Loran had soared high, the trees of the Moon Forest far

below him. The wind in his face felt refreshing, the silence and open air liberating. He peeled left, the Desolation in the distance, the western steppes far off on the horizon.

He felt he was done with that place for now.

Loran turned right, flapping hard, gaining height, then diving at the ground, gaining speed. He hadn't flown so freely since he was young, learning to fly himself. Aleas had begged him not to venture too far. To only fly at night, even. When prying eyes would not

see. Loran had failed to grasp what the panic in his eyes was for, until the men from Var'n Rodan had arrived. Then everything made sense.

The Moon Forest loomed large, and Loran opened his wings wider to soar over them, almost brushing the treetops with his feet. He landed at the side of the Moon Pool, folding in. Undoing the belt, he slid his black trews down his legs, stepping out of them. He was careful not to lose his dagger as he laid them over a low branch, and stepped into the water.

The water was cool in the late autumn evening. He sat on a low rock shelf he had sat on a dozen times, unfolding his wings and laying back in the water, letting the spray from the low waterfall to his right soak him through.

He sat like that with his eyes closed for what felt an eternity. Pondering, thinking, wondering. His mind full of questions and empty of answers. Filled with pictures of her face.

Would she understand? She must, would surely realise, that he could never stay here? What if his rage bubbled over and somebody else got hurt needlessly?

He smelled her perfume before she landed. Rose water and lemongrass. Heard the rustle of her dress, the flap of her feathers. Smelled the wine on her breath, even.

He opened his eyes and sat up, water cascading down his wings and back. She stood at the edge of the Moon Pool, watching him.

"You left without saying goodbye."

Loran looked down at his reflection in the water, ripples

contorting his face.

"I can't stay here." He said quietly, without looking up.
She waited.

"I don't belong here. You must realise that?"

"Ok, well. Give me some time to pack and say my goodbyes. Where will we go?"

Loran looked up at her.

"We?"

"Yes, we. You and I are one now. We may not be bound, but we are together. Where you go, I go." She'd decided on the flight here that she would not be without him. That things could never return to how they were before. She felt more awake, more alive, now, than ever before.

Because of him.

"I cannot let you…" he started.

"Try and stop me. You're mine, Loran. We stick together. No arguments."

Loran stared at her, words failing him. Somehow, after all this time alone and apart from his father, suddenly he was surrounded by people and loved ones.

And she was at the centre of it all.

"Ok," He conceded. "I suppose I could get used to being in the Citadel."

She nodded slowly, reaching up behind her to unbutton her dress at the neck.

"What's the water like?" she asked, letting the dress drop and stepping out of it. She hung it on a tree and hooked her thumbs into her undergarment, sliding it down her legs. Loran watched her, his groin stirring at the sight of her.

"Quite nice…" he managed, smiling slowly.

She stepped, naked, into the water and waded up to him. Her wings started to look instantly bedraggled in the spray. Loran stood, his arousal obvious.

"You won't be able to fly now your wings are wet." He whispered.

"I wasn't planning on going anywhere for a while." She

whispered back.

THIRTY EIGHT.

Deep in the bowels of Liana Palace, Torna let the waters of his bowl clear. He gritted his teeth and growled in frustration like a wounded hound. Outside, the wind howled, lashing the walls with sand.

Damn that Daemon.

Everything had been proceeding accordingly. His cunning had secured Fian's position in the palace of Isiarus.

L'Shaan reborn.

She should have destroyed the Avians, and the seraph would have destroyed her.

But no. The Daemon had arrived to stick his beak in where it wasn't wanted. Torna had watched in the waters as the battle had turned, that useless excuse Vororr being sweettalked.

Persuaded to be lenient.

And now he had real work to do.

Overthrowing Vororr would be twice as hard now. He would need all his cunning and guile to pull it off. Fortunately, cunning and guile were his stock in trade.

"What news?" Jana said, striding into the room, her black dress flowing behind her, blonde hair in a long braid.

"Not good." He droned, telling her of the battle lost, the wraiths defeated.

Her husband slain.

Jana fluttered her wingtips in frustration.

She really had looked forward to killing him herself.

It was just like Pyrus to go and get himself killed, and deprive her of her last vestige of revenge, the old arse!

These long months in this wilderness had only been sufferable at Torna's insistence of revenge for Meryl's death. Why

Pyrus ever felt the need to send her son on such a dangerous task as he had was always a mystery. The thought of his body mutilated, his needless death, had taunted her days and troubled her nights ever since.

"What now." She snarled.

Torna laughed.

"Patience, my pretty, patience. I have another cunning plan for the Avians, and this Daemon, especially. A plan that will leave them devastated. A plan I have devised over many years for just such an occasion. And when it finally comes to fruition, They won't have a chance."

He waved his hands over the water, the image clearing again.

"For soon, Godswar will be upon them…"

END

Printed in Great Britain
by Amazon